For the girls who were there with me —
the good, the bad, and the ugly.
You know who you are.

The Nannies

The Nannies

by Melody Mayer

Delacorte Press

Published by
Delacorte Press
an imprint of
Random House Children's Books
a division of Random House, Inc.
New York

Text copyright © 2005 by Cherie Bennett and Jeff Gottesfeld
Front cover photograph © by Johnny Hernandez/Stone/Getty Images

All rights reserved. No part of this book may be reproduced or transmitted in
any form or by any means, electronic or mechanical, including photocopying,
recording, or by any information storage and retrieval system, without the
written permission of the publisher, except where permitted by law.

The trademark Delacorte Press is registered in the U.S. Patent
and Trademark Office and in other countries.

Visit us on the Web! www.randomhouse.com/teens
Educators and librarians, for a variety of teaching tools,
visit us at www.randomhouse.com/teachers

Library of Congress Cataloging-in-Publication Data
Mayer, Melody.
The nannies / by Melody Mayer.
p. cm.
Summary: Kiley, Lydia, and Esme, three teenagers from very different
backgrounds, befriend one another while working as nannies for wealthy
employers in Beverly Hills, California.
ISBN 0-385-73283-X (trade pbk) — ISBN 0-385-90300-6 (glb)
[1. Nannies—Fiction. 2. Friendship—Fiction. 3. Self-confidence—Fiction.
4. Wealth—Fiction. 5. Beverly Hills (Calif.)—Fiction.] I. Title.
PZ7.M4619Nan 2005
[Fic]—dc22   2004028252

The text of this book is set in 11.25-point Berkeley Oldstyle.
Printed in the United States of America
September 2005
BVG   10 9 8 7 6 5 4 3 2 1

PENFIELD PUBLIC LIBRARY

The Nannies

Kiley McCann: Milwaukee, Wisconsin

"My name is Kiley but my friends call me Krazy, with a *K*."

"Wow."

Kiley McCann could tell by the way her interviewer had said "Wow" that she was impressed. Perfect. Kiley crossed her miniskirt-clad legs and shook chestnut hair off her face with a practiced gesture. From the corner of her eye, she could see the red light of the video camera that was recording every word.

"I'm totally wild," Kiley declared.

"Really." The multiply pierced interviewer leaned forward in her orange director's chair. "So, Krazy, what kind of music are you into?"

"Classic rock, totally," Kiley assured her. "Platinum, of course. 'Coy Miss Interruptus' is my fave. And Hendrix. Hendrix is the best."

"Are you experienced?"

"Very." Kiley dropped her eyes to half-mast. "I'm up for anything. Anytime. Anywhere."

"Well, wow all over again." The woman put down her clipboard and stretched, exposing two taut inches of stomach above her how-low-can-you-go jeans. Then she dead-eyed Kiley. "You're totally full of shit."

Kiley blushed—*blushed!*—which was not at all the look she was going for. "No I'm not," she insisted.

"Please. You're a goddamn seventeen-year-old poser. Don't yank my chain."

Face burning, totally busted, Kiley slumped back onto her stool. So much for passing herself off as a girl hot enough to get selected for a new reality TV show.

When her best friend, Nina, had picked her up at three a.m. to drive to Milwaukee, Kiley had felt so hopeful. Halfway there, they'd made a pit stop, where Nina had applied smudgy black eyeliner and three coats of mascara to Kiley's face. Ditto lip gloss. Then Kiley donned the microminiskirt, stiletto boots, and sheer camisole that Nina had swiped from her slutty sister Heather. Infused with donuts and truck-stop coffee, they returned to the car; Kiley rehearsed her wild child act the rest of the way to Milwaukee.

At first, the ruse seemed brilliant. When they arrived before dawn at the Milwaukee Center for the Performing Arts, where the interviews were to take place, there was already a four-deep line that snaked around the building. Over the next hour, while the sun rose, cute guy after cute guy chatted them up. That never happened in La Crosse, where Kiley's hair was invariably in a messy ponytail and the rest of her in the Gap chinos/T-shirt/Converse All Stars combo she favored.

2

And then, a miracle. One of the show's associate producers canvassing the line singled her out and handed her a card that allowed her to be interviewed immediately. The producer escorted Kiley past the long line of glaring stares and right through the glass doors of the center.

It had all seemed too perfect. Apparently, it was. Damn.

The young woman peered over rhinestone kitten glasses. "So Kiley, oh, I mean *Krazy*," she said, sneering. "When I asked '*Are You Experienced?*' I wasn't referring to your sex life. It's the name of a—no, *the*—seminal Jimi Hendrix album."

"Oh."

All around the rehearsal hall, which had been converted into an interview room, the show's staff chuckled at Kiley's gaffe.

"Let's cut to the chase here, Miss Susie Cream Cheese. You're from . . ." She scanned Kiley's application.

"La Crosse," Kiley offered meekly.

"Where the hell is La Crosse?"

"Down the river from Eau Claire."

"Oh well, isn't that soooo helpful." The staff exploded in laughter again.

Kiley cleared her throat. "Okay. I may have embellished my application a *little*."

"A *little*?" The producer ran three fingers through her Day-Glo red punk hair as she glanced down at her clipboard. "Starred in *Girls Gone Wild* video. Hitchhiked solo around Southeast Asia. Snuck into Eminem's hotel room." Her eyes flicked back to Kiley. "This would be at his big La Crosse concert?"

Kiley stood, slutty Heather's too-tight boots biting into her toes. She faced the chubby cameraman, who was still taping her humiliation. "You can turn that off now," Kiley said with as much dignity as she could muster. She headed for the door. "Sorry to have wasted everyone's time."

"Excuse me. Sit, please!" the producer called. "We're not done."

"What's the point?"

"I said *sit*." The producer stabbed a finger at the chair. Kiley stopped. Turned. Walked back to her chair. Folded her arms and stood there as the producer went to confer quietly with two middle-aged men.

Kiley couldn't hear them. She felt ridiculous, on display in Heather's stupid "do me" outfit. What ever had made her think she could bluff her way onto *Platinum Nanny*? In the tradition of *The Apprentice,* the show would feature an on-air competition— to become the live-in nanny to the kids of superstar rock 'n' roller Platinum.

Prior to the announcement of auditions, Kiley had barely heard of Platinum. That was when Kiley did what Kiley did best: her homework. Research revealed that Platinum was a vintage rocker whose outrageous behavior had made tabloid headlines in the late eighties and early nineties. Now the singer had supposedly reformed and was the mother of three children by three different fathers. Her who's-my-daddy? family lived in Beverly Hills, California, on an estate she'd purchased from David Bowie.

As part of her research, Kiley had borrowed every Platinum CD she could find; Nina had even burned some bootleg recordings from Kazaa. Of course, now that Kiley had blown the interview, it wouldn't have mattered if she'd memorized Platinum's entire catalog.

The whole thing had been the longest of long shots anyway.

It wasn't as if Kiley had a sudden urge for her fifteen minutes of TV fame, or to enjoy the lifestyle of the rich and infamous by proxy. What Kiley wanted—needed, was desperate for—was to live in California and become a Californian.

When Kiley was in fifth grade, her parents had brought her to San Diego for an uncle's wedding. Between her dad's job at the La Crosse Brewery and her mom's job as a waitress, money was always tight. In fact, that trip had been their first and only family vacation that hadn't involved the car, multiple six-packs for Dad, and self-prescribed herbal anxiety medication for Mom.

The San Diego trip was a once-in-a-lifetime thing. Maybe that was why Kiley found it so magical. Her father had stayed sober. Well, mostly. Her mother chilled out on kava kava. Well, mostly. They'd gotten along like the Brady Bunch.

Best of all, they stayed in an apartment that overlooked the ocean. That first evening, as Kiley watched the setting sun paint a canvas of cirrus clouds red and purple as it slid into the Pacific, she felt a magical sense of calm. The smell of the sea, the way the salty air felt in her lungs . . . everything was clean and new and *possible*.

Her family was not the type to go on educational outings. Or any kind of outings, for that matter. But in San Diego, they went to Sea World. And drove up to the Long Beach Aquarium. They were supposed to go on the visitors' tour of the Scripps Institution of Oceanography, but Dad decided to see the Padres play a home game. So Mom took Kiley alone.

Disaster struck in the parking lot when Mrs. McCann had a panic attack. Kiley could often talk her mother down from these incidents. But that day, no way would her mother even leave the car. So Mom stayed behind while Kiley joined a large tour group—everyone assuming that the ten-year-old with the ponytail belonged to one of the grown-ups.

If that first night on the apartment balcony had been the courtship, the tour of the Scripps Institution sealed the romance. Kiley fell in love with the sea the way other girls fall in love with horses or boy bands. She made up her mind: she'd become an oceanographer or a marine biologist. It would be a career so far removed from La Crosse and the brewery and her mother's panic disorder as to be on another planet. It was perfect.

Back in La Crosse, Kiley turned herself into an amateur expert on the oceans. When she was a high school sophomore, she ordered the Scripps catalog. Reading it was bliss . . . until she reached the page that listed tuition. For California residents, the cost was reasonable. For out-of-staters, there were two numbers after the dollar sign and before the comma, and they weren't 1 and 0.

Who was she kidding? No way could her parents afford to pay for Scripps. Even with loans and a scholarship, she'd be lucky if she could afford La Crosse Community College. Her only hope was to apply to Scripps as a Californian. Which was ridiculous, since she wasn't one, and had no way of becoming one. Until two weeks ago, that is, when Nina had raced over to Kiley's house with the news she'd just heard on TV—*Platinum Nanny* was holding a regional audition in Milwaukee.

There it was: a shot at California . . . albeit the longest shot in the history of long shots. But now, not only had she blown it, she'd probably end up part of the *Platinum Nanny Bloopers and Stupors Extraspecial Episode,* immortalized on the air for all America to see.

The boots were killing her. What the hell. She sat down and

pulled them off just as the producer returned. "You're really seventeen?" she asked.

"Yep." Kiley crossed one leg over the other and rubbed a throbbing foot.

The producer extracted a pink plastic file card from her clipboard and offered it to Kiley. "You know what this is?"

"Parking validation?" was Kiley's retort. Why not? She didn't have to impress anyone.

"Take it. You're in."

Kiley sat there, boots in hand, certain she had misunderstood. "B-but I lied," she stammered. "I made everything up—"

"Yuh, we kinda got that," the producer said, her brittle laugh revealing a lethal-looking tongue stud. "Little Miss Wisconsin Virginator who tried to bluff her way into *Platinum Nanny*. They'll eat it up in flyover country. Congrats."

"You mean I'm really a finalist?"

"Not unless you take this damn card."

Kiley grabbed it. "Oh my God. Thank you!" She jumped up and hugged the young woman, boots still in her hand. "Thank you!"

"You're welcome. Now go home to La Whatever-it-is and get packed for Hollywood."

Lydia Chandler: The Amazon Basin, Brazil

"Cup his scrotum," Lydia Chandler suggested, which made Dr. Butkowski turn the same bloodred shade as the fresh monkey meat he'd eaten at lunch.

Lydia rolled her eyes. She'd have thought that the visiting doctors would read up on the mores and folkways of the indigenous populations of Amazonia before they came to South America. But most of them arrived utterly ignorant; expecting their penchant for charity work in the depths of the rain forest would suffice to charm the natives into their graces.

Dr. B. was simply the latest variation on the theme. On the motor-launch ride upriver, the portly physician had waxed poetic about his thriving medical practice in suburban New Jersey; how he'd volunteered for Doctors Without Borders because he wanted to use his medical training to Help Mankind.

Yeah. Like *that* would last here in the land of no electricity and no toilets. In fact, it was evident that the stomach-churning, puddle-jumping bush flight into Amazonia, followed by the long boat trip up the Rio Negro, had taken a toll on Dr. B.'s beatific mood. Or maybe it was hearing the word "scrotum" from a sixteen-year-old girl clad in cutoffs and an ancient Houston Oilers football jersey that she'd macheted into a sleeveless belly shirt. Or maybe it was being scrutinized by a five-foot-two, mostly naked Amazon tribesman whose penis was tied up to his abdomen with a cord. Or, all of the above.

"This man is an Amarakaire tribesman," Lydia explained, only a trace of her native Texas accent left after eight and a half years in the bush. "Ama warriors greet strangers by cradling their testicles. I suggest you do it promptly, and with a big ol' friendly smile on your face. Trust me. You don't want to piss him off."

"I—I—s-s-s-ee here—" the doctor sputtered.

Lydia gave a long-suffering sigh. This was all her parents' fault. They *sucked*! She engaged in this stupid exercise every month at their behest—escorting a visiting medical missionary up the Rio Negro, with stops at every little village along the way. It was especially irritating because each tribe had its own shaman whose herbal medicines were capable of competing with nearly anything an American doctor might have in his pharmaceutical black bag of tricks. In fact, lots of the drugs that required a prescription back home were derived from flora right here in the Amazon.

But Lydia knew if she didn't play tour guide, her parents wouldn't fork over her allowance—not that there was much to buy in the Amazon basin, anyway. Without said chip, however, her thrice-yearly visits to Manaus—where she scooped up every American fashion magazine in sight—would be a worse waste of time than these doctor-escort jaunts. When luck was with her in Manaus, she was even able to order Sephora cosmetics, which were held for her at the American Express office until her next visit. (Half the time, the makeup never arrived, but it was better than regular mail. She'd tried that delivery system, but the parachute pack dropped from the mail plane had gotten snared in the jungle canopy. The next day, she swore she saw squirrel monkeys mincing around in MAC lip gloss.)

Lydia glanced at the tribesman. He was blinking rapidly, never a good sign. She put her hand on Dr. B.'s arm. "He's an Ama, doctor. *Cradle his balls.* Unless you want him to eat you."

"Eat me?" Dr. Butkowski squeaked.

"If you're into that kind of thing—they're pretty much ambisexual. They're also cannibals. Although less than they used to be."

The doctor licked his parched lips. "Now see here, I can't just—" Suddenly, the small Amarakaire warrior's right hand flashed out, heading directly for the doctor's crotch.

"My God!" the doctor yelped as the warrior made contact. The tribesman smiled, revealing a mouthful of stained, broken teeth. Meanwhile, Butkowski looked as though he wanted to sprint all the way back to Paramus.

"Okay doc, handshake's accomplished, do your thing. I'll be over there." Lydia tilted her head toward a dried-mud-and-rough-hewn-wood hut. She held up the latest issues of *Vogue* and *In Style*. "Thanks for the magazines you brought me."

"You're welcome. But Lydia, I don't know this man's language. Aren't you going to interpret?"

"I could. But he'd be offended. Sexism Without Borders, you

know," Lydia quipped. "You'll be fine. You're not the first Western doctor he's ever seen."

The doctor nodded warily as a group of curious warriors formed a ring around the doctor and their brother.

Lydia headed off toward the hut. "One more thing, doc," she called over her shoulder. "Don't be surprised if they have deviated septums. Some really strange shit goes up those nostrils."

She pushed into the empty hut, kicked aside a nest of fire ants, leaned back on a log, and opened *In Style*—knowing it wouldn't be long before the July humidity turned the pages to mulch. Reading these magazines was always bittersweet. She loved the glimpses of her former life, but each article and advertisement reminded her that she was trapped in the Amazon with her parents for another 469 days, until her eighteenth birthday. At which point she would be happy to doggy-paddle back to America—piranhas be damned—if she had to.

"Oh, great," Lydia muttered as she stared down at *In Style*'s featured city: *Hot Nights in Houston—the Best Places to Shop, Eat, and Party.*

Houston. *Her* Houston.

Though it had been more than eight years since she'd been ripped from her privileged life, she recalled it perfectly. Her home in the tony River Oaks neighborhood had been as large as a castle; she'd been the resident princess. Everyone would tell her how pretty she was, with her long blond hair and startlingly pale green eyes. A future Miss Texas, they'd said. Lydia and her oil-money-rich mother used to go on monthly shopping expeditions to Neiman Marcus, where she'd parade outfit after outfit for the admiring clerks. When Lydia couldn't decide which one she most wanted, her momma just bought her all of them.

And the *toys*. Her grandparents had an Italian master crafts-man hand-tool a dollhouse for her that was an exact miniature of her family's mansion. Even the teensy furniture inside was identical. For her seventh birthday, her parents had rented out an amusement park so that Lydia and two hundred of her clos-est school friends could ride the rides and play the games with-out waiting in line. The games had been rigged so that every child won, and the prizes had all been ordered from F.A.O. Schwarz, the best toy store in the world.

It still shocked Lydia that these exact same parents, who had bestowed this perfect life upon her, had ripped it away. It hap-pened after her father's heart attack. He was only thirty-seven when he keeled over in the operating room at the M. D. Ander-son Cancer Center after performing thyroid cancer surgery on an accountant who was later implicated in the Enron scandal.

That heart attack changed everything. Her father recovered, as did the accountant, but the incident made her parents take a long, hard look at their lives. Also at their daughter, who was nagging them for another palomino pony so that her first one wouldn't be lonely. That self-examination led to some kind of joint spiritual epiphany: their privileged Texas lives were empty and meaningless. Which was how it came to be that six months later, the Chandlers sold their worldly possessions, donated the proceeds to Doctors Without Borders, and moved south. Way south. Dr. Chandler would practice medicine in the bush. Mrs. Chandler would be his learn-on-the-job physician's assistant. Which was fine for them. Hey, they picked it. But Lydia had not. What really bit Lydia's butt was that her parents were the rare ones who, once they decided to Help Mankind, never looked back.

Hours later, after Dr. New Jersey finished ministering to the natives and Lydia piloted the boat back downriver to the squalid hamlet that she called home, sweet home, she trudged into her family's hut. She never failed to notice how its square footage was roughly equal to her old walk-in closet.

"Airdrop today, there's one for you," her mom said. She was busy sterilizing some medical equipment on a bed of hot coals. "How'd it go with Butkowski?"

"The usual," Lydia replied as she reached for some dried and salted snails—junk food in Amazonia. "Love was in the air, though; one of the Amas fell for him." She pawed through the mail and spotted the aerogram addressed to her, in her aunt Kat's loopy handwriting.

Before Lydia's parents had lost their minds, Aunt Kat had been the blackest sheep of the Chandler clan. An excellent athlete, Kat was the best female tennis player in Texas by age fourteen, with a feature story in the *Houston Chronicle*. However, when she came out as a lesbian at fifteen, no such press coverage ensued.

Kat didn't let the moralizers stop her. She attended the University of Texas as a broadcast journalism major, captained their tennis team, and left after her sophomore year to join the women's circuit. She reached the round of sixteen at the U.S. Open twice, but sustained a serious knee injury at twenty-four that sidelined her forever. After she retired from competition, she went to work as a tennis commentator for ESPN.

Kat's longtime domestic partner, the Russian tennis star Anya Kuriakova, had been a chief rival for years. There were good-natured titters when Kat and Anya announced that they were a couple; their marriage in Massachusetts had made national news. Now, Kat did her broadcast thing, and Anya coached promising young Russian players. The couple lived in a Beverly Hills mansion with a son and daughter who'd been conceived with the aid of a sperm donor. Which meant—sexuality aside—that Lydia's aunt and her family were now basically living Lydia's old life.

Lydia tore open the aerogram and scanned the usual news of home and family. But she nearly choked on a snail when she got to the next paragraph.

"ESPN has made me a terrific offer to double my on-air time. If I accept, I'll have to travel quite a bit more. Anya and I have decided it's time that we hire a nanny for the kids—I've always been more the hands-on mom type, you know. So I thought you might want to come back to the States and take the job."

Holy shit. A lifeline. One that led to 90210.

The engine in Lydia's brain kicked into high gear. Her parents had to say yes. If they tried to stop her, she'd hike into the rain forest and go on a hunger strike. She'd threaten to get it on with an Ama—not that any of them found her skinny, pale flesh, or the lips that had never been pierced by sticks, very appealing. But still. She'd do whatever the hell it took to get out of the jungle.

Goodbye, rain forest. Hello, Beverly Hills.

3

Esme Castaneda: Echo Park, California

A sheep, Esme thought as she stared at her reflection in the cracked mirror over her dresser. There was space for her to stand between her single bed and the dresser; together, they practically filled her tiny room.

You look like a damn sheep.

Ignoring the jagged part created by the cracked mirror, she brushed raven hair off her face, then straightened the neckline of the soft pink sweater she'd found at Goodwill. She liked this sweater a lot—it clung to her curves and cast a soft glow on her ochre skin. She knew it made her look pretty. So pretty. She loved and hated that, at the same time.

"Oye, chiquita, what's up? You lookin' fresh!"

Esme had been thirteen and living in Fresno when she'd heard those words shouted by a golden boy who leaned out the driver's-side window of a spit-shined, cherry red Cadillac. She kept walking, heading home from Our Lady of Mercy School. But the boy trolled along in his car, still calling to her.

"Pretty little *linda. ¿ Qué pasa?*"

Esme recognized him; she'd seen him around the neighborhood. He was so cute: bulging muscles, full lips, heavy-lidded eyes. She didn't need to examine the colorful dragon tattoo on his right bicep to know he was a banger, a Diego (after a different boy who'd come to Fresno from San Diego—the guy was now doing life at Vacaville for murder, but the Fresno gang he'd organized still thrived).

There were two gangs vying for control of Esme's neighborhood: the Diegos and the Razor Boys. This handsome Diego boy—Esme knew he could have gotten any girl, one of the older ones who already knew how to work their curves and paint their lips and do whatever it took to keep a guy interested. So why was this movie star Diego paying attention to *her,* a knobby-kneed kid in a stupid Catholic school uniform?

When Esme was born, her parents were sharing the cheap three-bedroom home of Esme's maternal aunt, uncle, and their five kids. Spanish was spoken at home and at church; Esme didn't learn English until she started kindergarten. She mastered it quickly, though. It was like a puzzle to her, and she loved to solve puzzles. On the rare occasion when her parents were forced to converse with a *norteamericano,* Esme was their translator.

All Esme's cousins went to Our Lady of Mercy, so Esme did, too. But even with aid from the church, it was difficult for the parents to afford the tuition. The adults did without so that the kids could stay at that school; that's how important it was to them. Esme's mom cleaned houses and her father was an off-the-books day laborer. The adults were hopeful that God and the church would keep their kids from joining gangs.

And their hopes were realized. For a while.

But Esme's cousin Ricardo soon threw down with the Razor Boys. He wore baggy black pants and black tees with the right sleeve rolled up to show off his new RB sign, a python tattoo. He started bringing home hundred-dollar bills from selling coke. The adults prayed he'd come to his senses, but it didn't do any good. Ricardo said the frigging church wouldn't put food on their table or buy them a decent car or him new Nikes. His father threw him out of the house. He never came back.

Esme had been ten then. She missed Ricardo—he was her favorite cousin. She'd see him sometimes, with other RBs. He became a gang *patrón*—a big guy—fast. But when he saw Esme, he looked right through her.

It wasn't long after that when the terrible thing happened. Esme's father, Alberto Castaneda, had stopped for a beer at a tavern with his friend Carlos. Some white boys came in, flying on crystal meth and looking for trouble. One of them dumped his drink on Carlos. The boy wouldn't apologize; Carlos wouldn't accept the insult. He threw the first punch. But the meth made the white boy superstrong. His friends joined the fight. Esme's father stopped Carlos from getting killed by stabbing one of the white boys in the gut.

Alberto didn't wait around to find out what happened. There were too many witnesses, and he was in America illegally. So he ran with his wife to the Echo Park section of Los Angeles, to live with distant cousins. Esme was left in Fresno. The plan was to wait for the trail to grow cold, and then bring Esme to Los Angeles.

Esme missed them, a lot. But there were letters and even the occasional phone call. After a few months they found decent jobs working off the books for a Hollywood producer and his wife. It was a long drive from the Echo to the producer's Pacific Palisades estate, but they were treated well and got paid every Friday. In cash.

On the day that the handsome Diego boy called to Esme from his badass car, it had been a year since her parents had left her in Fresno. The pain of it had numbed down to a dull ache in Esme's chest. But she never let it show. To prove that she didn't need anyone, she became self-contained and self-sufficient, a quiet girl, a good girl who got good grades. The nuns told her how smart she was, how much potential she had. She could go to college. Do anything. Be anyone.

Though Esme and her friends had started sneaking lip gloss and rolling up the skirts of their uniforms and flirting with boys in the park, they'd giggle and run away together if a boy came on too strong. After all, they were just seventh graders. They had classmates who were already in gangs, and four girls in their grade were already pregnant. But Esme and her friends were light-years from either sex or gangs. They knew they didn't want to be mothers; they saw what gang membership had done to Ricardo. Both were dangerous.

Looking back, sometimes Esme thought it was the dangerous part that had made her talk to that Diego in the Caddy that day. And then, to get in his car, with one hand on the door handle in case he tried anything. His name was Nick. He was sixteen. He didn't do more than hold her other hand. She felt so grown up, sitting there next to him in that fine car.

She started looking for Nick after school—she loved showing

him off to all her friends. He invited her to parties, and she went. The Diegos accepted her. Some of them called their girl-friends "sheep" and said that ho sheep were only good for one thing. Sometimes they even hit these girls in front of everyone to prove how macho they were. Esme saw how the girls put up with it, because their boyfriends set them up with apartments. Many of them had babies; some had more than one. All of them were still teenagers.

But Nick wasn't down with any of that. Even when he and Esme got more intimate, he treated her with respect. When he saw that Esme was interested in his tattoos, he got one of the gang members to show her how it was done. She asked to han-dle the needle, and quickly became a skillful tattoo artist. She did tattoos for any Diego who wanted one. They paid her. She didn't allow herself to think about where the money came from, or how Nick had paid for that fine ride of his, or the gifts he be-stowed upon her—jewelry and expensive perfume that she hid from her aunt. After she left the house, she'd change into the sexy clothes he bought her and trick herself out like the hottest sheep. By the time she gave him her virginity, she was so in love that she would have done anything for him.

Then one day, she had to prove it.

Girls were made part of the Diegos in two ways: by being jumped in—fighting all the girls in the gang at once—or by sex-ing up as many boys as a roll of a pair of dice. Snake eyes? You were lucky. Double sixes? Get ready for the train. Esme was pet-rified that Nick would ask her to do one of these two things. But he didn't. Instead, he taught her how to drive.

She loved it. She loved him. One night, after they'd had sex, Esme was lying in his arms. He said he wanted to go for a ride and wanted Esme to drive. She felt so safe, cuddled next to his heartbeat, him smoothing hair off her face and kissing her forehead, that she said yes.

Esme was behind the wheel when it went down. Nick was in the passenger seat, two more Diegos in back. The RBs strode out of the neighborhood Taco Bell carrying tostadas to go, laughing about something. Nick called to them: "Eh, Razor Boys? Diegos *rifan*! Diegos rule!"

The gunshots were deafening. Four RBs fell, their Taco Bell salsa mixing with their blood on the sidewalk. One stumbled down the block before he fell, too. A sixth RB got away.

The car took off. Esme felt it wasn't really her foot on the gas or her white-knuckled hands on the wheel. Nor was it really Nick who sneered at her, "How you like that payback, little ho sheep?" before he pushed her out of the car, his friends laughing and jeering from the backseat.

Esme still liked puzzles; the pieces of this one came together in less time than it had taken Nick to murder her favorite cousin, Ricardo. Making her his girlfriend, taking her virginity, teaching her to drive, making her drive his car, it had all been a setup to hurt Ricardo's gang in the worst way possible. He had used Esme to do it, just because he could.

She'd called her parents immediately and said she had to come to Echo Park immediately. She was out of Fresno before Ricardo's coffin was in the ground, but discovered that the Echo Park neighborhood of Los Angeles was just as rough as where she'd lived in Fresno, just as gang-infested. Same shit, different toilet.

But she did everything she could to put her past behind her.

For two years now, she'd gotten almost straight As, stayed far away from the gangs, and tried to forget the terrible thing she'd done. She'd even found a best friend, a guy named Jorge Valdez. He was one of the Latin Kings, a group of guys who fought for the rights and prosperity of the universal Latino movement. In Jorge's case he did it through poetry, and the hip-hop lyrics he wrote for some local rappers. His raps were always about bettering *la Raza,* staying in school, or cautionary tales about gangsta life. When she was with Jorge, she could almost forget.

But sometimes, at the oddest times, it came back to her. Like now, as she got ready to meet her boyfriend, Junior. Twenty-two and a *veterano,* a gang veteran, Junior had gotten out of the life. The homies respected him because he respected them. He'd become a paramedic, the one who'd come to the Echo when other paramedics would rather sit on their fat asses and eat donuts than make a run to the latest gang bang.

Unfortunately, Junior and Jorge didn't get along. Junior thought Jorge was a coconut—a Latino trying to be white. Jorge had an equally low opinion of Junior. Ever since she'd hooked up with Junior, she and Jorge had been drifting apart. She missed him, but not enough to put up with his negative attitude toward Junior.

It was something, to be the girlfriend of one of the most powerful boys in the neighborhood. Esme enjoyed the status it gave her, and she liked to please him. Pleasing Junior meant dressing like a girly girl; he liked to be proud of his woman in front of his friends. Usually, Esme liked it, too. But not when she remembered. *"How you like that payback, little ho sheep?"*

"*Esme, Junior está* in the house. He says to come *rapidamente,* please!" Esme's six-year-old cousin Maria sang out in Spanglish from downstairs.

"*Gracias,*" Esme called back.

Junior was driving Esme to pick up her parents at the Goldhagens' estate. The television producer and his wife had recently sold their place in the Palisades and moved to an even larger property in Bel Air. The good news was that Esme's parents had a shorter drive to get to work—a half hour with not too much time on the freeway. But today, their ancient Chevy had broken down, so they'd taken the bus. Now, Junior and Esme were going to bring them home.

Esme came downstairs and kissed Junior while Maria watched, wide-eyed. Junior winked at Maria. "Someday you'll have a boyfriend too, pretty girl." Maria blushed and bolted, which made Junior chuckle sweetly.

They followed the directions that her father had given her— 134 freeway to the 101, then over the hill at Benedict Canyon. It dropped them into Bel Air, which was like visiting another planet. Row after row of mansions on lush properties, perfectly landscaped by people like Esme's father. Some of the homes were hidden behind high iron gates, where visitors had to be announced before the gates to paradise would open.

There was just such a closed gate guarding the Goldhagens' new estate. When Esme and Junior pulled into the driveway, they were stymied. No guard, and apparently no intercom system. Junior got out of his car to search for a way in, but it was fruitless. He peered between the bars to see if he could see anyone. Nothing. Esme joined him, but to no avail. Normally,

Esme was a model of efficiency, yet she hadn't remembered to bring the Goldhagens' telephone number. No way was it listed.

It was so humiliating standing there that Junior kicked the gate in frustration before slamming back into the car. The idea of driving all the way back to Echo Park, Land of the Have-Nots, for the phone number, and then again to Bel Air, Land of the Haves, made them both feel small.

When Esme heard the approaching sirens, she wondered where the fire was. She had no time to adjust that thought before two Bel Air community patrol cruisers roared into the driveway behind them and smoke-skidded to a stop.

"Both of you! Out of the car! Hands in the air!" came over one cruiser's bullhorn.

Holy shit, Esme thought. *They mean us.*

4

"Where are they going to meet us?" Jeanne McCann fretted as she and her daughter Kiley strode past the endless gates in Terminal One at Los Angeles International Airport. It was late Sunday afternoon; the airport was insane. It seemed like everyone and his mother was on his way to or from a flight.

"Baggage claim," Kiley told her mother for the third time. "There'll be a guy waiting down there for us. Don't worry."

"How will we know it's him? What if he's late? What if he doesn't show up at all?" Mrs. McCann asked. She and Kiley dodged past a large Sikh family—the men in big turbans and beards—and then avoided a girl with green hair wearing a see-through shirt with nothing on underneath but massive implants. "Did you *see* that, Kiley?"

"Couldn't miss it, Mom. Calm down. Everything is going to be fine."

"Kiley, what if there's no one here from that show of yours?"

"There will be, Mom."

"But if they aren't there, where are we supposed to go? Kiley? *Kiley?*"

Danger. Red alert. Kiley heard her mother's rising vocal tone and knew that she was but moments away from a full-blown, stop-her-in-her-tracks anxiety attack right in the middle of LAX.

If only her mom would get an actual prescription for her condition! But Mrs. McCann had been raised in the Christian Science Church and didn't believe in medicine. Family legend had it that when Jeanne McCann had fallen from a tree at the age of six and broken her arm, no doctor had been called. Kiley's grandmother and her daughter had prayed for the arm to heal, and it had.

Well, Kiley had done plenty of praying herself—about a decade's worth, in fact—that her mother would get a grip and see a doctor who'd prescribe some heavy-duty pharmaceuticals. Those prayers had gone unanswered, and the panic attacks had worsened. Mrs. McCann did try herbal remedies; the way she saw it, herbs did not count as chemical intervention. Nor did they work particularly well.

Kiley gently pulled her mom to one side of the corridor and let the bodies slide past them. "Just take some deep breaths. Nice and easy. In and out."

Mrs. McCann leaned against the wall, eyes closed, breathing. Kiley could see the pulse in her mother's neck slow a bit. "Better?"

Mrs. McCann nodded and opened her eyes. "Thanks, sweetie."

Kiley was still amazed that her mom had agreed to come

on this trip. Since Kiley was only seventeen, the producers of *Platinum Nanny* had insisted that a parent accompany her. Should Kiley actually win, her mom would either have to stay in Los Angeles or sign legal guardianship over to Platinum. Kiley had downplayed the giving-Platinum-legal-guardianship thing. One step at a time, she figured.

She gave her mom a reassuring smile. "Ready to go?"

"Absolutely." Mrs. McCann hoisted the strap of her bag up her shoulder. They joined the flow of traffic again, dodging as an airport golf cart went by. "Kiley?"

"Yeah, Mom?"

"Do you know the name of the hotel? Have you checked to see that there's really a reservation for us?"

Kiley gritted her teeth. "Yes and yes."

They trudged on. Five minutes later, they'd negotiated a people mover and an escalator that deposited them on the baggage claim level.

Kiley spotted the gorgeous young guy in the tieless black suit right away. He held a sheet of cardboard with McCann printed in thick black letters. For the first time since they'd left La Crosse very early that morning, Kiley relaxed. Doing her best to reassure her mom that everything was under control was hard work.

Mrs. McCann waved her arm at the driver. "We're McCann!"

The young man nodded. "Great. Welcome to L.A. Let's get your bags. Everyone else got here five hours ago. Where'd you come in from, anyway?"

As the driver led Kiley and Mrs. McCann to their baggage carousel, Kiley's mom launched into an extended, adrenaline-fueled monologue about La Crosse, including a proud boast about the town being the home of the world's largest six-pack of beer.

This was true. At the brewery where Kiley's father worked, water for the beer was stored in six huge cylindrical water towers. The towers were painted like beer cans, complete with the La Crosse Brewery logo. Aside from the periodic floods that swept through downtown, that six-pack was La Crosse's claim to fame.

Minutes later, bags in hand, the cute driver led Kiley and her mom to his black sedan. He loaded the bags into the trunk and ushered his passengers into the backseat. Then he snaked the car through airport traffic, heading for the exit. "We'll make the Hotel Bel-Air in about twenty minutes. Don't worry."

The traffic was bumper to bumper; Kiley wondered how they'd possibly be at the hotel so quickly. Instead of turning north toward the 405 freeway and Beverly Hills, the driver went south toward San Diego.

Mrs. McCann panicked. "Excuse me, young man, I think you're going the wrong way!"

"We're taking a shortcut." The driver flashed a movie star grin in the rearview mirror. Moments later, he pulled the limo alongside a helipad, where a six-seater chopper waited with its engines roaring.

"We're riding in *that*?" Kiley asked, incredulous.

"You betcha." He rolled down the window as two people from the show approached his door. Kiley recognized the young producer with the multiple piercings who'd interviewed her in Milwaukee. Except now her hair was black.

"Hey, great, you're here, let's go, we're late," the producer bellowed over the chopper's noise, then faced the driver. "Get their bags inside, dammit!"

27

Kiley turned to her mom. "Are you okay with this?"

Mrs. McCann's hand fluttered to her chest.

When the cameraman shoved his camera against the window of the sedan, Kiley took it as their cue to exit on the opposite side. The cameraman kept filming as they made their way into the chopper and strapped themselves into two empty seats.

"You ladies ready?" the pilot asked as the producer climbed aboard. "Doors closed. We're good to go." The pilot flipped a few switches and handled the controls; instantly, the helicopter jerked straight up into the air. "We'll be cruising at two thousand feet," he told his passengers. "ETA at the Hotel Bel-Air in eight minutes. Service with a smile."

Moments later, the chopper was heading north, high above the 405 freeway; Kiley could see the traffic at a dead standstill in both directions. Mercifully, her mother had been scared silent.

"Mrs. McCann?" the cameraman said. "You look a little green."

"Mom?"

Her mother closed her eyes and started to hyperventilate, lips pressed in a thin line. This was not good. Kiley spotted an airsickness bag tucked behind the pilot's seat. She grabbed it and placed it in her mother's hands.

"Breathe into that, Mom." Her mother complied. The camera guy grinned and kept shooting, which pissed Kiley off. She splayed her hand over the lens, not about to let her mother be humiliated on national TV. "Stop. Now. I mean it."

The producer frowned. "Look, let's get this straight," she shouted over the noise of the helicopter. "You signed up for this gig. You don't get to tell us what to film. Check the contract!"

Jeanne McCann opened her eyes. "I'm so sorry," she whispered to no one in particular, the paper bag in her lap. The camera guy produced a bottle of water and handed it to Mrs. McCann. She took a couple of careful sips.

As they headed north, Kiley pressed her face against the helicopter's curved window. The west side of Los Angeles sprawled beneath them—they were passing over UCLA. The view was jaw-droppingly beautiful, clear enough to see well out into the Pacific, where aqua water stretched to the horizon.

The ocean. *Her* ocean.

Think Scripps, she reminded herself. *I am here for a reason. But I don't have to put up with these people being assholes to me or to my mom.*

She turned to the producer. "Can I ask you something?" Kiley took her cocked eyebrow to mean yes. "In La Crosse—that's in Wisconsin, by the way—we do this thing called introducing ourselves to each other. How it works is, one person says her name, and then waits for the other person to say hers. And then they shake hands. Hi, I'm Kiley McCann." She stuck out her hand toward the producer. "You're—?"

The producer offered an eye-roll, then a limp hand. "Bronwyn Brown. Associate producer."

"Nice to meet you, Bronwyn. I think it's time that I told you the real reason why I came here."

"What?"

Kiley let a small smile curl over her lips. "I came to win."

5

"Ms. McCann, Mrs. McCann, welcome to the Hotel Bel-Air," said the young man at the front desk. Tall and rangy, he had the chiseled good looks of a soap opera boy toy. Did they only let gorgeous guys into L.A.? "Your welcome packet from *Platinum Nanny* is in your room."

"Are the other girls here?" Kiley asked, glancing around for her competition.

The desk clerk shook his head. "They're on a shopping trip to the Beverly Center. Of course, with the traffic out there, you might be the ones ahead of the game." He smiled broadly at Kiley with Chiclet white teeth.

"Are our bags in our room?" Mrs. McCann asked.

"Of course, Mrs. McCann," the desk clerk said smoothly. He handed over a set of key cards. "Suite four-oh-one."

"You're *sure* our bags are there?" Mrs. McCann asked.

"I'm certain of it," said the desk guy, without any hint of irritation. Kiley noticed his nameplate: David.

"Thanks again, David," Kiley said. At the mention of his name, David's kilowatt smile went into overdrive.

"Happy to be of service. Anything we can do to make your stay more pleasant, you let us know. James will show you to your suite."

Kiley turned. James—another tall hunk of burning love, in the same dark gray suit that David wore, offered Kiley a dimpled grin and a sweeping gesture. "Right this way."

James led daughter, mother, and the omnipresent *Platinum Nanny* cameraman out of the elegant reception area into the lush gardens for which the Hotel Bel-Air was famous. As he walked, he relayed a brief history of the hotel, running down the list of celebrities who called the place their second home.

Impressed, Mrs. McCann didn't interrupt him. Even more impressive to Kiley was the care that had been taken in constructing the place. The architects had designed the hotel with low-slung buildings that seemed to be part of the surrounding hillside. And the greenery was world-class, better than anything Kiley had ever seen on television.

"This place looks like the Garden of Eden," Kiley told James.

"Adam and Eve didn't have five-star twenty-four-hour room service," James pointed out, and stopped at a solid white door with a gold plate that read 401. "Shall I?" He held up the access card that fit into the door.

"I'll do it," Mrs. McCann said. "This way we'll know if it sticks."

"Excellent," James agreed, without a hint of superciliousness.

Mrs. McCann slid the access card into the door. It opened easily.

"Enjoy," James told them. "Call if you need anything at all."

"And if we lose the little card thing?" Mrs. McCann asked.

"Just let them know at the front desk, ma'am." With one last dazzling smile, James departed.

Kiley and her mom stepped into their suite, a spacious and impeccably decorated two-bedroom apartment. There were Persian rugs on the floor, original late-twentieth-century gouaches on the walls, and a gorgeous floral display on the coffee table. The living room featured a big-screen TV, state-of-the-art computer, and flat-screen monitor.

"This is amazing," Kiley said, heading into a full kitchen, furnished in Swedish modern. A basket of fresh fruit rested on the marble counter. Kiley opened the fridge; it had been stocked with food. "Wow is an understatement, huh, Mom?"

Mrs. McCann stuck her head through the open doorway. "It ought to be double wow. I read the sign on the back of the front door. It's two thousand three hundred dollars a night. That's more than I earn in a month. And our luggage is definitely here. I checked."

There was an awkward moment of silence. Then Kiley impulsively hugged her mother. "Let's try to enjoy the lap of luxury, okay? Want to go for a swim?"

"I think I'll just lie down for a bit," Jeanne McCann replied. "I saw a manila envelope on the bed," she added. "From your show."

Kiley went to the bedroom—the packet was on the pillow. She tore it open; inside was a DVD. Kiley inserted the disc in the bedroom's combination TV/DVD player and it started automatically. Loud rock and roll filled the air, followed by concert footage of Platinum. Then Platinum herself grinned at the camera, her signature platinum blond hair reaching her waist. Her tanned skin was silken perfection, her makeup so well applied that she looked as if she was fresh-scrubbed. She wore white.

"Hello," Platinum said, with the faintest tinge of a British accent. "Welcome to *Platinum Nanny*. I'm so glad that you're here. What you are about to experience will change your life, and change the face of television forever. It also should result in a perfect nanny for my three children."

Platinum went on to explain that a series of challenges would eliminate contender after contender, until there was but one *Platinum Nanny* candidate remaining.

"And now," Platinum went on, as captioned images of all the contestants flashed on the screen, "here's your chance to meet the other contestants."

Kiley peered intently at the screen.

Cindy Wu, age eighteen, San Francisco, California. Incoming freshman at Stanford University.

Naomi Steinberg. Nicknamed Steinberg. Age nineteen, Rye, New York. Performance artist.

Tamika Jones, age eighteen, Carson, California. Rap artist.

Veronique Lecouturier, age twenty-two, Paris, France. Professional nanny.

Jimmy Jackson, age eighteen, Starkville, Mississippi. Star quarterback.

Her own face. Kiley McCann, age seventeen, La Crosse, Wisconsin. Incoming senior, La Crosse High School. And then, to her surprise, her mother's. Jeanne McCann, age forty-three, La Crosse, Wisconsin.

33

Platinum returned to the screen. "I just wanted to extend a welcome to all of you. Especially to Kiley's mother. Can't have little Kiley without a chaperone!" She winked at the camera, and then the screen went blank.

Kiley turned to see her mom in the doorway, staring at the TV, too. She had a sick feeling in her stomach. Suddenly, it all made sense. "Know what, Mom? I'm the joke."

"Huh?"

"The joke," Kiley repeated. "That's why I'm here. I'm the high school kid who had to bring her mom."

"It's a little late for regret, Kiley." Her mother sat next to her on the bed.

"What was I thinking? I never should have done this."

Mrs. McCann got in her daughter's face. "You are a lot of things, Kiley, but a quitter isn't one of them. You just turn that joke right back on them."

"And just how am I supposed to do that?"

"Just because I was sick on the ride over here doesn't mean I didn't hear what you said."

Kiley sighed. "What?"

"That you came to win, Kiley." She took both of her daughter's hands in hers. "You came to *win*."

6

Esme had enough experience with police to know just what to do: follow their orders exactly. She edged out of Junior's car, making sure her hands were visible at all times. Meanwhile, Junior slid out the driver's side.

"Hands on the hood! Both of you!" A cop was bellowing at them over his cruiser's bullhorn.

Esme felt ridiculous, putting her hands on the hood of the car. It was something out of a bad movie—the cops ducking behind their open car doors, guns at the ready for the shoot-out with the big, bad criminals. Right. If only they knew that they were accosting a paramedic and an honor student.

At one cop's signal, the others leaped forward and patted down Esme and Junior for weapons, screaming at them not to move. Esme suffered through the pat-down with as much dignity as possible. She knew that for some police, it was a sick power game. But here in Bel Air? When all she was doing was picking up her parents at work?

"What the hell is going on here?"

The voice shouting those words from the other side of the security fence had so much authority that everyone—Junior, Esme, and the four officers of the Bel Air law—looked to see who was doing the shouting. It was a tall, bearded man in his late forties. He wore faded jeans, a tennis shirt, and a blue Los Angeles Dodgers baseball cap.

"Possible intruders, Mr. Goldhagen," the older cop explained.

Esme had to risk it, though she'd never actually met her parents' boss. "No way! I'm Esme Castaneda! I'm here to pick up my parents!"

Mr. Goldhagen gave the cops a look that was both pleasant and pointed. "Fellas?"

The uniformed men exchanged a sheepish glance. "Just doing our job," the youngest cop said, but he slid his gun back into its holster.

The cops returned to their cruisers as Mr. Goldhagen pushed a hidden button and the iron security gate swung open. Junior glared at him. "What's up with your gate, man?"

"I apologize, it doesn't seem to be working properly. I'm Steve Goldhagen, by the way." He held his hand out to Junior.

"Raoul Hernandez," Junior said, reluctantly shaking Mr. Goldhagen's hand. Esme knew that there was no way he would reveal his G-name, Junior. Junior got the moniker for his older brother, who'd died in a shoot-out. It was that shoot-out that had made Junior "drop the flag"—leave the gang.

Mr. Goldhagen motioned to Esme to come through the open

36

gate. "I've heard a lot of great things about you from your mother. I'm sorry that this is the way we're meeting."

Esme managed a slight nod.

Junior was still fuming. "All we wanted to do was get past your damn gate. You trying to get us killed?"

"I really am sorry," Mr. Goldhagen said. "We just moved in and the gate's been acting hinky. There's no buzzer or telephone box down here; we see everything on closed-circuit TV up at the house. I pushed the button up there, but something didn't work. I got down here as fast as I could."

"Not quite fast enough," Junior said, his eyes hard.

Esme laid a hand on Junior's arm. "He apologized," she said softly.

"Would you two like to come in?" Mr. Goldhagen offered.

Junior shook his head.

"You can wait here then," Esme said. "I'll get my parents."

"This neighborhood makes me nervous," Junior told Esme under his breath.

But Mr. Goldhagen overheard, and shoved his hands deep into the pockets of his jeans. "How about I have my driver take Esme and her parents home? I really am sorry for what just happened."

"Thank you, sir. But Raoul will wait for me." She turned to her boyfriend. "Right, Raoul?"

Junior took a few steps backward and shook his head. "I'm outta here." He strode back to the car, started the engine, turned the car around, and headed back toward Benedict Canyon. Esme found this as humiliating as their stop by the cops. How could Junior just leave like that?

"Hey, I don't blame him," Mr. Goldhagen said, trying to lighten the mood. "I'd be upset, too."

Except that would never happen to you, Esme thought.

Mr. Goldhagen guided Esme toward a golf cart parked just inside the gate. "Is that young man your boyfriend? He seems a little tense."

"Yes to both. It makes him mad when someone judges him without even knowing him."

Mr. Goldhagen nodded. It was a five-minute ride up the winding hillside; there were moments when the driveway was so steep Esme feared that gravity would drag them all the way down to the Pacific. But Mr. Goldhagen kept the accelerator on the floorboard. Somehow, they made it, and stopped at the top. He pointed behind the house. "Your parents are out back, working in the guesthouse. Just follow the signs. Nice to meet you, Esme."

"You too, sir."

Mr. Goldhagen waved and started up the cobblestone path that led to the front door of the most magnificent mansion Esme had ever seen, including on TV and in the movies. It was built of natural woods, with huge, soaring windows, sloped roofs, and a series of cascading reflecting pools that produced a constant, lulling white noise. For the briefest moment, Esme felt a hot flush of jealousy. No way would she ever get to live someplace this beautiful, no matter how hard she worked in her life.

Then she shrugged, knowing she should be content with what she had. She'd been an accomplice to a crime—an unwilling accomplice but an accomplice nonetheless—and was still walking around a free woman. Her father had assaulted an Anglo—in defense of a friend but assaulted him nonetheless—

and was walking around a free man. She knew they both could easily be doing hard time.

Esme followed a gravel path around the mansion. Then she saw something that made her stop: two dark-haired little girls who looked to be about six, playing on a swing set. They were watched by a thin woman in a Vassar College sweatshirt who was easily fifteen years younger than Mr. Goldhagen. Leashed to the bench on which she sat was a champagne-colored poodle with a pink bow in its hair, and matching pink nail polish on its nails.

One of the girls singsonged a Spanish nursery rhyme as she pumped back and forth on the swing:

> *Uno, dos, tres, cho!*
> *Uno, dos, tres, co!*
> *Uno, dos, tres, la!*
> *Uno, dos, tres, te!*

Esme couldn't help herself. She came right back with the re-joinder she'd sung so many times when she was a child herself:

> *Bate, bate, chocolate!*

The girls stopped swinging and turned to Esme, as did the skinny woman.

"Who are you?" the woman asked.

"Alberto and Estella Castaneda's daughter—"

"Esme!" the woman filled in with a smile. "I'm Diane Gold-hagen. What a pleasure!"

So, this was Mr. Goldhagen's wife. The closer Esme came to

39

her, the more beautiful Esme could see she was. High cheek-bones, full lips, and thick blond hair.

"Nice to meet you, ma'am," Esme said dutifully.

"Please, call me Diane," the woman said. She turned to the children. "And these are our twin daughters, Easton and Weston."

Esme was surprised; her parents had never mentioned that the Goldhagens had young children, let alone identical twins. The only difference between them was that one wore a pink T-shirt and the other a blue one.

"No es verdad." The little girl in the blue T-shirt ran to Esme and grabbed her sleeve. *"No me llamo* Easton. *Me llamo Isabella, pero mi madre me llama* Easton *ahora. Qué significa* Easton?"

"Esme, you speak Spanish. What did she say?" Diane asked.

The little girl had said that her name was Isabella and that she didn't know why her new mom had named her Easton. Esme had no idea, either. But there had already been enough cultural friction for one day.

"She said she adores her name," Esme lied.

Diane's face lit up. "Really? That's so great! You know, it's been quite a challenge, not speaking their language." She lifted a pocket English-Spanish dictionary. "I'm trying, but I'm pretty hopeless."

Esme nodded, curious. Obviously the girls were Latina; Diane and Steve Goldhagen were not.

"It's a long story," Diane went on. "I was in Colombia—Cali, Colombia—on a UNICEF trip. We certainly weren't planning to adopt. But then these two little girls were introduced to me." She turned and smiled at the twins. "And I lost my heart."

"I can see why," Esme said. It was true; the girls were incredibly cute.

"So I called Steven and he said yes—he was in the middle of a hellacious shoot so I'm not sure he was tracking." Diane laughed nervously. "We already have Jonathan, he's eighteen. And Steven always said he didn't want more kids."

The toy poodle at her feet barked and jumped into Diane's lap. "I'm sorry, Cleo," the woman cooed, petting the dog, "I should have counted you, too." Diane smiled at Esme. "Cleopatra thinks she's a child, it's so cute. I'm not the kind of woman to have a fussy little dog, really I'm not. Cleo was an anniversary present from Elizabeth Taylor last year. She introduced me to Steven."

Esme nodded. She had no idea why the woman was telling her any of this.

"Anyway," Diane went on. She swept her arms toward her new daughters. "A canine baby isn't the same as a real baby— that's what I told Steven. The paperwork was accelerated and . . . here are my girls! I brought them home yesterday."

She motioned for Esme to sit next to her on the wrought-iron love seat. Esme sat and looked in wonder at the children. Their lives had to be so different now. "What happened to their parents?" Esme asked quietly.

"I've decided that's their story to tell—or not tell. Not mine."

Esme nodded. If she ignored the overdone poodle, she might actually be able to like this woman.

"Excuse me, Mrs. Goldhagen." A uniformed maid had just hustled toward them from the main house. With a pang, Esme realized that somewhere on the property was her mother, probably wearing the exact same uniform.

"Yes, Selma?"

"The groomer is here from Puppy Love's Traveling Show," the maid said. "They want to know can they park the groom-o-bile by the front door?"

"The side door, please, Selma," Diane said as she untied Cleo's leash and handed the pooch over to the maid. "Oh, I'm expecting Gelson's to deliver the groceries," she added. "If you could please supervise and make sure the filet mignon ends up in the downstairs freezer this time? And put the live lobster in the tank until Mr. Richard needs them for dinner, would you?"

"Yes, certainly," Selma agreed. The dog growled at her, baring its teeth.

"Stop, Cleo!" Diane scolded the pooch. "Have them switch her bow and polish to zebra-striped for this month, okay? Wouldn't that look cute?"

"Very cute, ma'am," the maid said dutifully, then trotted off with the dog.

Diane turned back to Esme, a finger to her lips. "Where was I? Oh, right. I was just thinking . . . you're Mexican—"

"American," Esme corrected.

"Of course, sorry. But your parents—well, you can't imagine what a godsend they are to us, we couldn't function without them—they're Mexican."

"Yes. From Ciudad Juarez."

Diane suddenly smiled. "I should take advantage of you while I've got you here. My high school Spanish is horrible. Could you tell the children that we'll go inside in ten minutes so that they can have a bath before dinner?"

"Sure." Esme turned to the girls. *"Escucha, Isabella. Cómo se llama su hija?"*

"Juana."

"Qué bueno. Escúchame, todo los dos. Vamos a la casa en diez minutos. Necesitais tener un baño. Y después, hay comida, a las seis. Bueno?"

"Sí," Isabella declared. *"Cómo se llama?"*

"Esme. Esme Castaneda."

"Qué bueno, doña Esme. Yo entiendo y comprendo ahora. Es muy difícil con una madre que no habla español. Hay mucha gente en los Estados Unidos que hablan español como usted?

"Demasiado. Soon, you will learn English," Esme told her. *"Necesitas trabajar con su inglés."*

"Sí," Easton said. Weston nodded. Then Easton put her head down on Esme's lap. Esme stroked her hair, thinking how much the twins looked like her little cousin, Jacqueline.

Ricardo's sister Jacqueline. Dead Ricardo. Murdered Ricardo.

7

"My girls seem to have fallen for you," Diane commented as the kids went back to the swings. She sighed. "I need to learn Spanish. It's so hard to make the time, you know? I mean, I work ten, twelve hours a day sometimes. I was overscheduled before I adopted them."

Esme nodded, curious. "What do you do?"

Diane ran a hand through her hair. "Oh, Lord, there's so much." She began ticking things off her perfectly French-manicured fingers. "There's my work with UNICEF—most people don't know it still exists. I'm on the board of the Getty Center, and the Jewish Federation, of course. And I'm one of the chairs for Susan Pelcarovic's EU-phoria Ball every year—we raise money to support international culture. Then there's the gym, facials, manicures—just basic upkeep. There just aren't enough hours in the day."

Esme tried to keep a pleasant look on her face. So, Diane didn't work at an actual job. What had her so overextended was volunteering and personal grooming.

"The girls will learn English quickly, you'll see," Esme told her. "Faster, if you don't speak Spanish."

"I don't want their adjustment to be too difficult," Diane said.

Adjustment. Esme found that notion hilarious. These children had just landed in an America where the streets really *were* paved with gold.

"You can always ask my mom to help. Her English is better than my dad's."

Diane nodded. "I hate to bother them."

"Well, there are a zillion Spanish speakers in L.A. you can call. And I'm available for emergency translation. Anyway, I guarantee that in three months their English will be functional. In a year, they'll speak it better than we do. And they'll tell you so, too."

Diane gave Esme an admiring look. "I just might take you up on your offer." She stood. Esme stood, too. "Anyway, your parents are doing some painting in the guesthouse. It's up that red-brick path past the tennis court. It was so nice meeting you, Esme." She held out her hand again.

"You, too," Esme replied, shaking it.

When Diane started up toward the main house with the girls, Esme followed the path. She passed the tennis court, where a college-age guy and girl were hitting together. With their perfect tans and tennis clothes, they looked like a magazine ad for rich, white perfection.

A few hundred feet past the tennis court was the guesthouse.

It was actually more like a second home, with its own parking area, a basketball hoop, a veranda with white wicker rocking chairs, and two orange trees flanking the entrance.

"Mama? Papa?" Esme stepped inside. The odor of fresh paint was overwhelming.

"*Yo estoy aquí!*" She followed her father's voice to the guest-house bathroom. At the moment, he was contemplating an old-fashioned toilet with a rubber plunger.

"Where is Junior?" her father asked in Spanish.

"A long story," Esme replied, waving away his question. "Mr. Goldhagen is having someone drive us home."

Her father put a hand to his lower back and winced. "Ay. Can you take this?" he asked, holding the plunger out to her. "I need to help your mama carry paint up from the basement. You know what to do here."

Esme had dressed for Junior, not for manual labor. "But Papa—"

"Don't 'But Papa' me, Esme. The sooner we finish, the sooner we can go."

Esme took the plunger from her father. She'd fixed their toilet at home many times—it wasn't as if they could afford a plumber. Crouching, she felt behind the toilet for the water valve to check if her father had turned it off. It twisted easily to the right, which meant he'd forgotten. After turning it as far as it would go, she stood and gave the bowl a few good pushes with the plunger. Then she pulled on the antique overhead chain, to make the toilet flush properly.

It flushed, all right. But *up* instead of down. Esme was forced to jump back to avoid the fountain of raw sewage that sprayed down onto her sandals.

"Shit!" she exclaimed.

"Exactly," said a deep voice behind her.

She whirled around. A fantastic-looking guy with short brown hair, startling blue eyes, and the rangy build of a born athlete stood outside the bathroom door. It was the guy from the tennis court—he still held his racquet. The girl he'd been playing—blond hair in a ponytail, sapphire eyes, and a heart-shaped mouth—stood a few feet behind him. The guy had a bemused smile on his face.

God, he was hot. Why the hell did he have to be so hot?

"Whoever you are, go away," Esme said, her face burning with embarrassment.

"I can't, I live here. Need some help?"

Esme scowled. "No." Stepping gingerly through the muck, she leaned over and lifted the top off the tank. It was filled to the brim.

"I think you forgot to turn off the water," the boy said.

"No, I didn't," Esme snapped. "Your valve is messed up. Do you know where I can find some pliers?"

"Gee, I don't think he has any pliers in his toolbox," the blond girl said, oozing attitude. She snaked an arm around the boy's waist from behind.

Bitch.

"Is there a main shutoff outside, at least?" Esme asked the guy.

He shrugged. "No idea."

"Excuse me." Esme squished past the couple and went outside to locate the water line that fed into the house. She quickly spotted the old-fashioned crank and twisted it, but it didn't budge. Another hard spin made it give way. Several revolutions later, the water to the house was off.

Next she went back inside to search for supplies to clean up the disaster she'd created. When she got back to the bathroom with her arms full of ancient copies of the *Los Angeles Times,* the handsome guy and his golden girlfriend were gone, thank God. But almost as bad: Mr. Goldhagen and his wife stood there. Esme's heart dipped to her crap-covered sandals. What if she got her parents fired because of this screwup?

"I'm really sorry about the mess," Esme began. "I made sure the water valve was closed, but . . ." She glanced down at the sewage. "I'll take care of everything. I promise."

"Don't worry about it," Mr. Goldhagen said. "We've already called a pro. One of the neighbors told us this toilet hadn't been used since Cary Grant owned the place."

Cary Grant. An old movie star, though Esme was fairly certain she'd never seen any of his movies.

"Anyway, Esme," Mr. Goldhagen went on. "The reason we wanted to talk to you is . . . my wife noticed how good you are with our kids."

"Selina's giving them a bath," Diane added. "When I peeked in, she told me that the girls keep chattering on and on about their new friend, Esme."

Esme smiled. "That's sweet."

"And obviously you're bilingual," Mr. Goldhagen said. "Which is key. So, we were thinking you might like to spend more time with the girls. We'd pay you, of course. Sound good?"

Not really. Yes, the twins were cute. But they reminded her too much of her cousin Jacqueline. And she already had a job doing tattoos in the Echo. Why would she want to change?

"I don't think so," Esme said. "Thank you for asking."

"Are you sure?" Diane asked. "Because I was thinking of putting a job listing up at UCLA and USC: Bilingual nanny, five hundred a week, plus guesthouse and use of a car."

Esme was lucky if she cleared two hundred dollars doing tattoos. "Did you say five hundred dollars a week? To look after the girls and clean your house?"

"Oh no, no cleaning," Diane assured her.

"You're interested," Mr. Goldhagen surmised.

"Maybe."

"Then let's take it one step at a time," Diane suggested. "What if we do a two-week trial? That way, we can all see if it works."

Esme hesitated. It was so overwhelming—one minute the police were barring her and Junior from the estate, and the next she was offered a job. "What happens with school, in the fall?"

"Well, if things work out, we'll arrange your hours around classes," Diane said. She turned to her husband. "I guess she'd go to Bel Air High School."

Mr. Goldhagen nodded. "You probably wouldn't want to leave all your friends. You could always drive back to . . ."

"Echo Park," Esme finished for him, realizing that her parents' employers weren't exactly sure where their employees lived. "We live in Echo Park."

The prospect of choosing Echo Park High School over Bel Air High School almost made her laugh. The only school friend she'd miss would be Jorge. There would be no hardship in leaving behind detectors and gang wars and drive-bys on school property.

Diane tented her fingers. "You'd live right here. With a functioning toilet, I promise. We'll give you a cell, and one of the cars so that you can get the girls where they need to go. The Audi, Steven?"

Mr. Goldhagen nodded. "The Audi."

A cell phone *and* a house *and* an Audi *and* five hundred dollars a week? She had to be dreaming. There had to be a catch.

Suddenly, Esme thought of Junior. What would he think if she said yes? That she was turning her back on her homies? That she had sold out? A flood of guilt raged through her. And shame. She had almost done it: turned her back on who she was, what she was, and where she came from, just because some rich white people were dangling prizes like she was a contestant on some game show.

"I'm honored you'd think of me," Esme said stiffly. "But I can't do it."

"Of course she can," said a strong female voice from behind the Goldhagen clan. It was Esme's mother, Estella Castaneda. She stood in the doorway holding two five-gallon cans of paint. "Not only that, she starts tomorrow."

"Oh. Oh, God. Oh, baby!"

Kiley's eyes snapped open. She had no clue where she was. But as her eyes adjusted to the darkness, lit only by a night-light in the bathroom, she saw her opulent suite. Right. Sunday night. Los Angeles. Hotel Bel-Air.

"Ohh. That's so good!"

Voices came through the wall behind her bed that separated her from the next suite. Evidently, someone—no, two someones—were making better—and noisier—use of their bedroom than she was.

"Oh, oh, oh . . . !"

God. How embarrassing. She was just glad that her mom couldn't hear this. Kiley rolled over and tried to ignore the symphony of lust.

"Ohhhhhhh!"

Jeez, what the hell were they *doing* in there?

Kiley crammed the pillow over her head to block out the sound, but it seemed like the moans and groans got louder to compensate. They went on, and on, and on.

And on.

In the morning, bleary-eyed Kiley and her mother ordered a room service breakfast—the very first of their lives. It arrived on a white-draped silver cart: lobster omelets draped with orange marigolds, fresh squeezed juice, and a selection of just-baked breads and pastries. The handsome waiter—was there any other kind of hotel help in Los Angeles?—explained in a French-accented voice that the marigolds on the omelet were edible.

Bon appétit.

When the meal was finished, Kiley checked her watch. She was supposed to rendezvous in an hour in the lobby with the producers and other contestants, which gave her enough time to walk around the sumptuous hotel grounds and maybe buy some postcards for her friends back in La Crosse, in case today turned out to be her last day in paradise. Her mom wanted to stay in the room, so Kiley pocketed the security card and stepped outside.

At that exact moment, a guy came out of the suite next door.

That suite. It had to be *that* guy.

He was drop-dead gorgeous. The limo driver, David in hotel reception, and James the bellboy were dirtbags compared to *that* guy. About six feet tall, he looked like Brad Pitt circa *Thelma & Louise,* a movie Kiley and her mom had once watched to-gether on the small TV in her parents' bedroom, because Dad was passed out drunk in the living room. Holy shit. No one should be that good-looking. If there were only so many good-looking genes in the world, some poor guy was butt ugly so that this guy could look like . . . well, like *this*.

"Hi, neighbor," he said, grinning at Kiley. "I'm Tom."

Yep. The voice matched. *"Ohh. That's so good!"*

Tom's fun and games of the night before flew into Kiley's head, accompanied by psychographics of him with some lucky bitch. The girl, who was probably as perfect-looking as Tom, was probably still asleep in his bed, wearing nothing but a belly ring and a satiated grin.

He held out his hand to Kiley—a large, strong hand with really large, long fingers. "And you are—?"

"Kiley," she managed, in a strangled voice. She shook his hand as quickly as possible.

"What brings you to the Hotel Bel-Air?" Tom asked.

Great. He wanted to be friendly. But the pornographic thoughts Kiley was thinking made "friendly" pretty impossible.

"I . . . have to go," Kiley blurted out, and strode off toward the hotel gift shop.

Of course, it turned out he was going to the gift shop too. "This hotel is beautiful, isn't it?" he asked, as if she hadn't just made a total ass out of herself.

Brilliant conversationalist that she was, she nodded.

"And the food. Killer."

She nodded again.

"Do you work out?" Tom asked, as if he and Kiley had been carrying on a friendly little chat. "Because they'll give you a free pass to the Century Club in Beverly Hills."

"I don't do gyms," Kiley said. "I swim."

"Hey, in my book, that's working out."

Right. Of course it was. She sounded like an imbecile.

"You know, I can show you the indoor pool, if you like," Tom offered. "The outdoor one is kind of overrun with 'check me out' types. But if you want—"

"Oops. I . . . just remembered. I left something back in my suite." Kiley turned and fled. She didn't stop until she was safely back inside suite 401, where her mom was sprawled on the couch watching *Good Day L.A.* Kiley recognized one of the hosts from a syndicated TV dating show.

"That didn't take long," her mother commented.

"I changed my mind."

"Okay, sweetie."

"Right."

Kiley went into her bedroom and closed the door. She was met by an antique mirror over her dresser; she couldn't help but study her reflection. Reddish brown hair caught up in a pony-tail. Average height, average weight, average, average, average. Maybe she looked cute when she wore Heather the slut's clothes and piled on the makeup. But that wasn't the real her.

Still, she couldn't help it. She leaned toward her reflection and tried out some of the dialogue she'd heard through the wall the night before.

"Ohhhh. Oh, yes."

God. She felt like an idiot and she looked like an idiot. But she couldn't help wondering what it would be like to have a boy carry her away to the place he'd taken that girl last night. A boy, say, like Tom.

9

Thwack.

"Stretch at top of serve, Oksana!" Anya yelled. "Stretch at top!"

Lydia lay on a chaise longue clad in a bikini the size of three postage stamps. She had a Stoli 007 in hand—the moms, as she had come to think of her aunt Kat and her spouse, Anya, had a very European attitude toward drinking, which was just fine with Lydia. At the moment, she lay twenty feet from an aquamarine swimming pool shaped like a tennis racquet. A hundred feet beyond that was the tennis court where Anya was coaching seventeen-year-old Oksana Kharlamova, currently seeded sixty-first in the world. Both Russian natives were so used to speaking English that they were conducting the lesson in their adopted tongue.

Lydia stretched and practically purred with satisfaction. Though she'd been back in the USA for a mere twenty-four hours, her eight and a half years in the rain forest already seemed like a bad dream. Oh sure, the airplane's approach to LAX had been surreal—instead of thrilling her, the city sprawl from the ocean to the eastern horizon had given Lydia the willies. But Kat had met her plane and there was no reason to battle baggage claim, since all Lydia's worldly possessions fit neatly into the threadbare backpack she'd carried on board.

After getting caught up on the family gossip, and telling Kat a bit about her life in the Amazon, Lydia had fallen asleep on the ride home. Kat hadn't awakened her until they were in the driveway of her home in Beverly Hills; Lydia had stepped from the limo to find herself in front of a boxy white stucco mansion. It featured four massive pillars playing sentry to elegant gold-inlaid double front doors.

This was Kat and Anya's home. Now, *her* home.

Immediately, she was shown to the guesthouse where she'd be living, a cozy one-bedroom place just steps from the back door of the main mansion. Kat offered food, but all Lydia wanted was more sleep. She fell out instantly, on a king-sized oak bed with a lavender silk canopy.

Six hours later, she awakened, ravenous.

She went to the main house to find the kitchen, which took a while. In the state-of-the-art stainless-steel and mosaic-tile room, she encountered a slim young woman in yoga pants. The woman said her name was Alfre—she was Kat and Anya's nutritionist. Would Lydia like some fresh carrot-beet-orange juice?

Actually, Lydia preferred a giant, greasy cheeseburger laden with sliced pastrami, just like the ones she remembered from her favorite childhood diner in Houston. Also, a truckload of crisp french fries and an extrathick vanilla milk shake. All the foods she'd dreamed about while munching on roast monkey in the land of the Amarakaire.

Ask and ye shall receive. Though it was nearly ten o'clock at night, the nutritionist summoned the chef. Twenty minutes later, Lydia was eating exactly what she'd ordered. Then she'd gone back to bed, awakened, and ordered the exact same meal for breakfast. It was served to her no questions asked on the outdoor patio, along with the latest edition of *Vogue*.

Perhaps best of all, there were no kids yet to look after. Her two cousins, soon to be in her charge, would not be back from camp until Thursday. As for Kat, she'd departed that morning for Bristol, Connecticut, to attend some big powwow with the ESPN brass. Lydia had nothing to do but spend the morning lounging around . . . which brought her to where she was right now: poolside, drink in hand.

Bliss. Lydia took another sip of the 007 and mentally toasted her new life. Anything she could possibly want was available; all she had to do was pick up the small phone that sat on the glass table to her right. Press one for a maid. Press two for the chef. Unfortunately, there was no "Press three for a hot guy," but that could be taken care of on her own. And soon. She hadn't been about to lose her virginity to some five-foot-nothing Amazonian warrior with brown teeth. But she was sure she could find just the right American warrior prince to do the manly deed.

She closed her eyes, embraced by the sun. Long live Princess Lydia.

"Your aunt works me very hard."

Lydia opened her eyes to see Oksana plop down on the chaise next to hers. She wore white shorts and a blue-and-white Nike sports bra, her sun-bleached blond hair tied back in a

57

braid, her skin golden. Over her shoulder was a white towel monogrammed with Kat and Anya's initials.

"You are Lydia, yes?" Oksana had only the slightest Russian accent.

Lydia nodded.

"I am Oksana. Your aunt Anya is my coach."

"She's not my aunt," Lydia explained, propping herself up on her elbows. "She's my aunt's partner."

Oksana gave a small shrug and sipped from a water bottle before she spoke again. "Then she is aunt, too." She pointed to the monogram on the towel. "*K* for Kat, *A* for Anya. They have told me about you. You live in jungle before this, yes?"

Jungle, rain forest, whatever.

"Something like that."

"How are you liking Beverly Hills?"

Lydia smiled. "I am loving Beverly Hills." She reached for her Stoli 007. "Would you like a drink?"

Oksana shook her head. "Not during season. Only between Thanksgiving and ten days after New Year's. Forty-five days of normal." She patted her taut, muscular stomach. "What are you doing now?"

Lydia's smile grew. "Not a damn thing."

Oksana draped the towel back over her shoulder. "I must go shower. But later . . . maybe you would like to do something instead of nothing. I will go to De Sade tonight. Would you like to come with me?"

Lydia knew about De Sade. A few months ago, one of the visiting doctors had brought *Los Angeles* magazine to her—it had featured De Sade, the hottest new club on Sunset Boulevard. She'd practically committed the issue to memory. And now, here she was in Los Angeles with a rising young tennis star who'd just invited her to go clubbing there.

"I'd love to." Then, Lydia frowned. "But I don't have anything to wear . . . unless cutoffs and a Houston Oilers shirt count." She gestured toward the blue floral bikini she was wearing. "This belongs to one of the moms, I'm not sure which."

"Not a problem, I loan you clothes," Oksana said.

Lydia would have preferred to zip off on a major shopping spree. But there was the little problem of money. As in, she didn't have any.

"So tonight," Oksana went on, "we go to Koi for dinner. Then to De Sade, my treat. You are game?"

"I am *so* game," Lydia agreed.

Was life great or what? It was about damn time.

10

Lydia tried not to stare across the outdoor terrace of Koi, where a handsome guy with short cropped hair had just stood up from his table. So did the leggy girl with whom he'd dined.

"That guy looks like Tom Cruise," Lydia told Oksana.

Oksana followed Lydia's eyes. "That *is* Tom Cruise."

Lydia almost dropped her Coke. "No way. He's so *short.*"

"Is movie magic."

"I wouldn't know," Lydia confessed. "I haven't seen any of his movies. I just recognize him from magazines."

Oksana's perfectly plucked eyebrows headed north toward the terrace's retractable rooftop. "No movies in jungle? I can't imagine. What did you do for fun?"

"I got really good at fishing for peacock bass using pig guts as bait. And there were the cannibals—there are a few left. They were always good for a few laughs," Lydia mused. "And the witch doctors have a cool little show they put on where they drink sheep piss to give them extra strength."

"You are joking."

"Not."

"Amazing," Oksana marveled. "This must be big change. Are you having good time?"

Good didn't begin to cover it. Lydia felt like piercing her lip with one of those long sticks that Amazonian women considered a fashion statement just to make sure that this wasn't some big ol' dream. Here she was, at Koi, surrounded by models, actors, and assorted beautiful people. More than that, from the smiles and approving looks she'd gotten on her way to the table, everyone thought *she* was one of them.

Part of it had to be due to the twenty-minute shower she'd taken after lying out all day by the pool. For the first time in eight and a half years, Lydia felt truly clean. Part of it had to be the clothes that Oksana had lent her: a Rock & Republic jean skirt with stud detail, and a citrus-and-pink-mesh Betsey Johnson T-shirt. That she was actually wearing the designers she'd read about was a wonderful feeling. Oksana hadn't been able to come through with shoes, since her feet were so much bigger than Lydia's. But Lydia had raided the moms' closet for an incredible pair of Jimmy Choo baby blue python stiletto sandals. Lydia, who'd once lost a pet dog to a python, loved the idea of having them on her feet.

Dinner had been sushi, sushi, and more sushi. Lydia was accustomed to raw fish, but that fish had always been limited to whatever was swimming in the river near their tiny settlement, not mahimahi, salmon, and special California sushi rolls. It was only after two hours of gorging and people watching that Lydia and Oksana returned to Oksana's pearl gray classic Porsche Spyder.

"Tournament in Stuttgart," Oksana declared.

"What?"

"I reach semifinal. It paid for car. Want to drive?" Oksana offered Lydia the keys.

"Nah," Lydia told her nonchalantly, unwilling to admit that she had no idea *how* to drive. Porsche Spyders were scarce in Amazonia. As were paved roads. Or any roads, for that matter.

So Oksana motored them over to De Sade. The club was in an old warehouse off Hollywood Boulevard to the east of Katana. No sign, no nothing. Just a valet parking stand, a purple velvet rope, and an endless line of please-God-let-them-think-I'm-cool-enough-to-get-in types. A buff guy with coal black skin and muscles on his muscles stood by the door.

"That guy is the cool police, huh?" Lydia asked as the valet took the Porsche from them.

Oksana smiled. "Is important job."

Lydia scanned the line of hopefuls, each doing his or her best to look casual and not ooze desperation. Every girl had miles of tan skin, tattoos on their lower backs, and long, flat-ironed hair. The strict "this is what makes a girl beautiful" standard made Lydia chuckle. Amazonian women were usually naked from the waist up; if their breasts didn't sag toward their toes, they were considered unattractive. In the worst of the heat, Lydia had sometimes gone native herself.

"Come on," Oksana said, taking Lydia's hand. "We don't wait, trust me." She ducked under the velvet rope, still holding on to Lydia. "Hi, Greg," she called to the bouncer. "Is Maria here yet? Or Jennifer?"

"Ox, babe, what's up? Nah, not yet, but the night's still young." The big black guy enveloped Oksana in a bear hug, then grinned as Oksana introduced Lydia. "It's crazed inside. Some TV show is shooting."

Lydia hoped it was a show she had read about. One time the family had stayed in an actual hotel in Manaus because the budget *dormitorio* her parents favored was completely booked. The hotel had a satellite dish, and Lydia had parked herself in front of the TV for practically their entire stay. One station had showed a steady diet of reruns of American sitcoms—*Friends* and *Frasier,* mostly, dubbed in Portuguese. Lydia had adored *Friends.*

"Is it *Friends*?" she asked eagerly.

Greg cut his eyes at her. "Girl, that show is over and out. Where you been?"

"In the rain forest," Lydia replied.

Greg laughed. "Yeah. And I've been on Mercury working on my tan. Anyway, it's a new reality show. *Platinum Nanny.*"

"Oh sure," Oksana said. "Like *The Apprentice,* right? They will pick someone to be rock star nanny." She turned to Lydia. "Anya has given Platinum tennis lesson."

"Okay, back to the masses for me," Greg announced. "Take these and give them to the cashier." He pressed two guest passes into Oksana's palm and waved the girls inside, then went back to the block-long line of wannabes.

Oksana gave the passes to the cashier and led Lydia into the club. The massive open space was dimly lit by recessed golden domes. Crystal-beaded chandeliers hung from the fifty-foot vaulted ceiling. A DJ was spinning hip-hop; hundreds of bodies throbbed to the beat. Overhead, steel cages swung from the ceiling. In each cage, a stunning thong-clad girl or guy gyrated, flesh glistening.

Lydia spotted the TV crew immediately; they were shooting near the DJ's booth. A passel of flunkies with walkie-talkies ringed the camera crew. Curious, she motioned to Oksana that she wanted to go watch. The girls snaked through the dancing throng toward the television shoot. Lydia got close enough to see five girls and one guy dancing together. The guy was tall and broad-shouldered, with blond hair that flopped onto his forehead and a dimpled smile. Very tasty. Four of the girls were variations on Hollywood types, lots of skin and designer everything. The fifth girl, however, was a sweet-faced brunette in khakis and a T-shirt, with her hair in a casual ponytail. She definitely didn't fit in with the others.

A woman with a punk black hairdo motioned to one of the flunkies. He coaxed a middle-aged woman in beige knit pants, aqua floral blouse, and beige support sandals into the shot. Instantly, the hot guy pulled the older woman toward him and danced with her, ignoring the cute girls. The older woman moved stiffly, looking as though she'd rather be anywhere except where she was.

Lydia wondered what all this could possibly have to do with choosing a nanny; then Oksana tugged her away.

"Let's go dance!" She steered Lydia toward a red leather banquette and pulled out a hidden drawer underneath. "Put bag here."

The only things in Lydia's mini Chanel bag, also borrowed

from the moms, were a small Chanel lip gloss, a tampon, and one of the tiny vials of herbs that Lydia had brought back from the Amazon. Lydia extracted the vial, and tucked it in the back pocket of her skirt before stowing her bag. Oksana closed the drawer, locked it with a tiny padlock, and headed for the dance floor.

Lydia gave herself over to the music. After more than eight years of native chants and instruments, the hip-hop beat was intoxicating. One song segued into the next; they danced until a waiter clad in nothing but faded jeans, the better to show off his tanned six-pack and pierced nipples, offered Oksana a flute of champagne with floating raspberries. Then he offered one to Lydia.

"They know my drink!" Oksana called over the music.

"I thought you didn't drink until Thanksgiving!"

"No vodka, I meant!" Oksana hoisted her flute toward Lydia, then drained it. Lydia did the same. The music and the champagne kept coming; Lydia felt as if she could dance all night. Then, out of the blue, a male hand snaked around her waist. A bucktoothed guy who bore a strong resemblance to a tree rat pulled Lydia to him and started humping her to the music. But Oksana got ahold of the little weasel in her muscular grip. "She's with me, dickhead!" Oksana spat, then spun the rodent-man into the crowd.

Lydia smiled. It was sweet, really, though she could more than take care of herself. Back in the Amazon, size had nothing to do with deadliness. The fiercest warriors were inches shorter than she was. But they had an absolute willingness to kill and knowledge of how to do it in the most expedient way possible. Lydia had learned these lessons well—she hadn't befriended an Ama shaman for nothing.

"Thanks, Oksana. But if someone cute hits on me, back off."

"Someone cute, did you say?"

Lydia nodded. "*Very* cute!"

Oksana pulled Lydia close and kissed her. Seriously kissed her. Huh. Interesting.

The native Amas were bisexual; sex was a far more casual thing in Amazonia than in modern civilization. Not for Lydia, since she hadn't had any of it yet. But that didn't mean she wasn't open to new experiences. She had to admit, though, it was kind of weird getting her very first real kiss from another girl. It wasn't disgusting or anything, but no bells went off, either.

Oksana ended the kiss with her arms around Lydia's waist. "Nice?"

"Not bad," Lydia replied.

"We should go back to my place. Chateau Marmont."

Hmmm. If Lydia had simply been willing to file it under the heading of "Why Not Try It?" she might have taken Oksana up on the offer. The Chateau Marmont was supposed to be a really nice hotel, too. But peculiar as it seemed to share her first real kiss with another girl, it seemed utterly bizarre to lose her virginity to one. If that's what lesbians did. Lydia wasn't exactly sure.

Princess Lydia decided to hold out for her prince—he'd better hurry the hell up—and declined Oksana's invitation. If the tennis player minded at all, she didn't show it; the two girls danced the night away.

11

God. Kiley didn't get panic attacks, but she wasn't immune to anxiety. It always hit her in the stomach, and it was hitting her now. She climbed into the limo with her mom and the other contestants. They were on their way to the Brentwood Hills Country Club for the first elimination challenge for *Platinum Nanny*. Kiley had no idea what the challenge would be—it had been kept completely under wraps. All she knew was, she had to survive.

The day before had been fun. Eliminations hadn't yet begun, and the producers had sent everyone to get their hair cut, colored, and styled at JosephMartin on Rodeo Drive in Beverly Hills. They had wanted to give Kiley red streaks and hair extensions. A stylist had shown her a photo of some chick from a men's magazine with the same streaky waist-length hair, her tits and butt stuck out to the camera.

It was so *not* Kiley. She'd been adamant on the no extensions, but had given in on the streaks. A flunky had blown her hair perfectly straight, and she'd been forbidden to wear it in a ponytail, thank you very much. Nor could she see it; the producers had wanted to get her reaction on camera.

After hair came makeup. All the contestants were taken to Valerie Beverly Hills, the famous cosmetics salon at the busy corner of North Canon Drive and Little Santa Monica Boulevard, whose twenty-foot-high windows reflected the endless parade of Jags, Beemers, and Hummers that snaked along the street.

The first thing Chamomile—Kiley's makeup artist—asked was if she'd ever had her eyebrows done. When Kiley said no—that she didn't even know what that *meant*—Chamomile looked like someone had shot her through the heart. But she'd scrutinized Kiley's brows and started to pluck.

Kiley winced. Chamomile said something about suffering for beauty and moved on to the eyebrow stencils. These stencils—each was named for a famous movie star; Kiley was outfitted with the Julia Stiles—were put over the eyebrows, then a stiff brush dipped in high-pigment eye shadow was used to color inside the stencil, resulting in alleged movie star eyebrow perfection.

Following the Stiles stencil, Chamomile brushed Kiley's brows with clear gel on a mascara wand, which was supposed to make them shiny and "hold them in place." Kiley said her eyebrows had never gone anywhere on their own, so she didn't know why they needed to be held in place. No one in the salon found her comment at all amusing.

After the eyebrows came makeup. As before, Kiley wasn't allowed to view herself, but the cameraman from *Platinum Nanny* filmed every moment.

Finally, with cameras on, Kiley was spun toward the mirror. She actually gasped, since she didn't recognize herself. She had on even more makeup than when she'd been interviewed for *Platinum Nanny*. But it was subtler, too. She looked . . . well . . . pretty. She wished she could show her mother. But Mrs. McCann was being made over at a different salon.

Next stop: Fred Segal's in Santa Monica. The show was buying each contestant one outfit, with a price limit of a thousand dollars. Kiley found that number hilarious; for half that, she could get an entire Old Navy wardrobe, plus shoes.

A Fred Segal clerk who normally would not blink in Kiley's direction treated her like royalty. Item after item came off the rack—designers Kiley had only read about, like Carlos Miele and Tom Ford and Tracy Reese. Kiley finally settled on a pale green watered-silk Chloe camisole trimmed with forest green and pink ribbons. It was almost too beautiful to—

Suddenly, Jeanne McCann had appeared in the store aisle. Kiley's jaw fell open. They'd cut and streaked her mother's graying hair, which was now soft brown with blond highlights feathered around her cheekbones. The hair, an elegant silk pantsuit, and understated makeup made her mom look both younger and chic. The lovefest reunion of mother and daughter was all caught on camera.

Now it was a day later. As the limo cruised west on Sunset Boulevard, it stopped at the corner of Barrington for a red light. Kiley looked out the window; above them was a fifty-foot billboard that featured an impossibly gorgeous male model, golden rippling muscles above bulging Calvin Klein underwear. He was looking past the camera, as if he was watching a beautiful woman undress for him.

No way. The model was Tom from the suite next door. *That* guy.

69

"How hot is *he*?" Tamika asked rhetorically. She was checking out the billboard, too.

"I'm starved," Steinberg put in. "And I'd love to eat him for lunch."

Cindy shook her head. "It's an illusion. He probably doesn't look half that good in person."

Oh yes he does, Kiley thought. *In fact, he looks even better.*

But she had no intention of telling the other girls that the guy was living right in their midst. Not that Kiley would ever have the nerve to do anything about it. But right now it still felt as though he was her intimate secret, even if she never saw *that guy* again.

12

While it was fun for Lydia to loll at her aunt's pool, the surroundings lacked a certain something in the male scenery department. That's why she decided that the Brentwood Hills Country Club was definitely a step up. The very exclusive, very expensive club was tucked into the hills between Brentwood and Pacific Palisades. The moms had a family membership, which meant that now Lydia was a member, too. Later on, Anya had told her, Lydia would be escorting the children to the club's "Nanny and Me" activities. But for now, Lydia was a free woman.

After a sumptuous breakfast of bagels, Norwegian lox, and scrambled eggs from Nate 'n' Al's restaurant in Beverly Hills—Lydia had tired of pastrami cheeseburgers—it was easy to summon the moms' driver and ask for a lift to the country club.

The driver was aggressively skinny, with short, spiky dirty blond hair and great cheekbones. His name, he told her, was X. Then he took one look at the chain-fringe-pocketed Frost

French jeans Lydia had purloined from the moms, and said she could not possibly wear those jeans with those sneakers, because the proportions were all off. That he was so obviously gay, and so obviously knew what he was talking about, sent Lydia back to the moms' closet for some Marc Jacobs pumps that X declared to be classic leg-lengtheners.

Lydia decided that having a driver on call—especially a driver with such excellent fashion sense—was far better than a driver's license of her own. She'd never have to deal with traffic, and she'd always arrive in a style to which she was quickly becoming reaccustomed.

The country club pool was a busy place: moms chatting, industry people talking about scripts, teens doing a designer variation on an Ama fertility dance. At a nearby patio, waiters served upscale hot-weather fare; lobster bisque, grilled pigeon salad, and caramelized onion tart with anchovies were the specialties. A waiter explained to Lydia that if it wasn't on the menu, she could get it anyway. Just ask.

Plus, there was the stargazing. By eleven o'clock in the morning she'd recognized Scarlett Johansson (not nearly as pretty in person) and Jessica Simpson (who looked even better).

She'd just caught sight of Mena Suvari when a buff lifeguard strolled past Lydia's chaise. She'd approached him earlier when he was on a break, to ask if he might get her a cocktail, since she'd left her ID in Peru. He'd laughed and said he'd be fired if he got a drink for a minor. But if she wanted Sprite . . . The spin he put on "Sprite" was clear: he might not be able to bring her a Flagman appletini, but the Sprite could be fortified and no one would be the wiser.

At the moment, Lydia was sipping her second well-fortified

72

Sprite. She called to him as he walked past her. "You seem to get a lot of breaks."

"New shift," he said, cocking his head toward the lean young woman in a red Speedo who was ascending the lifeguard stand. "Besides, being social is part of my job. What's your name again?"

"Lydia. Lydia Chandler."

He shook her hand. "Nice to meet you again, Lydia Chandler. I'm Scott Lyman—wait, I already told you that before. You're new, right?"

"Got here yesterday."

"From?" He pointed a playful finger at her. "Someplace in the South, right? I recognize the accent."

Lydia almost laughed aloud. "You could say that."

"Welcome to L.A., Lydia from the South. You found a great place to spend the day. But I know better places to spend the night." Then he winked.

Even a girl who'd gone through puberty catty-corner to a dung heap—that would be her—would find that line-and-wink combo cheesy. But Scott's sinewy swimmer's muscles were far too promising to let a little thing like IQ or personality get in the way.

Lydia leaned on one elbow. "You want to have sex with me, right?"

Scott practically choked on his own spit. "Well, yeah, I mean . . . you get right to the point, huh?"

Lydia shrugged. "Where I come from, people don't beat around the bush, they live in it. What are you doing later?"

Scott gave her a lazy grin. "You mean what are *we* doing later? How about if I get your digits?"

Digits. That had to mean her phone number, Lydia figured. She borrowed a black marker from the woman on the next chaise longue, who was editing a script. Then she took Scott's hand, ready to write her number on it. But he jerked it away at the last moment.

"Can't. Forgot. I've got to do this TV thing that's taping over there." He cocked his head in the general direction of the outdoor bar. "It'll show."

Lydia sat up. "Turn around then."

He did craning to see what she would do. Lydia pulled down the back of his sky blue Gottex swim trunks just far enough to scrawl the number of the cell phone her aunt had given her. She then capped the marker and tossed it back to the woman from whom she'd borrowed it.

Scott wagged a playful finger at her. "You're a bad, bad girl."

"Thank you. So what show?"

"New reality show. *Platinum Nanny.*"

"Yeah? They were shooting at De Sade last night," Lydia said. "I was there with a friend."

"For a new girl in town, you get around. I'll call you. I'm gonna get awesome exposure from this. Hey, you wanna come watch?"

Since Lydia was already enjoying his awesome exposure, she allowed as how she might do just that.

The host of *Platinum Nanny,* Amber "A.M." Mahaffey, was also its executive producer. She'd been an MTV veejay fifteen years ago, back when Platinum had been in her prime. A.M. parlayed that gig into a career as a television executive. *Platinum Nanny* had been her idea; her close personal relationship with Platinum had made the whole thing possible. Or, as cynics might point out, it was a last-ditch effort to resuscitate Platinum's and A.M.'s careers, both of which were currently on life support.

Kiley stood with the contestants near the shallow end of the pool, wearing the navy Speedo the show had given her. The other four girls had been provided with bikinis that ranged from tiny to almost nonexistent. Jimmy had been given cutoff jeans covered in Confederate flags. It was all a setup, of course—it hadn't taken Kiley long to figure out that reality TV was as carefully planned as a scripted show, with each person's role clearly defined: the Brilliant and Obnoxious (Cindy), the Competent and Sexy (Veronique), the Buffoon (Jimmy), the Alt-Artist (Steinberg), the Streetwise (Tamika), and finally, the Innocent . . . which would be her. She was sure that when the show was edited and aired, the producers would emphasize those roles. From multiple seasons of *Survivor*, Kiley knew the lamb always got tossed to the wolves. It did not bode well for her longevity on the show.

13

Esme had driven past the Brentwood Hills Country Club on occasion, stared at the Jaguars and Beemers that turned onto the private driveway, gazed at the magnificent grounds secure behind high wrought-iron fences and gates. But she never imagined she would be inside those gates herself.

Now, just three hours into her two-week trial period as the Goldhagens' nanny, Esme was not just inside the gates, but inside the club's playroom for children. It was the size of an elementary school gymnasium. But unlike a school gym, the crowded playroom featured every toy and activity imaginable. There was a trampoline and miniature golf, a climbing wall, an arts and crafts corner, and more Legos in one pile than Esme thought humanly possible.

But Easton and Weston were ignoring all these attractions. Instead, they sat in front of the big-screen, high-definition television, mesmerized by *Dora the Explorer*. It made Esme smile.

Part of *Dora* was in Spanish, but most of it was in English, which made the show an excellent way for the twins to learn their new language. And if the kids ended up addicted to TV, they'd certainly been adopted by the right parents.

Esme checked her watch; the kids were scheduled for a private swimming lesson in five minutes. She coaxed them away from Dora and led them out of the building and toward the pool. People smiled as they passed. Esme figured the smiles were either to demonstrate how liberal and inclusive they were, or because they thought her sister was J.Lo.

She found the pool. Unfortunately, it was the wrong one, for adults only. A waiter directed her to the family pool, on the other side of the breezeway. But before she could herd the girls in the right direction, Easton spotted the TV camera crew near the diving board.

"TV! TV!" Easton shouted. She jumped so high that her Harry Winston twenty-four karat gold-and-diamond E pendant—a gift from some Hollywood big shot—flew up and hit her on the cheek.

Weston picked up her sister's chant. "TV! TV! *Yo quiero* TV!"

Obviously, something was filming. But they couldn't stick around to find out, since Esme had less than three minutes to get the kids to their lesson. She tried to explain to them that they could come back later, but neither kid would take *"más tarde"* for an answer.

Stuck, Esme phoned her boss and asked for guidance.

"Let them have fun," said Diane. "We'll worry about discipline later."

Weston pointed to the camera. "TV! *Como* Jimmy Neutron!"

Esme sighed and closed her cell. It would take a while for the kids to appreciate the difference between animation and live action.

"Hey. Your twins are so cute! They look just like you."

Esme's hackles rose at the comment from an unseen someone behind her; it was just so typically Anglo—another way of saying that all brown people looked alike. She turned and scowled at a slender girl with a deep tan, pale eyes, and long, choppy, white blond hair.

"I don't think so," Esme retorted, her voice chilly. "I'm their nanny."

"Oh, cool. I'm a nanny too!" the girl said, clearly not in the least offended by Esme's frosty tone. "The kids I'm taking care of are out of town, though. Lucky me."

Esme almost smiled. She couldn't stay mad, the girl was just so ingenuous. "Do you know what they're shooting?"

"*Platinum Nanny.*"

Esme had seen the promos for *Platinum Nanny*—there were billboards all over town touting the show. So she stood on tiptoes to better check out the contestants—each girl was better looking than the one before, the lone guy handsome in a whitebread all-American way, but *so* not her type in those stupid Confederate flag cutoffs.

Easton tugged on her arm. "Can I be on TV?" she asked in Spanish.

Esme chuckled. *"Más tarde, cuándo tu tienes a menos que veinte años. Ahora, tu estás demasiado joven."*

"You said something about when she's older, right?" the blond girl asked.

Esme nodded. "You speak Spanish."

"A little," the girl said. "Homeschool. Where I've been living for the last eight years, no one spoke English but my parents and me. And when I say no one, I mean no one."

Odd, Esme thought. The girl had no accent, except maybe a twinge of Southern. Where could she have come from where no English was spoken?

"I'm Lydia Chandler," the girl said, with a friendly smile. She held out her hand.

Esme shook it. "Esme Castaneda."

"Nice to meet you, Esme." Lydia nudged her chin toward the contestants. "See the brunette in the one-piece? I'm rooting for her."

"You know her?"

Lydia shook her head. "But she looks like she doesn't belong up there, you know? I know how that feels. Plus, I think they've got her mother on the show—that woman over there. My momma would bump uglies with a witch doctor before she'd go on a reality show."

"Bump uglies with a witch doctor?"

"Did you just say—" Esme began.

"Look at that." Lydia's attention was still focused on Mrs. McCann. As Esme watched, a producer tried unsuccessfully to coax her out of her bathing suit cover-up. When that didn't work, she got Mrs. McCann to put on a truly ridiculous floppy orange polka-dotted sun hat.

Esme tried to picture her own mom on a show like *Platinum Nanny.* It was like trying to picture her as president of the United States. No, wait. Her mother as president was much more likely, even if it was constitutionally impossible.

"My mother would never do it, either," she told Lydia. "Not in a million years."

"See?" Lydia asked cheerfully. "We already have two things in common. I think we ought to be friends."

Esme hardly knew what to say. She remembered back in Fresno when she'd been around eight years old, a girl had come up to her at school and asked out of the blue if Esme wanted to be her best friend. Instead of feeling flattered, Esme had wanted nothing to do with her.

But that wasn't her reaction to this girl, who was startlingly beautiful, very direct, and kind of quirky. So even though it was obvious to Esme that they came from not just two different worlds but two different planets, something made her say, "I think so, too."

14

"We're about to get started. Slather on the sunblock. I don't want any lawsuits!" Bronwyn instructed the contestants.

Kiley rubbed sunscreen onto her arms and tried not to stare at Cindy. God, she had the most amazing body. So did Veronique, and Tamika, and Steinberg, all of whom were showing miles of skin. It left Kiley feeling pasty and self-conscious in her stupid one-piece, wishing she had spent less time at Pizza-Neatsa in downtown La Crosse and more time in the pool.

Neither Kiley nor any of the other contestants knew what A.M. had planned for this first elimination. But it was obvious the challenge would have something to do with water. A flunky adjusted A.M.'s body mike, then moved out of the shot as the camera's red light went on.

"Welcome to the Brentwood Hills Country Club, the most exclusive country club in the world. If you have to ask if you can join, you can't. If you have to ask how much it costs, you can't afford it. Whoever is selected as Platinum Nanny will spend a lot of very fun days here, since Platinum is a member." A.M. eyeballed the contestants. "It bears repeating that being Platinum Nanny is a lot of responsibility. You might even be called upon to save your children's lives. Scott?"

Scott Lyman stepped up to A.M. with a boyish grin; A.M. snaked an arm around him. "This hunk of manhood is Scott, one of the club lifeguards."

Scott faced the camera. "This is my fifth year here," he said. "I'm a former Olympic swimmer in the backstroke."

Cindy broke into applause. The rest of the contestants followed, including Kiley.

"Thanks," Scott said. "How many of you know mouth-to-mouth?"

Veronique was the only one who raised her hand.

"If you're teachin', I'm learnin'," Tamika called out sassily.

"That's exactly right, Tamika," said A.M. "Scott here is going to teach all of you official Red Cross mouth-to-mouth. Then, we're going to have a little competition." She turned to Jimmy. "You okay with that, Jimmy?"

The boy from Mississippi turned beet red at the thought of a lifesaving lip-lock with Scott, but kept his cool. "Bring it on," he growled.

A.M. laughed. "You're a good sport. But actually, we've got a different teacher for you. Meet Annette." A petite female lifeguard stepped up next to Scott. She looked like a young version of Catherine Zeta-Jones.

"Ooowee!" Jimmy exclaimed. "Annette, show me the way."

• • •

Easton tugged on Esme's hand. "Pee-pee!" She held her crotch through her babystyle bottle-green capri pants with a look of desperation.

Esme took advantage of the contestants' mouth-to-mouth lesson to get the girls to the bathroom, where they were fascinated by the automatic toilets, wanting to flush them over and over, tearing off pieces of tissue and watching them disappear. They explained to Esme that in Colombia they'd done pee-pee in the dirt outside their rural orphanage. They said it so innocently and without embarrassment that Esme knew it had to be true. And here they were a few days later, in this real-life fantasyland called rich people's America.

Lydia made room for the three of them when they came back, and pointed to the buff lifeguard. "Think that guy is cute?"

"Not my type," Esme told her.

"At least he's not five feet tall and naked," Lydia replied philosophically.

Esme shook her head. This girl said the strangest things.

"Coming through, coming through." The crowd parted so that a production assistant could lead a group of men into the circle of contestants. They ranged from young-and-morbidly-obese to cadaverous-and-old-enough-to-be-your-great-grandfather. All of them wore decrepit, moth-eaten clothes. Easton and Weston held their noses and told Esme in Spanish that the men smelled bad.

"I hope no one in this crowd understands Spanish," Esme whispered to Lydia.

"Body language always tells the story," Lydia pointed out,

since the two kids were fanning the air in front of their faces and laughing at the same time.

Once the commotion settled, A.M. addressed the contestants again. "Now we're going to test those mouth-to-mouth skills! Unfortunately our TV audience doesn't have smell-o-vision, or you'd understand that for the last three days, these men have consumed nothing but garlic, kim chi, and beer. Their clothes have been marinated in a pigsty."

A.M. began matching up victims and contestants, pushing the most ancient geezer at the girl in the navy tank suit. "Kiley, this is Ralph," she said. "Meet your drowning victim."

"Kiley—cute name," Lydia commented as the girl folded her arms and nodded. "See, she's not freaked out."

Meanwhile, with the exception of Kiley and Cindy, all the contestants appeared on the verge of nausea. Jimmy was greenest of all, because Annette had been replaced by a toothless man with three days' worth of gray stubble on his chin and a festering sore on his forehead.

"Contestants: you never know what you'll be called upon to do when you're a nanny. You're about to demonstrate what you learned on your victims. Scott and Annette will judge your technique. And Platinum is watching even as I speak, via a live feed to her home. Hello, Platinum!" A.M. waved to the camera. "Platinum will consider Scott and Annette's opinions, but ultimately—if you know Platinum—she makes her own decisions. Oh, one last thing. Mom?" A.M. motioned for Mrs. McCann to join her. "I think we all know Kiley's mom by now. Since your daughter is the youngest one here, we thought she might benefit from a little hometown cheerleading. You up for it?"

"Sure."

"Good. She's going to need it. The Platinum Nanny will have to be very fit; kids can wear you out. So contestants, before you demonstrate your mouth-to-mouth skills, Scott will lead you in a little workout. Scott?"

The lifeguard stepped forward. "Contestants, follow me. Try to keep up. We've got paramedics ready just in case."

Paramedics? Kiley gulped hard.

"Spectators can see what our home audience sees by watching the monitor," A.M. added as a big-screen TV was wheeled out onto the patio. She pulled a whistle out of her pocket. "Contestants ready?"

She blew the whistle. "Go!"

15

Scott charged forward, the contestants in hot pursuit. Jimmy kept up easily, Cindy right behind him, the others trailing. Kiley found herself dead last. Other than swimming, she was definitely not a jock girl; she huffed and puffed to stay within shouting distance of the pack as Scott sprinted for the golf course.

"Shit." Tamika suddenly stumbled, turning her ankle as she did. Kiley flashed past her, sucking wind. They'd covered at least a half mile when Scott suddenly stopped by a twenty-five-foot portable tower. From it hung seven different ropes.

"Climb up, ring your bell at the top, then climb back down!" he bellowed at the contestants.

Rope climbing? Kiley felt desperate as she wheezed her way to the tower. She couldn't climb a rope. A few million people would get to watch her demonstrate her weenie arm strength on national television.

But Scott pointed to a rope and Kiley grabbed it, gritted her teeth, and started to hoist herself up hand over hand. By the time she was halfway to the top, Jimmy and Cindy were already on their way back down. Kiley struggled to hang on; it felt as if her arms were going to be yanked loose from their sockets.

"Might as well pack it in, jailbait," Jimmy jeered as he passed Kiley.

Other than Tamika, who hadn't even approached the tower, Kiley was still in last place. But she hadn't come all this way to quit. She dug deeper, groaned with the effort, and hoisted herself to the top of the tower. A quick bell ring, then she scrambled halfway down and made up a little time by dropping to the ground. She skinned both knees, but got up and ran on. Up ahead, was a set of low-slung barriers.

"Go under!" yelled one of the assistants.

Kiley dropped to the ground, eating dirt as she snaked along, but made up some lost time on Steinberg and Veronique. Next were hurdles, followed by a cable swing over a muddy pond. Kiley willed her burning arms to hold her, but her grasp slipped and she slid into the muck. She scrambled out, blackened with mud, and tried again. This time, she succeeded, but by the time she got back to the pool, she was still in fifth place.

"Swim!" A.M. ordered. "One lap each, backstroke, breast-stroke, crawl!"

"Go, Kiley!" she heard her mother shout. "Swim!"

Kiley grinned. Swimming was her long suit. She dove into the water, flipped, and started her backstroke. It was just her and the water, in perfect harmony.

By the time Kiley finished the medley, she'd passed contestant after contestant and moved into second place. Only Jimmy was ahead of her, and just by a couple of seconds.

"Out of the pool and revive your victim!" A.M. bellowed.

As Kiley scrambled out, her fully clothed "victim" leaped in. For a split second, Kiley froze. What the hell was she supposed to do?

"Jump back in, Kiley, go-go-go!" her mother boomed.

Go-go-go? She was so exhausted she wanted to die-die-die. But she launched herself back into the pool anyway, stroking toward her victim. The crowd and the camera crews moved to the edge of the pool to watch; a lot of people cheered for Kiley. She was the first one to catch her victim, drag him out of the water at the shallow end, and start mouth-to-mouth.

"Nice job, Kiley!" Scott encouraged her.

Ten minutes later, A.M. ended the competition. Kiley had "revived" her victim to Scott's satisfaction. The other girls were at varying stages of mouth-to-mouth. Jimmy was still in the pool. His victim had turned out to be a fabulous swimmer; Jimmy couldn't catch him.

"Need some oxygen, Jimmy?" A.M. said with a smirk.

And now you *might as well pack it in,* Kiley thought.

A.M. turned back to the crowd. "Thank you, folks, for being such good sports. Watch *Platinum Nanny* starting next week to see who survived this competition!"

The crowd broke up. Lydia nudged Esme. "Was that girl Kiley cool or what? Let's go meet her."

Esme froze, feeling uncomfortable and out of place. "No, I really can't, I—"

Too late. Lydia sidled over to Kiley, and Weston was holding Lydia's hand. Esme had no choice but to follow.

"Hey," Lydia told Kiley. "You were fantastic."

"Thanks," Kiley said. "Are you one of the production assistants?"

"No, just a face in the crowd. Lydia Chandler."

"Kiley McCann." Her eyes shot over to the older woman. "That's my mom."

"Yeah, we heard. She's cool." Lydia lightly touched Esme's arm. "And this is Esme—"

"Castaneda," Esme filled in. She tried to pry Weston's hand out of Lydia's, but the child wouldn't budge. "Meet Weston and Easton. I'm their nanny."

Lydia took a moment to study Kiley's face. "Did anyone ever tell you that you look like Lindsay Lohan before they glammed her up? I saw this photo spread in *Teen People* a couple of years ago, and I swear you look just like her."

"I wish," Kiley said, laughing.

"What are you supposed to do now?" Lydia asked.

Kiley wrung some water out of her drenched hair. "Get some first aid for my knees, I guess. Then go back to the hotel and make private tapes about how we feel about the other contestants. Then they'll make the elimination decision."

"Then?"

"The world's hottest bath. After that, if I'm still in the comp—"

"You will be," Lydia assured her.

"I hope," Kiley said. "Anyway, I guess I'll watch TV tonight with my mom. If I'm kicked out, we'll go home."

Lydia put a hand on her hip. "You're not going home. And I

know you don't really want to watch TV with your mom all night, do you?"

"No," Kiley admitted. "Not really."

"So how about all three of us go out and party?" Lydia suggested. "I was thinking about having sex with that lifeguard, but that can wait."

"Shhh!" Esme hissed, eyes darting down to the children. The two little girls looked up, wide-eyed.

"Why? It's not like it's a dirty word," Lydia told her.

"I'm on two-week probation at my job." Esme kept her voice low. "I don't want to mess up, okay?"

Lydia nodded. "Sorry. From now on, I'll edit if they're around." She smiled down at Weston, whose little hand still clutched hers.

"*La nueva chica tiene pelo muy bonito,*" Weston said, gazing upward at Lydia.

"She's in love with your hair," Esme translated.

Lydia smiled down at Weston. "*Gracias.*"

"*Usted es una estrella de las películas?*" the little girl asked Kiley.

"She wants to know if you're a movie star," said Esme.

"Tell her no, but thanks," Kiley answered as she shrugged into a terry cloth robe an assistant thrust at her. "The lifeguard. Is he your boyfriend, Lydia?"

"Nah. We just met," Lydia explained cheerfully.

"You're going to have sex with a boy you just met?"

"Maybe. But he can wait. I have a friend who can get us into De Sade. You know that club?"

"No, but—"

"Then we should go clubbing tonight."

Esme could not picture herself "clubbing" with these two Anglos. She loved to dance, but she and Junior always went to certain places in their neighborhood and saw the exact same people they saw on the streets during the day. Sometimes they'd venture to a private club in Long Beach or Alhambra, but most everyone at those places was Latino, too. It occurred to her that she really didn't have any Anglo friends. Besides, she still had to take the children home, return to the Echo, finish packing her things, and move.

The short version she gave to Lydia and Kiley was that she had to move into the Goldhagens' guesthouse that night.

"You mean like Steven Goldhagen who does all those TV series?" Kiley asked.

Esme nodded. "They just adopted these girls."

"Awesome. I have a driver," Lydia said. "He can pick y'all up. What time?"

Kiley said she was staying at the Hotel Bel-Air, and added that she didn't know how her mom would feel about her going out.

"You'll figure out a way," Lydia predicted. She turned to Esme. "Where does your boss live? I bet his place is out of control."

"I really don't think I can go this evening, but thank you for inviting me."

"Oh, sure you can," Lydia insisted. "You're free at night, right?"

Esme couldn't lie. "Unless they ask me to watch the children. But I should be around in case they need me."

"Give me your cell phone." She put her hand out for Esme's

phone, then punched in her own phone number. "Call and let me know. We want you to come."

Kiley nodded.

Esme took the phone back, with no intention of calling. There were only so many life changes she could make all at once. Partying with girls from another planet would have to wait.

16

Esme lay in Junior's arms and tried to ignore the hip-hop pounding through the thin wall that separated Junior's bedroom from his living room. But it was no use. The sound system's bass made the bed vibrate; the volume was so loud that Esme was sure they could hear every word in Fresno.

"I hate that music," she said, nestling into Junior's muscular chest. "Why do you let them listen to it in your house?"

"You know why, Esme."

She did, but that didn't mean she liked it. Junior had worked endless overtime and borrowed money to purchase the small bungalow on Allison Avenue in the Echo. Members of his old gang, Los Locos, knew it meant they always had a place to go. His rules were strict: no drugs and no weapons. But it still meant that at least two or three Locos were always crashed out in the living room. Esme and Junior rarely had any real privacy.

What's more, the whole Echo knew that Junior's was a Los

Locos house. Junior had installed bulletproof glass in the front windows. Every time a car backfired, Esme jumped.

Junior craned his neck to read the clock radio on the scarred nightstand. Esme knew it had to be close to five o'clock, which made her heart clutch. She was due back at the Goldhagens' home, with all her gear, at six. Their driver had offered to wait for her or return to pick her up.

But Junior wanted to drive her himself, maybe to prove that he wasn't intimidated by Bel Air. Her suitcase was already in his car. But she had little inclination to go. Moving to the guest-house would make afternoons like this a thing of the past. The Goldhagens had made it clear to her: no male visitors. Besides, the thought of living in that foreign land made her throat close up. She didn't belong there and she never would.

"I changed my mind," Esme muttered. "I'm not going."

"Yes, *chica,* you are." Junior sat up and reached for his jeans.

She shook her head stubbornly. "Why would I want to clean up after some rich Anglos?"

"You're not their maid, Esme, and you know it." As Junior pulled on his T-shirt, Esme saw the triple lightning bolt on his muscular forearm, the sign of Los Locos. There was another tattoo that she'd designed and inked across his back—her own name, entwined with thorns and vines.

"It doesn't matter. It's not me."

He pushed into his Pumas. "For two weeks, you can try it."

Why was he pushing her? It was not the reaction she had expected; she'd been sure that Junior would be angry with her for leaving the Echo.

"You go, Esme." He sat on the bed again. "Here, I worry about you every moment that I'm not with you."

She folded her arms. "I can take care of myself."

"The hell you can." He grabbed her arm, too hard. "This is not a game, *chavala*. There's bad shit going down between Los Locos and some badass boys from Pacoima. I don't want you to be a part of it." He rose, stuffed his wallet into his back pocket, and strapped on his watch. "Get up. We have to go."

Esme stood, dragging the sheet with her. "I'm not one of those stupid sheep, okay? Don't treat me like I don't have a brain."

Junior turned, eyes blazing. "Then stop acting like you don't have one. Esme, this is a chance for you."

"A chance for *what*?"

"To make some money, go to a decent school. Have a *vida* that's not completely *loca*!"

Esme narrowed her eyes and remembered something her friend, Jorge, had said to her. "I can have a life without selling out, you know. Jorge already got accepted early decision to Cal on a full scholarship."

"You aren't Jorge, Esme. His father is a public defender. Your father doesn't even speak English."

Esme took another tack. "Why should I move to that place when you wouldn't even set foot on their property? You—"

"*Basta de cuentos!*" Junior made a sharp "that's enough" gesture with his hands. Then his voice softened. "Look, I understand you're scared. But you can't let that stop you."

"Like hell I'm scared! I just—"

"You're going. If I have to drag you into my car, you're going. Get dressed."

Junior slammed out of the room. Esme sat on the edge of his bed, wrapped in the sheet that still smelled of him. If she had been the type of girl to cry, this would have been the moment. But that hadn't happened since before the day she'd helped to murder her cousin Ricardo; she wasn't about to start now.

But she still bit her lower lip. There was only one reason Junior would treat her this way: he didn't love her anymore.

17

"What time is it?" Mrs. McCann asked as she checked the latch on Kiley's suitcase.

"Five." Kiley stood before the dresser mirror, brushing her hair before putting it up in her usual ponytail. Screw A.M. if she didn't like the way Kiley wore her hair. A.M. was not going to decide who the nanny would be.

"We have a few minutes," Mrs. McCann went on. "Is this outfit okay?"

Her mom wore orange-sorbet slacks and a yellow-and-orange-print summer-weight sweater, with big yellow plastic earrings and necklace. The La Crosse Kmart ensemble made Kiley wince. Then she was ashamed of herself.

"It's nice, Mom."

"My watch is a little slow," Mrs. McCann said, resetting her Timex to synch with the antique clock on the marble mantel. She scanned the living room to make sure she hadn't left anything. "I looked in my room, under the bed, in the bathroom . . ."

Kiley grimaced. She was nervous about the elimination, so her mother was getting on her nerves even more than usual. In exactly fifteen minutes the contestants were to meet in the hotel's club room, where A.M. would announce which five were still in the running for *Platinum Nanny*. She knew she'd done well at the mouth-to-mouth event, but she also knew Platinum's reputation for flightiness. Why not get America talking by sending her home?

Please don't let them eliminate me.

"What if our clock is slow, Kiley?" her mother asked. "What time does your watch say?"

"Five. Did you take your kava kava?"

"You don't need to worry about me, sweetie," her mom assured her.

From past experience, Kiley knew that wasn't true. Every time she'd thought that her mom had overcome her anxieties, they would erupt again, often due to nothing. Still, she didn't want her mother to feel bad, so she just changed the subject.

"Do I look okay?" Kiley gestured toward her khaki capris and white tank top.

"You always look okay, sweetie," her mother said. "Which is more than I can say for some of those girls you're up against." She took a tissue from her purse and blew her nose. "Evidently they never heard of leaving a little something to the imagination. We should go now, just in case. I'll call the valet for our—"

"Done. I did it when you were in the shower." Kiley had been told that all the contestants' luggage would be held in the lobby while A.M. made the announcement. Then, the cameramen would follow the loser on the walk of shame to retrieve his or her bags, and then to the shuttle bus to the airport. The loser would be on the first flight out.

"We don't want to be the last ones. Maybe I should have worn a different outfit. Do you think I should have worn a different outfit?"

"No, Mom."

"I think I should have worn a different outfit." Her mom's hand fluttered, fanning her face. "We'd better go, sweetie. Just in case the clock is wrong."

Kiley nodded to placate her mother but knew they had plenty of time, and she was reluctant to leave the suite. When else would she ever stay in a hotel as beautiful as this? What if all that awaited her was bad news? What if she was about to do the walk of shame and never see Tom again?

Tom. Why was she even thinking about him? It was ridiculous. So what if he had made small talk with her? It's not as if it meant anything. That her whole body had felt like mush when he'd shaken her hand was just a hormonal thing. He was a model; he was supposed to make girls feel like that, to sell whatever it was he was selling. He was probably just another shallow, brain-dead, self-absorbed L.A. jerk.

In fact, the only reason she wanted to see him was to prove to herself that she could look him in the eye, shake his hand again, and act normal.

That was all. Really.

The Hotel Bel-Air club room was done in dark leather and mahogany, like something from a British manor house. When Kiley and her mom entered, the other five contestants were already in their director's chairs, sitting in a semicircle around where A.M. would address them. Tamika's right ankle was wrapped in an ACE bandage.

Kiley took the last empty chair, on the far left side. Behind the semicircle of contestants was a floor-to-ceiling, wall-to-wall photograph of Platinum, her long blond hair blowing off her face. Steinberg, who was seated to Kiley's right, leaned over to her.

"You check out Veronique?" she muttered.

Kiley looked at the French girl, who wore a hot pink scoop-necked tank top that displayed her amazing, if unnatural, chest.

"She could put an eye out with one of those things," Steinberg went on. "Notice how she snagged the center seat. That's so if A.M. asks questions, everyone else has to turn their head. But she's always face-on in the camera."

"I never would have thought of that," Kiley marveled.

"She's a bitch," Steinberg said, "but she's a smart bitch."

"Mom? Where's Mom?" Kiley heard Bronwyn call out.

"Here!" Mrs. McCann waved her hand. She'd found a folding chair near the food service table that held donuts, bagels, and soft drinks.

"Mrs. McCann, Jayce here is going to take you into another room," Bronwyn went on. "She'll interview you on camera about who you think is going to be eliminated and why. Then you can watch the elimination on a monitor, and we can get your reaction."

"Fine." Mrs. McCann stood, gave Kiley a quick thumbs-up, and left with Jayce. Kiley heaved a sigh of relief. Maybe the kava kava was working.

Steinberg leaned toward Kiley again. "Your mom is such a good sport."

Kiley was about to thank her when Bronwyn stepped over to the center area. "People, listen up. This is how it will work. A.M. has already recorded her spiel about how this is the first elimination, blah, blah, blah. You all taped your segments this afternoon about how you feel about each other, who hates who, all that. We'll edit that stuff in. All we're filming now is the decision of who stays and who goes. If you're out, you'll get like two seconds for your tearful goodbyes. Then follow Jennifer— Jennifer, raise your hand."

A flunky in overalls raised a lackadaisical finger.

"Follow Jennifer to the lobby, pick up your suitcases, go to the courtesy van, have a pleasant life, buh-bye. You can see your magic moment on TV next week. Everyone got that?"

Please don't let them eliminate me.

A.M. strode into the room in a Ralph Lauren suit, apparently with nothing on underneath—the businesslike sex-kitten look. A flunky hooked the body mike to her lapel as she took her place at the center of the semicircle. The massive photo of Platinum loomed behind her.

Kiley's stomach lurched. This was it.

"Four, three, two, and—" Bronwyn pointed at A.M., who smiled at the camera.

"Welcome back to *Platinum Nanny.* We're at our first elimination. As you know, Platinum watched the challenge live and then reviewed the tape. She wants to know that if anything happened to her kids in the water our contestants could save them . . . and look hot in a bathing suit at the same time."

A.M. grinned and waited for the requisite chuckle. "I have the results in this envelope. If I call your name, you are still in the running for *Platinum Nanny*. Take one of these from me"— A.M. held up a platinum star—"and proceed to the ballroom. If not, *ciao*."

A.M. waited a pregnant beat, then opened a sealed platinum envelope. "The first contestant still in the running for *Platinum Nanny* is . . . Veronique."

The young French woman didn't look at all surprised as she slid off her stool, took a platinum star, and headed out the door. *Figures,* Kiley thought. Veronique was already a professional nanny. Plus, she had TV-friendly breasts. Four more names.

Cindy Wu.

Steinberg.

Oh God. Kiley felt as if she was going to barf. Now it was just Tamika, Jimmy, and her.

"Tamika."

The black girl looked stunned; after spraining her ankle, she hadn't even finished the obstacle course.

"This isn't *Survivor,*" A.M. explained. "Don't *ever* assume you know who will stay and who will go, because it's all up to Platinum." She eyed Kiley and Jimmy, who was grasping his muscular thighs in a death grip. "Our final possible Platinum Nanny is . . ."

Please, please, please . . .

"Kiley McCann."

Kiley sagged with relief. Jimmy didn't bother with goodbyes; he just shuffled off, a camera following him to record his misery. Kiley didn't feel bad about it, either, because Jimmy was a jerk. Then she hugged a still lingering Tamika, the contestant she felt closest to, and practically danced out of the room. She was one step closer to her goal, Scripps, the ocean. It was definitely worth celebrating. And as much as she loved her mom, watching TV with her in the hotel suite that night was not going to cut it.

Clubbing. With those girls she'd met. Hell, yes. Now all she had to do was convince her mom to let her go.

18

ADOPTION GIFTS

Two bilingual Lizzie dolls with outfits designed by Stella McCartney. From: Governor Schwarzenegger and Maria Shriver.

Two remote-control Robosapiens. From: Uncle Ivan and Aunt Deborah.

Two Discovery Sky & Land telescopes. From: Jennifer Garner.

Two Lullabye Baby 34-inch Gund stuffed bears. From: Peter Engel.

Two pink Nanette girls' faux leather jacket-and-jeans three-piece sets. From: the staff at Spago.

The list went on, and on, and on. Esme sat on the living room couch of her guesthouse, writing thank-yous to famous people who had already sent adoption gifts to Diane and Steve. Writing to these famous people was surreal, but remarkably boring. Diane had dictated onto a tape what she wanted written. Esme had to listen to the cassette, write it out, and leave space for Diane's signature. A ten-year-old with neat printing could do what she was doing.

Over the past two days, the gifts had come piling in: it seemed like there was always a messenger's car or FedEx truck barreling through the broken front gate and up the driveway. There were more than fifty names and gifts on Esme's list; she'd written six thank-yous so far.

The bird in the old-fashioned cuckoo clock on the wall startled her with its call. But the time was wrong. So Esme got up, stretching a kink in her back, to take it off the wall.

She opened the back of the clock and examined the works— old clock oil had gummed up its movement. She unearthed a bottle of ammonia she'd seen under the kitchen sink and poured a little into a dish. Then she added water, got some cotton swabs and cuticle oil from the bathroom, and carried it all back into the living room.

There, she dipped a swab into the improvised cleaning solution and dabbed at the thick oil, lost in thought. This new life seemed part of an alternate universe. What was she doing in this magnificent guesthouse, writing thank-yous to people she knew from television and in the movies because her boss had told her to do it? Taking a job because her mother told her to take it? Because Junior told her it would be good for her? Hadn't she always prided herself on her independence?

The clock cleaned and oiled, she reset the time, then returned to the kitchen and poured the leftover cleaning solution down the drain. What was it that *she* really wanted? The only things in her life that were completely her own were the tattoos she designed. How should she go about making her life as much her own as those tattoos? She had no idea, none.

Finally, Esme returned to the thank-yous. But she found it impossible to focus. So she prowled through the rooms of the guesthouse, as moments from her first day on the job replayed in her mind. It had actually gone fine. After their return from the country club, she'd given the kids lunch, then played with them in the newly built sandbox, which was the size of a small desert. Afterward were baths, followed by new outfits from Pampolina: orange stretch-velvet pants and silk-screen T-shirt for Weston, lavender cords and T-shirt for Easton.

After that, Esme had taken the kids for burgers at Mel's Drive-In. Their burgers were served in cardboard racing cars, which the girls loved. She also ordered them a vanilla milk shake to share, topped with a mountain of whipped cream and two cherries. When the waiter brought it out, the girls just stared. Esme coaxed them to try it. Tentatively, they'd put their lips to the straws. One sip of milk shake and both little faces lit up; they didn't stop sucking until they'd drained it.

Once they got back home, Esme helped them change into their new Tracey Ross cashmere pajamas, which, according to the price tags that Esme had carefully cut off, sold for five hundred and sixty dollars. The kids fell into bed before eight o'clock, unable to keep their eyes open. But she did coax a "Good night, Esme" from them instead of *"Buenas noches."*

Diane had assured Esme that she'd be home in time to tuck

in her daughters. But she called at seven to say that she was running late at Yoga Booty, and Selina would stay with the sleeping girls until she got home.

Esme wouldn't have minded working overtime. The truth was, she was lonely. And bored. She went to the kitchen and found a box of cereal in the cupboard; someone had thoughtfully put fresh milk in the refrigerator. She ate her bowl of Cheerios standing at the counter, the sound of cereal crunching in her mouth deafening. And then she realized why: it was the silence. All her life, she'd lived on busy streets where automobile traffic rolled by, Latin music blaring from car stereos, and emergency vehicle sirens wailed at all hours. And then there were the police helicopters, *whup-whup*ping overhead, seeking out the latest criminal *del día*.

But here in Bel Air, it was absolutely still. No traffic. No sirens. No choppers. Only the occasional chirping of a cricket in the gardens outside. She shuddered. How could she ever sleep in this kind of creepy silence? She rinsed her cereal bowl and put it away. Went back into the living room and wrote a few more notes. When Junior finally called, she would tell him that she was writing damn thank-yous to—

Her cell rang. Esme snapped it open. "Junior?"

A throat cleared. "It's Mr. Goldhagen, actually. Steve."

Esme winced. "Yes, sir?"

"I just got back from my office. Diane tells me you were super with the kids today."

"Thank you, sir."

"Well, that's great, Esme. Listen, I'm up at the main house. I was wondering, there's this thing tonight at the Santa Monica Pier. An opening party for a new Cosmos film called *The Ten*, Kirsten Dunst and George Clooney. A courier dropped off a

107

bunch of passes at my office, but Diane and I are staying in tonight. I thought maybe you'd want them. Sort of as a welcome to our family."

Esme was taken aback. How were passes to a Hollywood party a welcome to his family?

"That's very nice of you, sir."

"If you'd like to use them, take the Audi," Mr. Goldhagen continued. "I'll put the keys and the passes in the mailbox."

"Thank you, sir—"

"Steve. Don't mention it. If you go, eat and drink them out of house and home. I hate those sons of bitches at Cosmos. Hey, Esme?"

"Yes, sir?"

"Ya gotta stop calling me sir. I think you're talking to my father." He chuckled and hung up.

Wow. A Hollywood opening-night party. Of course she knew about *The Ten*. Slated to be this summer's Cosmos Pictures blockbuster, it was about a mysterious revisitation of the ten biblical plagues on Southern California. In the movie trailer, Kirsten Dunst got her foot caught between loose boards on the Santa Monica Pier and couldn't escape plague number seven, the hailstorm.

Of course, Esme was sure that by the end of the film, Dunst would be alive. It was always the unknowns who got killed off; the famous actresses lived. Would Kirsten Dunst be at this party? Would George Clooney?

Suddenly, Esme felt excited. She had passes to a Hollywood party and a really expensive car to get there. She considered calling Junior. But he would be extremely uncomfortable at an upscale Hollywood event. Then she thought about the two girls she'd met at the Brentwood Hills Country Club. What were their names? Lydia and Kiley. They were probably long gone by now, out at some fantastic club where the music was rocking and the people were rich and gorgeous and no one from the Echo could get past the bouncers.

I can do this, Esme told herself. *Whatever happens, happens.* She found Lydia's number on her cell and pressed the "Send" button.

19

"That's it. Over there!"

Lydia pointed to a makeshift plywood barrier that blocked the main entrance to the Santa Monica Pier. A line of beautiful people waiting to be ushered into the party extended back nearly a hundred feet.

"I've been down here a few times with my home—my friends," Esme told the other girls. "I've never seen it walled off like this, though. How do you know about the pier, Lydia? You've never been here before."

"Italian *Vogue,* last summer," Lydia said. "I picked it up in Manaus. There was a photo spread of Heidi Klum in these amazing Vera Wang dresses. It was the only magazine I had for a month, and I couldn't read Italian."

The other girls grinned. On the limo ride to the pier, they'd swapped a bit of their histories. Lydia had regaled them with some amazing tales from the Amazon rain forest. Esme had carefully edited her own life story, simply saying that her parents had moved from Fresno to the Echo, and that she'd moved with them.

But she was feeling good. Great, even. When she'd called Lydia and Kiley, they'd been at House of Blues swatting away drunk frat boys from Arizona State who'd bet each other that they'd all get laid on their road trip to Los Angeles. Lydia and Kiley had zero interest in helping them fulfill their fantasy, so they were more than up for Esme's invitation. In fact, Lydia volunteered to have her aunt's limo swing by the Goldhagen estate so that no one would have to drive.

Esme had wanted to ask Lydia and Kiley what to wear, but didn't have the nerve. So she tried on everything she owned, then panicked when she realized she was standing in the midst of a sea of obviously cheap clothes. Finally, she pulled on some low-slung black pants and a very fitted red Lycra T-shirt, then stepped into a pair of mile-high strappy red sandals she'd bought at the "All Shoes $9.99" store. She added a slick of red lip gloss and left her hair loose and wild. It would have to do.

She looked at Kiley and Lydia as they joined the line. Kiley tugged self-consciously on a beautiful green camisole, purchased for her by *Platinum Nanny*. She wore it with her Levi's and a pair of Dr. Scholl's sandals, saying it was either the sandals or her Cons. Lydia, on the other hand, was decked out in a vintage Gucci print minishift with the middle cut out and borrowed Manolo Blahnik heels she said were called the Hourisan: silver gray leather heels with intricate chain ankle straps. Evidently, Naomi Campbell had worn them to the MTV Video Awards—or at least that's what Lydia said she'd read in *In Style*. Both dress and shoes had been borrowed from her aunt. Her celery-colored eyes were outlined in smudgy kohl black; there was some kind of styling stuff in her white blond hair that made it look choppy and hip.

Esme thought, *If ever there were three girls who looked like they do* not *belong together, it's us.*

Each arriving partygoer had to flash their invitation to security multiple times. First at the check-in table, where they also had to show ID. Then again, as they stepped through a metal detector. And one more time, at the temporary door to the pier itself.

"Metal detectors?" Lydia asked. "What are they afraid of?"

A guard overheard her. "Standard procedure, in case a stalker tries to get through. Just ask Letterman or Zeta-Jones. On second thought, I think they're inside. Don't ask them." He swung the door open, and the girls were in.

They were surprised to find their end of the pier practically empty, except for a knot of twenty or thirty people waiting just inside the door. From the far end of the pier came pounding rock music; they could see the Ferris wheel and roller coaster at that end in full operation, as two searchlights crisscrossed the sky. Obviously, the party was way down there.

A San Francisco–style trolley car, equipped with wheels instead of riding on a metal track, rolled up to them. A conductor called out over a loudspeaker, "Step back for departing passengers. Then, all aboard for the *The Ten* party. Next stop, West Pier! All aboard!"

A bunch of people got off the trolley; the girls climbed on. They stood at the rear, grasping a vertical metal bar as the conductor whooshed them along. It was a short ride, not more than two minutes. But they rolled straight into an amazing party. Not only were the floorboards packed with gorgeous people who all seemed to know each other, but both sides of the trolley-way were lined with carnival-style sideshows—fire eaters, jugglers, contortionists, and the like.

"Welcome to the *The Ten* opening-night party," the conductor announced as his trolley slowed. "We've re-created the moments from the movie just before the seventh plague. Minus Kirsten and her broken ankle, of course."

All around the three girls, people laughed as if at an inside joke.

"Have a great time," the conductor continued. "I'll be here every ten minutes to bring you back to Ocean Avenue. Please watch your step as you exit the trolley."

People piled off. Esme, Kiley, and Lydia were swept along by the crowd. Most people were heading for a sixty-feet-high movie screen that had been erected at the far end of the pier. Below it, a huge crowd watched in awe as the enormous hailstorm featured in *The Ten* swept up the coast from Long Beach, heading for Los Angeles. Jump cuts from the movie followed, set to heart-pumping music.

"Oh my God, it's us!" Kiley cried.

Esme and Lydia turned to see what Kiley was talking about. To their left was another enormous movie screen. The girls' images were on it. It was the weirdest thing: when they laughed in reaction to their projected image, they could see themselves laughing on the giant screen.

"There must be cameras mounted somewhere," Esme said. As if on cue, one zoomed in; her face appeared in close-up—the lips pouty, the eyes enormous. "I'm not sure I like it."

The image shifted over to Lydia, who posed and blew kisses

113

the way she'd seen Paris Hilton work a crowd that afternoon on a TV show called *Access Hollywood*. Hilton's picture had been in every recent magazine that Lydia got in the Amazon.

"Wow, look at that," Kiley said, nudging Lydia's attention back to the *The Ten* trailer. It was another scene from the movie, this one on a Los Angeles freeway. The locust swarm of the eighth plague was rushing east. A family was stuck in their SUV, a terrified little girl in the backseat cranking up the windows against the huge cloud of marauding insects.

"That's sick," Lydia declared. "Why would anyone want to watch other people die?"

"Umm . . . because it isn't real?" Kiley queried, amazed that Lydia was having such a strong reaction. "Because it's a movie? Like, say, *Titanic*?"

"I didn't see *Titanic*," Lydia admitted. "But I've watched six people really die. Two from snakebite. One from malaria. Two from dengue fever. And one sliced his heel on a rock in the Rio Negro and was eaten by piranhas before he could get to shore. How about you?"

"None," Kiley admitted, chastised. "I didn't think of it like that."

I've seen plenty of people die, Esme thought. But when she took in Kiley's stunned face, she decided to keep her mouth shut.

"Oh, ignore me," Lydia said, waving away the disagreement. "I'm still suffering from culture shock. Hey, y'all think we can get a drink out here?"

No sooner did she pose the question than a waiter in a Los Angeles Dodgers baseball uniform smoothly appeared, carrying a tray. On it were flutes of champagne, cans of beer, and plastic bottles of springwater.

"What's with the uniform?" Lydia asked him. She took a

champagne glass for herself, while Kiley and Esme both opted for bottled water.

"Dodger Stadium gets invaded by lice during a doubleheader with the Giants," the waiter reported. "World's biggest itchfest. Barry Bonds can't even get to the plate. Keep watching. They may show it on the big screen." The waiter moved off into the crowd.

"Esme?"

Esme froze. A deep male voice had come from behind her. Who could possibly know her in this place?

She turned to see the Goldhagens' handsome son a few feet from her, smiling broadly. What was his name? She didn't remember. She didn't *want* to remember. What she did remember was that when she'd met him, her feet had just been drenched by a wave of shit.

"Jonathan Goldhagen," he reminded her. "We met yesterday?"

"I know who you are," she said, sounding cross.

He grinned and cocked his head toward the smaller of the two movie screens. "I recognized you. You looked great."

Esme clamped her jaw. She was not about to thank him for his cheap compliment. He was rich, handsome, and so sure of himself, standing there in faded jeans and a white linen shirt that probably cost more than Junior made in a week. He was undoubtedly used to girls throwing themselves at his feet. Well, she did not intend to be one of them. But she didn't want to be impolite, so she introduced him to her friends.

Lydia wagged a playful finger at him. "I know who you are. You're a movie star. Right?"

Jonathan scratched his head sheepishly. "I don't know about that."

"Your first movie came out last winter," Lydia went on.

"Some indie thing that no one saw but got a really good review in *Cosmopolitan*. They said you were going to be the next Jake Gyllenhaal. Esme, don't you know who this guy is?"

Esme shrugged, guarded.

"It's no biggie, Esme," Jonathan said. "Like she said, no one saw the movie."

Esme didn't respond to that, because what could she possibly say?

"I'm not into the whole movie-star thing, anyway," Jonathan continued. "That's my dad's world, not mine."

"You probably got your big break because of him," Esme commented coolly.

Jonathan nodded. "I'd say no, but I'd be lying. Yeah, his name got me through the door. But I'm the one who played the role."

"Lots of people can act," Esme insisted, a bit surprised at her own venom toward this guy.

Jonathan held his hands up. "Hold on. Did I miss the part where you decided you hate me?"

"She doesn't hate you," Lydia assured him. "Most likely she's attracted to you and feels conflicted about it."

Heat rushed to Esme's face. "Since you know so much about him, Lydia, why don't you two go off together and yak about how wonderful he is?"

"He *is* very hot," Lydia said, quite serious. "But he likes you."

"You heard the girl," Jonathan added playfully.

He was just so smug, so sure of himself. She didn't want to look at him. Instead, Esme glanced back up at the big screen again, where the locust cloud was threatening Las Vegas. She was sorry she'd ever called Lydia and Kiley.

"You have a very outspoken friend," Jonathan told Esme.

"She's not my friend," Esme snapped.

"Oh, I am, too," Lydia insisted easily.

Jonathan scanned the crowd. "I'm looking for a waiter, but they seem to have disappeared." He put a hand on Esme's arm. "Want to take a walk? Let me get you something better than that water to drink." He nodded to Lydia and Kiley. "Will you excuse us?"

"It's not up to them," Esme pointed out. "And I don't feel like going anywhere with you."

"You're a big ol' liar," Lydia told Esme. "You know you want him."

How humiliating. "I don't—I'm not—" Esme sputtered.

"Go with him," Kiley suggested kindly. "He seems nice."

"You should listen to your friends," Jonathan put in.

"We'll meet up at the Ferris wheel. In an hour," Kiley said. "How's that?"

"Oh, I can get her home," Jonathan said easily, lightly touching Esme's back. He smiled. "After all, I know where she lives."

20

"Here you go, sir. Two Arnolds, spiked." The bartender in the Dodgers uniform handed Jonathan two tall frosty glasses.

"Thanks." Jonathan stuffed a five-dollar bill into the tip jar, picked up the drinks, and handed one to Esme.

"It's called an Arnold?" she asked, dubious.

"Arnold Palmer, actually," Jonathan explained. "Named after the legendary. Try it."

Esme didn't raise the glass to her lips. "The legendary what?"

"Golfer." Jonathan looked incredulous. "You never heard of Arnold Palmer?"

Esme shook her head. "Golf looks boring."

Jonathan laughed. "Yeah, some people think so. But I like it." He nudged his chin toward her drink and she put the straw to her lips. "Taste it. Half lemonade and half iced tea, spiked with vodka."

She did. "You're right. It's delicious."

She sipped more of the drink and glanced around. They were at a bar near the arcade; when Jonathan had taken Esme's elbow and guided her through the masses, the crowd had seemed to part like the Red Sea for Moses. Esme admitted—if only to herself—that she had liked the feel of his strong fingers on her, the authority with which he led the way. It was a different kind of authority than Junior had. Junior had earned it. Jonathan was born to it.

"So, how goes the nanny gig?" Jonathan asked. He waved at someone who recognized him, then immediately returned his gaze to Esme.

"I just started. I don't really know yet."

"They're sweet kids. But Easton and Weston? Whatever possessed Diane to name them that?"

In spite of her raised guard, Esme smiled. "I wondered the same thing myself."

"She meant well, I guess. Wanted them to fit in. But it just makes it harder on the kids, seems to me."

"I agree with you."

Jonathan smiled into her eyes. "Well, well, we seem to have a meeting of the minds on two things." He hoisted his drink. "A good drink named after a golfer you've never heard of, and the idiocy of renaming my new siblings. At least she didn't name them after fruit. Apple, Pear, Cantaloupe . . ."

Esme chuckled despite her best intentions.

He pointed a playful finger at her. "I heard that. Soon you'll have to admit that you actually like me."

"I don't *dislike* you," Esme said carefully.

"That's progress."

"Look, I'm sorry if I was rude before. I just . . . I work for your parents."

"Rudeness forgiven, and why would I care that you work for my parents?" Jonathan asked. "That would be like saying I can't be friends with the daughter of my director or my producer."

Esme looked out to the dark ocean. "It's not exactly the same."

"Sure it is." He put his hand on her arm. "Hey, no need to be so serious. We're at a hot shit Hollywood premiere party. Let's have fun. So, what says big fun to you?"

"Um . . . the Ferris wheel?" she asked. She'd always loved Ferris wheels and carousels, the tinny music and the simple pleasure of going round and round, always knowing you would end up safely where you started.

"As my lady wishes." He gave her a courtly bow and put their nearly finished drinks on the bar. Then he extended an elbow. She was about to take it when he grabbed her hand, yelled "Come on!" and they made a headlong dash for the giant wheel.

Whoosh! A few minutes later, they were flying. Up, up, up, over the pier, the ocean, and seemingly all of Los Angeles. To the east, the city spread out in all its glory. In the clear of the night, Esme could see from Santa Monica clear down to Long Beach. It was a glorious feeling. What was it? Freedom, that was it. She felt young. And pretty. And carefree.

"You look like you're about six," Jonathan said as the giant wheel crested and swooped downward again.

"I love this!" Esme called into the wind. Something about

being on the wheel made her feel so much less self-conscious. "So you're a big movie star. What were you in?"

"Just one movie so far. *Tiger Eyes*. It closed pretty much before it opened. Except for New York and Chicago and here, where it's still in the art houses."

A breeze pushed some of Esme's dark hair onto her face; she brushed it away as the wheel started another revolution. "What's it about?"

"This guy, Martin—his dad's a screwed-up ex-cop who messes with his head. So Martin ends up with a kill-or-be-killed mentality."

"You were Martin?"

Jonathan nodded. "He drops out of college and lives on the mean streets. Falls for a junkie hooker. His dad pulls it together and tries to save him, but he hallucinates that his dad is a murderer and kills him."

"That sounds awful."

"It took three weeks to shoot—I was depressed as hell," Jonathan admitted. "I mean, I told myself how lucky I was to get the gig. The guy who wrote and directed it is fresh out of USC film school—everyone says he's a genius. But I'm a pretty positive guy. Spending three weeks in Martin's skin sucked."

"And when you went home at night, could you stop being him?" Esme wondered.

"Home? My hotel room." Jonathan corrected her. "The Comfort Inn in Metairie, Louisiana, where we shot in August because it was cheap. We're talking seriously low budget. I dreamed Martin's nightmares every night I was there."

"That must have been very painful," Esme said.

121

He nodded, cocking his head. "You mean that."

Esme was confused. "What?"

"You didn't just say the words. You meant them," Jonathan explained. "I see it in your eyes."

Esme shrugged. "Maybe I know what it's like to have nightmares."

He studied her for a moment. "Do you?"

"Not about a movie role." She looked away.

"What then?"

What, indeed? Real life? Like he could ever begin to understand. She pushed the windblown hair from her face again.

"Objects moving in a circle are under the influence of changing force."

"Which means?"

She leaned close to his ear. "That we're moving in a circle. And that I took physics last year."

Jonathan laughed. But they were returning to earth, where Esme carefully guarded her life, her past, the truth. The wheel slowed to a crawl. People in the cage below them stepped off to rejoin the festivities.

"So what's bumming you out, Esme?" Jonathan probed.

She shook her head. "Forget I said anything. Can we go around again?"

"As many times as you want."

"Why are you being so nice to me?"

"I like you." Jonathan waved off the ride attendant as she tried to help them out. "One more time."

"Have fun," the attendant told them. Their cage creaked upward. Then, as the wheel filled with passengers and finally whooshed them skyward, that feeling of freedom rushed over her again. She found herself telling Jonathan that she was also kind of an artist, only with ink on skin. How she saw a tattoo as a sacrament, a sacred trust between her and the person who offered up their flesh. When she'd started out, someone had told her what she could and should draw. But now, she only did her own designs. "And I will never let anyone tell me what I can do again," she finished.

"So you're the independent type, huh?" Jonathan teased.

"Let's just say I can take care of myself."

"Okay," he agreed. "Let's." He put his hand atop hers. She leaned her head into him. It felt like the most natural thing in the world.

After two more rides on the wheel, they debarked and wandered through the crowded party, lost in each other, words tumbling. Jonathan talked about how he felt he didn't really know how to act; that he wanted to learn and do live theater, maybe even write plays of his own. Esme talked about how she wanted to study serious art, like sculpture and oil painting. They laughed and joked. Ate cotton candy. He gave her a piggyback ride. Esme felt like a Latina Cinderella, at the most perfect place with the most perfect boy.

But even for Cinderella, the clock struck midnight. When they walked back to the east end of the pier, and out through the same door they'd entered, everything that glittered was no longer gold. The streetlamps cast their light on the Santa Monica homeless as well as the Beverly Hills rich, the have-nots as brightly lit as the haves. There were two worlds out here. She belonged to one. Jonathan, to the other.

As the traffic inched by on Ocean Avenue, just thirty or forty feet away, they made their way to the valet station and joined a long line of people waiting for their cars. Cars in both directions slowed so that their occupants could gawk at the partygoers, in the hopes of maybe recognizing someone famous. Esme felt eyes even on Jonathan and herself.

"¡Oye chica, qué guapa!" shouted someone derisively from one of the passing vehicles. *Hey, girl, you're hot!*

Jonathan drove a Prius. By the time he piloted it to Bel Air, the night felt thick, its magic trapped and then suffocated. She was just a girl who worked for his rich parents. Not Cinderella. Fairy tales were stupid. And dangerous.

"You have a girlfriend," she blurted out, when he went through the broken front gate and pulled up in front of his parents' home. "The girl on the tennis court."

She saw his half-smile. But he didn't speak. Just lifted her hand to his lips and kissed it.

21

Behind Lydia and Kiley, a rock band on a raised stage launched into the theme song from *The Ten*.

> *"Imagine the end of life as we know it.*
> *I can give you shelter from the swarm.*
> *If you're afraid, try not to show it*
> *Tomorrow there will be a brighter dawn."*

"Catchy," Lydia said, checking out the band. "The lead singer is yummy, don't you think?"

Kiley didn't answer. She was watching the big screen at the end of the pier again, which was still showing scenes from the film. At that moment, a hot guy in an equally hot Ferrari was trying to outrun the oncoming hailstorm.

"Holy shit," Kiley exclaimed. "I know him."

"Of course you do, he's in all the magazines. He's a Calvin Klein model."

"No, I mean I *know* him know him. His name is Tom." Kiley quickly told Lydia the story of how she'd met the guy at the Hotel Bel-Air after her auditory up-close-and-personal with his sex life. "Then I saw his billboard on Sunset Boulevard. And now, he's in this movie."

"Sweet. I'd *definitely* have sex with him," Lydia declared.

"You have sex on the brain."

"True. But I'd rather have it on various other body parts. Have you had sex yet?"

Kiley was taken aback. "I . . . uh . . . had a boyfriend last year and we sort of—"

"You mean you don't know if you did or you didn't?" Lydia pressed. "Is that possible?"

"I think we did," Kiley admitted. "But I prefer to think that we didn't, because, well, it sucked. He was so nervous that I got nervous and then . . . I don't know."

"Okay, then you didn't," Lydia opined. "You should hook up with Tom. He's pretty near a perfect male specimen. And you already heard how he had that girl hooting and hollering."

Kiley put a hand over her face. "Talk about embarrassing."

Lydia nudged her hip playfully into Kiley's. "Come on, it got you all hot and bothered. You know it."

"Well, maybe I'm not ready for hot and bothered," Kiley retorted.

"And maybe you are."

Kiley scrunched up her face. "But how do you know? Seriously, how do you know?"

Lydia blew a strand of hair off her face. "I say go for it and live long enough to write a torrid memoir."

Kiley laughed. "That's one way of looking at it."

"And you know what suite he's in," Lydia added. "You could just go knock on his door."

The band quit playing; a female executive from Cosmos Films with world-class hair and an extremely short skirt started to introduce the stars of *The Ten*. As she named each one, and asked the audience to hold its applause for the end, they dutifully trotted out on stage.

"Allegra Royalton! Tom Chappelle! Tara Reid! Kirsten Dunst! And Mr. George Clooney!"

Kiley grasped Lydia's arm and pointed. "There he is. That's him!"

Lydia nodded. "Dang, girl, you have good taste. I can't believe you ditched him when he wanted to show you the pool."

Kiley made a face. "I know, I'm an idiot. I just got freaked out. I mean, after all that moaning and groaning and 'oh, baby'ing."

"You could have asked to join in. I bet he would have said yes."

Kiley hid her shock as best she could. "Trust me. Nice girls in La Crosse don't ask to, er, join in."

"Well, the good thing is, you can change," Lydia mused. "Anyway, once you win *Platinum Nanny*, you won't live in La Crosse anymore."

"What makes you so sure I'll win?"

"I'm a positive thinker. You got your mother to let you come out tonight, didn't you?"

Kiley looked sheepish. "Only because she fell asleep at eight."

Up onstage, the studio executive finished her spiel about how wonderful the cast was, how wonderful the crew was, and how wonderful the film is. Kiley gazed at Tom in disbelief that she actually knew him. Well, sort of. He'd offered to show her the indoor pool, anyway.

Lydia nudged Kiley's arm. "Let's talk to him."

"I can't do that!"

"Of course you can. But you'd better hurry. They're all leaving the stage."

Kiley felt Lydia yank her forward as her heart began to pound double-time. *Okay,* she told herself. *You can do this. Act natural. Casual. Cool. Oh, hi, Tom. Suite next door, remember? This is your first film role? Can I jump your bones?*

But by the time they reached the stage, Tom was stepping into an extralong stretch limo behind Tara Reid. The doors closed, and the limo took off for parts unknown.

22

"As you can see, Platinum's home is very . . . platinum."

A.M. led the five remaining contestants into the rock star's living room, and Kiley willed her mind to focus. She wasn't about to blow it just because she hadn't gotten any sleep the night before. Just because in her fevered dreams she and Tom had done everything she had ever imagined . . .

Stop that right now, she commanded herself. *You're acting like some starstruck groupie. It's not as if you and he have this big thing happening. You have nothing happening. You will never have anything happening. So concentrate on what's important before you get kicked back to La Crosse on your well-padded ass.*

"*Très gauche,*" Veronique sniffed as she eyed the opulence that was Platinum's home. Since the cameras were rolling, Kiley assumed that Veronique thought superciliousness was going to get her somewhere.

In Kiley's humble opinion, Platinum's mansion was a

marvel. The living room itself contained sufficient square footage to house the Bowl-o-Rama where her father's league played, including all forty lanes. Everything was done in shades of white. From the marble table and velvet couches to the fresh floral arrangements that decorated the mantel, everything was blindingly, endlessly white. Kiley didn't know that this many shades of white actually existed.

"She must have some clean kids. Or else they aren't allowed in here," Tamika muttered. She was limping slightly because of her injured ankle. Kiley chucked her chin at Tamika's body mike, reminding her that anything they said could show up on air. Tamika shrugged. "Screw that shit. If Platinum wants a wuss, I'm not her girl."

Kiley admired Tamika's attitude. Privately, she'd been wondering the same thing.

"Hey, where's your mom?" Steinberg asked Kiley as A.M. led them into what she called the Meditation Room. Capital *M*, capital *R*.

"No clue," Kiley replied. When they'd arrived, her mother had been whisked away to another part of the house.

The Meditation Room was what A.M. described as "Platinum's sacred space." A five-foot stone Buddha sat on an altar against one wall. Pungent incense burned at his feet. On the wall behind the Buddha was a giant cross inlaid with jewels, an equally big golden star of David, and a silver crescent moon. Other than the half dozen bamboo mats on the floor, the rest of the room itself was barren.

The tour continued. The kitchen was as white as the living room. There was a home recording studio lined with platinum albums, and a home theater that featured posters from the movies in which Platinum had appeared. The group was then ushered through the family room. Finally, A.M. took them to the nursery.

"As in children, not plants," A.M. explained. She chuckled at her own inventiveness.

Kiley was relieved to discover that there actually was a place for children; an entire wing, actually. But the toys in the playroom were too orderly, the DVDs all neatly arranged. There wasn't a GameCube or an Xbox in sight. Did any kids actually live here?

Suddenly, bright lights snapped on, and Platinum herself made a surprise entrance. She was over five foot eight in her stocking feet, which meant nearly six feet tall in the white three-inch heels that currently adorned her feet. Her long, white blond hair hung as straight as polished mirrors down both sides of her narrow face. Her unlined skin shone as if she was twenty, though Kiley knew she was forty-two by some accounts, forty-five by others. She wore white jeans and a white silk shirt. In her arms was her dog—a white Pomeranian.

Platinum handed the dog to A.M., then swept her arms wide to the quintet of nanny hopefuls. "Welcome, welcome, welcome!" She seemed to have a slight British accent, though Kiley knew from her research that Platinum was from Michigan. "It's so wonderful to finally—"

"Hold up, Platinum, little lighting problem!" the director called out. "We'll need to shoot that entrance again."

"Dammit," Platinum snapped. "Give me Lil' Shit!" Platinum grabbed the dog from A.M., then stomped out of the room.

Okay, this was very weird. Platinum had a British accent when the camera was on, but sounded like an American truck driver when it was off. Well, maybe it wasn't all that surprising. Kiley had read a *Rolling Stone* interview where Platinum claimed that twenty-three personalities lived in her brain, and that she'd had sex with more than a hundred guys on a single concert tour. The interview had been accompanied by a photo of Platinum in ripped jeans and a T-shirt that read SCREW YOU. OH WAIT, I AL-READY DID.

"Okay, good to go," the director called. "Four, three, two, and . . ."

Platinum entered again, Lil' Shit in her arms. "Welcome, welcome, welcome!" She was British again. "It's so great to finally meet all five of you in person, and to know that soon one of you will be taking care of my terrific children. Now, let me show you to your accommodations."

"That's a take!" Bronwyn called. The cameras stopped rolling.

Platinum shoved Lil' Shit at A.M. again. "Have someone take him out so he can take a dump." She looked around. "Who took my freaking glass of wine?"

"Um, I don't think you brought it in with you, Platinum," Bronwyn murmured. "We talked about that before."

"Screw you." Platinum turned out.

A.M. turned to the remaining contestants, the dog still in her arms. "Okay!" she said brightly, as if everything was going swimmingly. "Time for you guys to see where you'll be living. Jayce, take this animal outside. Girls, follow Bronwyn."

A few minutes later, Kiley and the other contestants stood with Bronwyn in Platinum's guesthouse. It looked like a fairy-tale cottage: blue clapboard shutters, rocking chairs on the front

132

porch, and flowers blooming in the red window boxes. Inside was a cozy living room with a couch facing a fireplace and scatter rugs on the burnished hardwood floors. Both bedrooms held twin beds covered in floral quilts. There was one bathroom and a small kitchen.

"Nice?" Bronwyn asked. All five contestants dutifully expressed their enthusiasm for the cameras.

"Little problem, though. There are only beds for four. But someone else will be eliminated before tonight—and then there's Mom."

She looked pointedly at Kiley, who waited for her to elaborate. Nothing. Did that mean they'd keep her mother at the hotel? Or did that mean they'd be going home, so it wouldn't matter?

"Ladies," Bronwyn intoned. "It's time for you to meet the most important people on this show. Platinum's children."

A.M. stepped back. Platinum entered, holding the hands of a boy and a girl. "These are my younger ones. This is Siddhartha." Platinum lifted the boy's hand. He had the face of an angel— pale blond hair and huge blue eyes. "He likes to be called Sid. He's nine."

"So?" Sid asked belligerently, as if someone was challenging him.

"Anything you'd like to tell them, then, Sid?" Platinum asked, sounding vaguely as if she was channeling Princess Diana.

"Yeah." He dug into his back pocket and extracted a plastic box that held a card deck. "No one can beat me at Yu-Gi-Oh. No one."

"Do you have Blue Eyes White Dragon?" Cindy asked.

Sid's face lit up. "Three of 'em. If I use Polymerization, I can get Blue Eyes Ultimate Dragon. That's unstoppable."

"I've got an Egyptian God card. We'll have to play sometime," Cindy offered.

Score a big fat bonus point for Cindy, thought Kiley, who had vaguely heard of Yu-Gi-Oh. Didn't it have something to do with Japanese anime?

"And this is Serenity." Platinum looked down at the girl. "She's about to turn eight."

Serenity was a cherubic miniature of her mom, save for her golden hair, which was a rat's nest of snarls. Though her clothes looked brand new, her skin was extremely dirty.

"Anything you'd like to say, sweetie?" Platinum asked her daughter.

"Yes. Don't call me Seri. It's Serenity. Four syllables, Se-ren-i-ty. I hate green food. And I'm allergic to water."

"No you're not, dear," Platinum said through a smile.

"Yes I am, *Mother.*" The little girl extracted her hand and folded her arms.

"We've been dealing with a bathing issue," Platinum explained.

"Yeah. She won't take one," Sid interjected. "That's why she's dirty. And she stinks."

"At least I don't wet my bed like someone in this room," Serenity shot back.

"So, you suck."

"So, you suck harder, bee-otch!"

"Don't worry," A.M. assured Platinum. "We'll edit all this out."

Kiley tried not to look as shocked as she felt. In her house, if she'd ever spoken like that, she'd have gotten her mouth washed out with soap. Literally.

"It's cool. I mean, fine," Platinum corrected herself, and patted both children on their heads. "It's important that the children feel free to express their emotions."

Uh-huh. Kiley worked hard to keep her face in neutral.

A handsome teen boy shuffled into the cottage. His dark hair was fashionably punk. He wore a black T-shirt, baggy jeans, and black sunglasses. He looked like a junior rock God.

Platinum gestured toward him. "And this is my oldest child, Bruce."

" 'Zup?" he asked no one in particular.

"Bruce is fourteen," Platinum said.

"Call me the Boss," Bruce put in. "I'm outta here. Peace out." Without a further word, he loped out of the cottage.

"Bruce is leaving this afternoon for David Crosby's rock and roll camp, so you won't be seeing him for a while," Platinum explained. "All the more time for you to concentrate on my little ones."

Kiley studied the two younger kids as A.M. and Platinum conferred. No one knew who their fathers were. She'd read that Sid's dad was Ian Cummins, who'd been lead guitarist of the British punk band Brighton in the eighties. He had overdosed in 1999 at the Chelsea Hotel in New York, in the same room where Sid Vicious permanently checked out. Serenity was reputedly the offspring of Platinum's then-haircutter. As for Bruce—well, one supermarket tabloid had done an in-depth investigative piece on why Platinum's eldest child shared the same name as an American rock-and-roll icon. But there was absolutely no evidence that the icon had ever met Platinum, and the tabloid eventually retracted its story.

A.M. was ready again. "Time for our next elimination, which will also be your first nanny assignment with Platinum's kids." She held up a top hat. "There are five assignments on slips of paper in this hat. Each of you will pick one. You'll have two hours to accomplish your task. Understood?"

Cindy got her assignment first. She had to arrange an outing for the younger kids that would enhance their creativity. "Piece of cake," she declared.

Tamika was next. She had to work with the chef to create a gluten-free weeklong meal plan, and then cook a gluten-free dish.

Steinberg. Write an original song for Sid and have him perform it.

Veronique. Meditate for twenty minutes with Sid in the Meditation Room. Which would be eighteen minutes longer than he'd ever lasted before.

Kiley pulled the last slip of paper from the hat:

Get Serenity to take a bath.

Serenity scowled at Kiley and turned to her mother. "Mom, can we go now? This is boring. Come on, Sid."

She grabbed her brother. He yanked away and gave her the finger, but followed her out of the guesthouse.

"My kids rock," Platinum said with a fond smile.

Your kids are brats, Kiley thought behind her well-maintained pleasant smile. *How the hell will I get your bratty, stinky daughter to take a bath?*

"But contestants," A.M. continued, "there's more! One of

you is going to be working for one of the biggest rock stars in history. That means it's expected that you know her."

"Yes," Platinum agreed, back to her well-bred voice. "That is important because—" She stopped midsentence. "Screw this." The British accent was gone. She blocked the cameras' bright light with her arm. "Turn that shit off for a minute." The cameramen obeyed, as Platinum turned to A.M. "Listen, screw changing my image or whatever. I sound like an asshole. I'm just going to be myself."

"But we agreed—"

"Well, now we disagree. They want fake, let 'em get Madonna." She looked around. "Who has my goddamn dog?"

"Jayce took him out to poop," a flunky reported.

"Oh, cool," Platinum said. "Then have Mrs. Cleveland grill him a steak. Okay, let's roll 'em, jerk-offs."

The cameras went back on; the crew moved closer to the circle of contestants. Production assistants passed out small white boards and erasable markers as Platinum and A.M. took seats on a pair of stools.

"Before you can go off on your missions," A.M. told them, "we're going to see what you know about your famous employer."

"And I'm, like, staring at you," Platinum put in, wiggling her fingers at them. "I can see into your brains. So don't screw this up." Her eyes raked over the contestants, lingering on Kiley.

"Here's how it will work," A.M. continued. "I'll pose a question. You write the answer on your board. When you get five answers correct, you can start your mission. If you don't get five right, you never start. Got it?"

They got it. Kiley noticed that Veronique was not looking confident. Neither were Tamika and Steinberg. Well, Kiley had done her homework back in La Crosse. Bring it on.

It turned out that Cindy had done her homework too. She nailed the first three questions, about Platinum's birthplace (Flint, Michigan), her childhood as a military brat (Where was Platinum living at the age of thirteen? Answer: Wiesbaden, Germany), and her brief stint at the American Institute of Dramatic Arts in New York (where she'd had a torrid affair that resulted in a senior dean's dismissal).

"What was the name of Platinum's first album?" A.M. asked.

All five girls scribbled furiously. When they flipped over their slates, four of them had written *Double Platinum*. Kiley had written *Crispy Baby Burns*.

A.M. made some marks on her clipboard. "All correct but Kiley Mc—"

"Hold on," Platinum stopped A.M. "Kiley's right. The others are wrong."

"But your first album was *Double Platinum*!" Cindy protested.

"*Solo* album," Platinum corrected. "I did a Four-one-five Records recording with the Symptoms live at the Deaf Club in San Francisco in 1978. Nice one, Kiley."

Yes! It was everything Kiley could do to not pump her fist in the air.

The questions kept coming. What date did Platinum's first album go double-platinum? Who starred with Platinum in the video that won the MTV Video Award in 1991? Who was president when Platinum threw up on the undersecretary of defense at a White House state dinner for Nelson Mandela?

Kiley had four right answers, Cindy three. Everyone else had either one or none, when A.M. posed one more:

"Who owned this estate before Platinum bought it two years ago?"

"Merde." Veronique cursed under her breath. Steinberg and Tamika stared blankly at their slates. Kiley and Cindy wrote the same thing: David Bowie.

"Cindy and Kiley correct," A.M. pronounced. "Kiley has five right answers, she—"

There was no need for A.M. to finish the sentence, because Kiley was already heading out the door in search of Serenity.

23

Serenity wasn't hard to find. She was sprawled on the grass just outside the guesthouse, staring up at the clouds.

"Hi, Serenity," Kiley said.

"Hi."

"What are you doing?"

"Looking at stuff in the sky."

"Want to come inside with me?"

"Whatever." The girl got to her feet, and Kiley had a momentary ray of hope that this wasn't going to be as arduous as she had thought.

"So, I hear you don't like to bathe much."

"I didn't say I don't like to bathe," Serenity corrected her. "I said I'm allergic to water. There's a difference."

Serenity headed for the house, so Kiley did, too. She switched over to mouth breathing. Sid had been right; his sister stank. They crossed the slate patio and entered the main house through sliding glass doors in the back. It led them into the white-on-white family room, which didn't look all that different from the white-on-white living room, save for a large white fireplace that had obviously never been used.

"Let's watch a movie in my room," Serenity suggested, tugging Kiley toward the stairs. "I've got a TV and a DVD player and both *Tomb Raider* movies."

"What a great idea," Kiley exclaimed, going for cheerful. "How about if we watch one, then you try a bath?"

Serenity put her fists on her hips and glared at Kiley. "What are you, retarded? Do you think I'm going to fall for that?"

Kiley was flabbergasted. The mouth on this kid was amazing. In a bad way. Meanwhile, she could see the cameraman smiling behind his camera as he recorded every mouthy moment. She cleared her throat. "You really shouldn't call people names."

"I didn't call you a name, I asked you a question. 'Are you retarded?' That's a question."

Kiley slapped a smile on her face and willed it to stay there. "You know, you're right."

"I know. I'm always right. Now let's watch a movie."

They went up to Serenity's very white bedroom. The bookcases were neatly organized, the plush white carpet freshly vacuumed. Serenity went to one wall and pushed a button. A panel slid back, exposing her TV and rows of DVDs.

The little girl squinted in the darkness and plucked one out. "Have you seen *Not Another Teen Movie*? It's so funny."

Kiley had seen it. It was rated R and extremely raunchy. "You're allowed to watch that?"

"Sure. Whatever I want. My mom says that movies never hurt anyone." Serenity popped the DVD into the player and

141

pushed some buttons; the film started. Then she settled into one of the white leather beanbag chairs on her floor. Kiley couldn't think of anything to do but the same. The camera guy put down his heavy gear. "I can't film this," he told Kiley. "The light sucks."

"Snickers? Licorice Whips? Bit-O-Honey?" Serenity had picked up a small white telephone.

"Are you asking me what I want to eat?" Kiley asked.

"What are you, deaf?" Serenity shook her head as she spoke into the phone. "Mrs. Cleveland, I'm watching a movie. I want the candy box. Bring it upstairs to my room. Now."

She hung up and focused on the movie, where a teenage girl was trying to hide a vibrator under the covers of her bed before her family barged in. "Know what that is, Kiley? It's a neck massager," Serenity said knowingly. "The reason it's so funny is that she's putting it under the covers."

Thank God for small favors, Kiley thought.

"My mom has an even bigger one. Actually, six of them. They're in her closet. Sid and I play with them sometimes."

The idle cameraman cracked up. Great. She was sitting in the dark with an almost-eight-year-old, providing entertainment. How was she ever going to get this girl into a bath? Kiley knew she had to do something. So she took the remote and pushed the "Pause" button.

Serenity whirled around, brows knit with irritation. "What do you think you're doing?"

"We need to talk."

"No we don't. You work for me, you know," Serenity snapped. "Stop the movie and turn on the lights. I want the world to see what an idiot she is," she told the cameraman.

142

Kiley fought for self-control as the lights came on. "No, Serenity. I don't work for you. And if I become your nanny, I still won't work for you. I'll work for your mom."

"So?"

"So, an eight-year-old does not tell the nanny what to do."

Serenity sprawled on the plush carpet, arms behind her head. "Ha. I always tell the nanny what to do."

"You had a nanny before?"

Serenity eyed Kiley balefully. "What do you think?"

On a whim, Kiley stretched out next to her. "I think you ask a lot of questions when you already know the answers. Here's one I want to ask. What makes you think you're allergic to water?"

"I don't *think*. I *know*. Want to watch a different one? How about *Texas Chainsaw Massacre*? It's really gross and cool."

"Maybe later." Kiley propped herself up on one elbow. "When did you discover you were allergic to water?"

Serenity stared at the ceiling without answering.

"Because I'm guessing that before you became allergic to water, you took baths and showers," Kiley went on.

Before Serenity could answer, a heavyset woman in a white uniform trudged in, carrying a large plastic box. She set it down and opened the lid. It was filled with every type of candy sold at a movie concession stand; there were even two containers of fresh-popped popcorn. "Drinks?" the woman asked.

"Strawberry smoothie," Serenity said. She found a Snickers bar. "What do you want, Kiley?"

Kiley ignored her, stood, and extended her hand to the woman. "Hello. I'm Kiley McCann."

"Mrs. Cleveland," the older woman said, shaking Kiley's hand. "I'm the cook. Something to drink?"

"Nothing, thanks."

"Shall I take this away, Serenity?" Mrs. Cleveland indicated the candy box.

Serenity wrapped her arms around it. "Nope."

Mrs. Cleveland nodded politely at Kiley and departed; Serenity was already rooting around in the box for more candy. "Did you see *DodgeBall*? That really funny part where the mean guy got so fat? If I ever get that fat I'll get my stomach stapled like Carnie Wilson. She's a friend of my mom. I don't think her surgery worked too good because she's still kind of fat. Let's watch the movie again. I'm sick of talking."

Kiley frowned. She was getting nowhere fast. "Hey. Did you know that the most beautiful woman in ancient Egypt used to take baths in milk?"

Serenity put the half-eaten Snickers on the carpet and tore open some M&M's. "Really? That's interesting."

"It makes your skin very beautiful. Maybe you'd like a milk bath."

"Sure. If we fill our swimming pool. That'd be fun. I want to have fun. We could invite a lot of hos over, like in *Risky Business*. Know what a ho is? I do. It's a girl who has sex for money. I know about sex, like how people do it. Want to hear?"

Kiley's head swam. "You shouldn't be watching *Risky Business,* Serenity. Or this movie either, for that matter. You're too young."

"No I'm not."

"Your mother really allows you to watch those movies?"

Serenity kicked her shoes into the carpet. "I told you, she doesn't care."

"Your last nanny said it was okay?"

"She was a doodyhead with a funny accent. She lived in the guesthouse. I did whatever I wanted." She grabbed the candy box again and peered inside. "Red licorice?"

"No thanks. So you mean you brought whatever DVDs you wanted up here? Alone?"

Serenity tore open the licorice package with her teeth. "Maybe I did and maybe I didn't."

Kiley pressed on. "How about your brothers? Did they watch with you?"

"Bruce knows all the good ones. His friends come over and they stay up really late downstairs in the theater room."

"Do you stay up with them?"

"They kick me out. They say I'm too little." Serenity got a sly look on her face. "But they don't know everything."

Kiley thought she might be on to something. "Did you sneak inside?"

Instead of answering, Serenity scrambled to her feet. "I like that thing where we fill the pool up with milk. I'll call Mrs. Cleveland so she can buy a lot of milk." She picked up the house phone.

"You *did* sneak." Kiley was sure she was right. She gently took the phone from the little girl.

"Okay. If I tiptoe into the back of the theater downstairs, Bruce and his stupid friends are too busy making out and they don't even know I'm there." She jutted out her chin defiantly. "I can watch scary movies if I want to."

"You like them?"

The girl shrugged.

"What's the scariest one you ever saw?" Kiley asked.

"I don't want to talk anymore." Serenity jumped up, upsetting the candy box. "Let's go to Sid's room and play air hockey. Come on."

But Kiley didn't move. "When I was a kid, I once saw this movie that scared me so much," she recalled. "While people were sleeping, creatures from outer space invaded their brains and turned them into zombies."

Serenity fake-smiled. "Come on. That's not scary because it isn't real. Not like getting chopped up in a shower."

"You saw a movie where someone got chopped up in a shower?"

Serenity nodded. "It's a true story, too. About this man who's psychic. That's the name of the movie. *Psychic.*"

Psychic? "You mean *Psycho?*"

The little girl looked guarded. "Maybe."

"A crazy man attacks a lady taking a shower," Kiley prompted.

Serenity nodded. "And this friend of Bruce's, I heard her say it's a true story."

Jeez. Kiley took a guess. "Did you get allergic to water after you saw *Psycho?*"

Serenity nodded again.

Kiley went and smoothed the snarled hair off Serenity's face. "Sweetie, that's just a made-up story. It isn't real."

"Yes it is."

Kiley dropped her voice low so that the cameraman's mike wouldn't pick it up. "Know what, Serenity? I know a secret about that crazy guy in the movie."

"What?"

146

She dropped to the girl's ear and whispered, "He only attacks if the person in the shower is alone."

Serenity bit her lower lip and considered this. "Otherwise he'd get caught, right?"

"Yup. So if two people are in the bathroom and one of them is on guard . . ."

Serenity cut her eyes at Kiley. "You first."

"What?"

"You take a shower first and I'll guard you," Serenity explained. "If you don't get killed, you can guard me when I take a bath. In milk."

Kiley smiled. There was nothing in the rules that said the bath had to be in water. "Deal. Do you want to call Mrs. Cleveland to bring the milk, or should I?"

"I'll do it." The girl looked up at Kiley and smiled.

Kiley smiled back. It was the very first moment that Kiley liked her.

24

Thank God Aunt Kat has good taste, Lydia thought as she surveyed the clothes she was wearing, found in her aunt's closet: a pair of Seven jeans and a white T-shirt that read NICE GIRLS RARELY MAKE HISTORY.

But Kat was coming back from Connecticut the next day, and so were the kids. Lydia knew she'd need to get these clothes back into Kat's closet and do something to augment her own very limited wardrobe. So she was off to Rodeo Drive for a shopping spree, courtesy of the emergency Visa card that Kat had thoughtfully left for her in the guesthouse.

As she was pulling on the jeans, the phone rang. She flung herself across the bed to answer it. "Hello?"

"Miss Lydia?"

"Yep."

"This is Janeese—one of the housekeepers up at the main house. Xander just returned. He's ready for you."

"Thanks." Lydia hung up and checked out her reflection one last time before heading out. She'd also borrowed choice cosmetics from Kat and Anya's marble dressing table. Aunt Kat was quite the lipstick lesbian; her makeup collection would make Lil' Kim weep with envy. Lydia had helped herself to Benefit BADgal black eyeliner, Yves Saint Laurent mascara, and some MAC lip gloss. She shook her head: Kat's cowgirl-shaped rhinestone earrings danced on her earlobes. Maybe they were really diamonds; she made a mental note not to lose them. But she was sure they were insured. Anyway, work started tomorrow. No more borrowing after that. She tucked the brand-spanking-new credit card into her back pocket.

X was leaning against Kat's Beemer smoking a cigarette. "Shop-Till-You-Drop is ready for action," X pronounced, getting into the driver's side. He stubbed out the butt as Lydia climbed into the front seat next to him. "You look delicious. If I was straight, I'd definitely—"

"If you were straight, I wouldn't have begged you to take me shopping," Lydia said. She kissed his cheek. "Straight men have terrible taste and hate to shop. That's what it said in *Marie Claire*."

X pulled the Beemer out of the driveway, then reached for an open pack of gum in the seat divider and popped a piece into his mouth. "Your aunts hate when I smoke. Want some?"

Lydia unwrapped a stick. "Live and let die," she said easily, as she watched the lushly landscaped homes roll past and mentally calculated how long they'd have to shop. It was two o'clock. They had to pick Anya up at four-thirty at an *Out* magazine photo shoot that was being done at the Normandie Room, a gay club in West Hollywood. So, they had only a couple of hours to shop. It wasn't much, but at least it would be a start. "So what's up with my little cousins? They nice kids?"

"That is a subject I do not intend to touch." X honked at a Jaguar in front of them. The female driver was yakking on her cell and oblivious to the changing light at the corner of Benedict Canyon and Sunset Boulevard.

"Why?"

"Because we would not just be gossiping about the family that employs us, dear heart. We'd be gossiping about *your* family. That's why."

A few minutes later, X pulled up to the valet stand on Rodeo Drive and Burton Avenue. A short Latino man in a red vest and black pants opened Lydia's door. Then he trotted around the car and handed X the parking stub.

"Behold Two Rodeo Drive," X sang out with a flourish of his hand. "Three blocks of the most expensive retail in the world."

"Wow," Lydia breathed, as she took in the sight of what she'd previously seen only in magazines.

"Exactly," X agreed. "This is where every little girl learns that she too can grow up to be a hooker who looks like Julia Roberts, and marry a rich man who looks like Richard Gere."

Lydia frowned. "I have no idea what you're talking about."

"*Pretty Woman*?"

Lydia shrugged. "Never heard of it."

"God, you have a lot to learn." X took her hand and led her past a long row of boutiques. Armani. Gucci. Christian Dior. Chanel. He stopped in front of a particularly posh boutique with one lone suit in the window. "Bijan."

"Huh?"

"The most expensive store in the world, dear heart. Named for the Iranian gentleman who owns it. That suit, for example?" He gestured at the suit in the window. "It probably runs somewhere around twenty, twenty-three thou, more for the custom alterations. Throw in two hundred for the cashmere socks, six-fifty for the hand-sewn shirt, seven-fifty for the Italian loafers, and you're talking twenty-five thousand easy for the ensemble, plus tax. That's minus underwear and necktie. Although if you can afford the outfit, you can afford to get laid by someone gorgeous who won't care that you're not wearing your Calvins underneath."

"Too bad he doesn't sell women's clothes." Lydia chuckled. "I could do some damage in there."

They kept walking until they reached a fairy-book tableau of romantic archways and bubbling fountains. A man in an old-fashioned livery costume greeted passersby near a latte cart. A group of Asian tourists snapped photos of each other with the fountain as a backdrop.

X shook his head. "The first rule of shopping on Rodeo Drive: No photo ops. Ever. It screams tacky tourist."

"Got it. Can we go scream Chanel?"

A short walk took them back to the boutique, where a very slender young woman dressed entirely in black slid over to them. Her bright green eyes surveyed Lydia's T-shirt with disapproval. "May I help you?" she asked in a French accent.

"Hey," Lydia replied, exaggerating her slight Texas twang. "How y'all doing?"

"We all are doing quite well," the saleswoman sniffed.

"Cool!" Lydia exclaimed. "I'd like to look around."

"Very well. I will be at zee register." The woman turned away.

"Bee-otch," X muttered. "She pegged you. Texas tourist on a budget."

"That's why I laid on the 'aw shucks' accent," Lydia explained. "We'll, just have to prove the bee-otch wrong, won't we?" She marched to a rack, found a twelve-thousand-dollar vintage pink-and-black-tweed suit, and held it up for X's approval.

"You've got taste," he told her. "Of course, you can't wear the skirt with the jacket, it's much too ladies-who-lunch-ish. I'd say, go with the jacket and jeans and do-me pumps; try the skirt with a tough-girl muscle tee and too much smoky eyeliner."

"Will do." Lydia went back to the racks and quickly gathered up two more suits, a black cocktail dress, and four silk shirts.

The French woman noticed Lydia's growing pile of clothes and raised her eyebrows in surprise. "Zee changing room?" she asked.

"Unless y'all want me to strip down right here," Lydia said brightly.

The clerk looked faint and opened a door to the dressing room. It was larger than Lydia's hut in the Amazon and featured three velvet-cushioned chairs, a silk brocade love seat, and a two-hundred-seventy-degree array of mirrors. "*Monsieur* would like to come in wiz you?"

"You know, *monsieur* would," Lydia said. "But if I strip in front of him, he just won't be able to help himself, if you know what I mean. And I'd hate to stain up that cute little couch."

She could hear X's laughter as she sashayed inside. It was just like being a little girl in Houston again as she tried on garment after garment. She couldn't make up her mind. So she did what she used to do in Houston—opted to buy them all.

Five minutes later, Lydia was at the cash register, watching the French clerk impassively total up her purchases: $24,428.44, tax included. Lydia handed over her credit card, feeling effervescent from the joy of shopping.

"We have time for one more boutique before we pick up my aunt, don't we?" Lydia asked X. "Let's do Christian Dior. No. Harry Winston. I need some bling of my own, seriously, and—"

"*Mademoiselle?*" the cashier interrupted. "Zere is a bit of a problem. Your card has been declined."

"It can't be declined, it's brand new," Lydia insisted. "My aunt just gave it to me."

"Maybe you've got a twenty thou limit," X mused as the clerk pushed the card back to Lydia. "How boring."

"Maybe so," Lydia allowed grudgingly. She picked up one of the suits and separated it from the pile, then gave the clerk the card again. "One more time, please."

But the same thing happened; the machine rejected the card. Lydia reduced her pile of clothes one more time. Same thing.

The clerk's face went from implacable to irritated to withering. "Perhaps you should check wiz your bank," she suggested. Then she walked away.

"Call Visa," X advised. "There's got to be some kind of screwup."

"Good idea," Lydia said. She took out her cell and called the number on the back of her credit card, following the voice prompts until she reached a recording that advised her of her credit limit.

"Your credit limit is one hundred dollars," said the robotic voice.

Red-faced, Lydia motioned X out of the boutique, where she

told him what she'd heard. "I can't even buy a pair of socks here for under a hundred dollars! Maybe my aunt meant it to be a hundred *thousand* dollars or something." She started to speed-dial Kat, then realized her aunt might be too busy packing up the kids for their return home. So she called Anya.

"Hello?"

"Hey, Anya? It's Lydia."

"What's up? This is bad time. We're just to finish shoot."

"I'll make it quick then. So, um, you and Kat know I don't have any clothes. And I was just doing a little shopping on Rodeo Drive—"

"Not with hundred-dollar limit, you're not," Anya told her.

"What?"

"Card is for emergency only. Like Kat told you."

Had her aunt mentioned that? Honestly, Lydia hadn't been paying a lot of attention, so thrilled had she been to have a credit card of her own.

"Well, not having clothes *is* an emergency," Lydia insisted.

"If you want to shop on Rodeo Drive you must to save money," Anya chided.

"How can I save money? You're only paying me three hundred dollars a week!"

"With car, house, and meals," Anya reminded her. "Hold on." Lydia waited while Anya spoke to someone; then she got back on the line. "Now I am glad you called. We do change of plans. My shoot runs long, so go back to house and make children welcome, please."

Lydia was confused. "But they're not home yet."

"I mean prepare for them. For tomorrow. Signs for rooms

that say Welcome Home. Some balloons, maybe. Ask cook to bake vegan soy cookies. Children are lactose intolerant. I prepare list of children's schedules. I will give to you later."

"Okay, *fine,*" Lydia agreed with a long-suffering sigh. "But what about clothes? Am I supposed to just keep borrowing yours?"

"What clothes of mine did you borrow?" Anya asked sharply.

Shit. "Never mind. I'll take it up with Kat."

"You will see, she and I agree on everything," Anya predicted. "Two bodies, one mind. We talk later."

She hung up. So did Lydia.

"Well?" X prompted. "Wal-Mart in East L.A.?"

Lydia shook her head. "I'd rather go naked," she muttered. "Not only am I broke, we have to go back home so I can have the cook make vegan cookies for the kids, whatever the hell vegan cookies are."

"They suck, dear heart," X said cheerfully as they headed back toward the valet.

"So does my life," Lydia said.

She had to face facts: She was a nanny. She was broke. Even if she was in a devoutly coveted zip code, she was still on the outside looking in.

25

Esme was heading down the path from the main house to the sandbox with Easton and Weston when she saw her mother approach from the other direction.

"Mama!" Esme exclaimed. It felt surreal that they both had the same employer.

"Esme." Her mother smiled like the sun. *"Y los niños. Cómo están hoy?"*

"Estamos muy bien," Weston said. Then she looked past Esme's mother and pointed to the tennis court. *"Yo quiero jugar al tenis con mi hermano Yon-o-tin!"*

Esme followed Weston's gaze to the tennis court, where Jonathan was rallying with a hard-hitting guy in his twenties.

"Esme?"

Esme turned back to her mother. "What?"

Mrs. Castaneda was gazing at her with a knowing look.

"What?" Esme repeated.

"*Qué pasa con* Jonathan?"

Esme flushed; her mother had always been able to read her like a book. "Nothing."

Her mother sniffed. "See that it doesn't turn into something," she said in English. Then she smiled, said goodbye to the girls, and headed briskly toward the main house.

"*Esme? Tenis por favor?*" Easton asked, tugging on her hand.

Esme looked at the court, where Jonathan whacked a cross-court forehand. He looked so perfect out there, like someone from *The Great Gatsby,* a book she'd devoured in eighth grade. Last night she'd dreamed of him, in a huge canopied bed with silk sheets strewn with rose petals. He'd kissed her, and undressed her, and—

Oh God. She couldn't possibly face him. She couldn't.

"No, you want to play in the sandbox, remember?" Esme reminded Easton in Spanish.

But Easton shook her head and charged off toward the tennis court. "Jonathan!" she cried, pronouncing her brother's name *Yon-o-tin.*

"Hey, little girl!" Jonathan waved. Then he noticed Esme and Weston, and gave them an easy wave, too. Moments later, Easton was out on the court, hugging his legs. Then Weston bolted from Esme's grasp and did the same thing. Esme, with no choice, followed them.

"They seem very attached to you," Esme said stiffly.

"Literally." Jonathan grinned.

"Sorry to interrupt your game."

His eyes met hers. "Actually, I was just thinking about you."

The way his words affected her, Esme felt like an elevator in free fall. "Yes, well . . . ," she managed.

His partner came up to the net. "Jon? You done for the day?"

"Yeah, let's knock off, okay?"

"We on for Friday?"

"Absolutely."

The other guy gathered his gear and left the court. "He's a pro from the Riviera Country Club," Jonathan told Esme. "He's trying to improve my serve. It's a losing battle."

Esme had no idea what to say to that. She had no frame of reference for a life that included a compelling desire to improve one's tennis serve.

"Ball," Easton chirped. She picked up a stray yellow tennis ball.

"Hey, she used English!" Jonathan exclaimed.

"Ball! Ball! Ball!" Weston cried, not to be outdone.

Jonathan got his tennis racquet and handed it to Easton, positioning her hands around the grip. "Like this," he said, and helped the child swing a two-handed backhand. Easton giggled with delight. "I'll have to get them kids' racquets."

"Actually, I think Andre Agassi and Steffi Graf just sent two," Esme said. "They're on my thank-you list."

"Excellent. Listen, toss a ball to Easton, okay?"

Esme picked up a tennis ball and bounced it to the girl. With Jonathan's help, she swung and made contact, which caused her to chortle with delight.

"*Más, más!* Again! Again!"

"Learning English through tennis. We may be on to something." Jonathan grinned.

For the next fifteen minutes, Jonathan helped Easton, and then Weston, swing at the balls that Esme would toss. He encouraged them after their misses and applauded their successes.

He was, Esme realized, great with them, sweet, patient, and kind. He didn't seem to resent instant siblings from another culture. Quite the opposite. What a good guy. But Esme didn't want him to be a good guy. She didn't like her heart's staccato beat when he stood near her.

When both twins were chasing down tennis balls, Jonathan sidled over to Esme and handed her a racquet. "Maybe you need help with your swing, too. Hold it like you're shaking hands." Then he turned her sideways, got behind her, and stretched her racquet back. "How does that feel?" His voice was low, his breath hot on her neck.

"Did you ask your girlfriend that the other day?" Esme asked.

"What girlfriend?"

"The girl you were—"

"Jonathan?"

It was Diane Goldhagen, standing outside the tennis court fence. Esme quickly stepped away from Jonathan and made sure that her boss couldn't see her reddening face.

"Hey," Jonathan said easily.

"How are the girls doing, Esme?" Diane asked. Her voice sounded stilted, as if she had seen something she disapproved of but was too polite to point it out.

"We were going to the sandbox but they wanted Jonathan to give them a tennis lesson." Esme tried to be reassuring.

"That's fine. Hello, my angels!" she called to the girls. They turned and looked at her for a brief instant, then went back to gathering up balls as if she didn't exist. But since Esme had started her job, Diane barely saw the twins; she was always out. So she couldn't really blame the girls for not responding.

Esme figured she should play the good nanny, so she hustled

159

over to them. "*Niños, es su mama!* Go see your mother," she chided, ushering them toward the fence. They took exactly two steps in that direction, froze, and scuttled back to Esme. Their silence was deafening.

"Give 'em time," Jonathan said.

"Right," Diane agreed, though Esme could see how hurt she was. "Well, Esme, I'm off to a meeting at the Getty, then I'll be at Yoga Booty, and after that I've got a facial at Sea Mountain Spa."

Esme nodded.

"Oh. The cutest twin handcrafted rocking ponies were just delivered from the Olsen twins. Let Easton and Weston decide where they want to put them," Diane continued. "I added them to the new thank-you list; there's a hard copy on your kitchen table."

"Fine," Esme said. "I'll take care of it."

"Great. So, call my cell if you need me. Bye, my angels!" The twins paid no attention. They were too busy pegging each other with tennis balls. Diane attempted a smile, then left.

Anxiety washed over Esme. "I should have made the girls go to her. And I never should have . . ."

"What?"

Let you flirt with me. I have a boyfriend. I haven't even told you that. So why do I want you to take me in your arms and—

"No," she said aloud, forcing herself to ignore him. She turned to the girls. "Come on, *niños*. Let's go to the sandbox."

26

"Where the hell is Platinum?" A.M. boomed at a flunky wearing headphones.

"I don't know, A.M., I can't find her," the girl replied helplessly. "I called the house, the studio . . ."

A.M. rolled her eyes. "That's so damn typical."

Kiley looked around, taking in the surroundings. The four remaining contestants had been taken by minivan from Platinum's estate to the Universal Studios lot in Burbank—a stop-and-go trip because of the traffic; it had taken nearly an hour. There had been speculation in the van that the challenge had something to do with the famous Universal Studios theme park and City Walk. But instead of going to that park, they went through the security gates of the actual movie studio, and only stopped when they reached an exterior movie set that had been made to look like a street in downtown Manhattan.

Platinum herself was supposed to be on hand for this challenge—the girls still didn't know what it was going to be—but they'd been waiting a half hour and the rock star still hadn't shown up. So they'd been left to cool their heels on a few benches that had been set out near the food service table.

A.M. checked her watch. "We'll give her a few more minutes, then we'll get started." A makeup girl rushed to A.M. and touched up her powder, while the stylist sprayed gloss on her hair.

Kiley took a water bottle from the food service table, screwed off the top, and guzzled some down. It was just her, Cindy, Veronique, and Tamika, since Steinberg had bit the dust the day before. When Sid informed Steinberg that he hated to sing, she'd written a rap for him instead. But when it came time to perform it in front of his mom and the group, Sid had mooned the cameras and all of America. That put Steinberg on the next plane to New York.

After they had completed their Platinum-savvy exam, the others had succeeded in their missions, more or less. Tamika had created a gluten-free dish for the kids, though when Platinum sampled it, she said it tasted like ass. Veronique managed to keep Sid in the Meditation Room for twenty minutes; Kiley didn't want to know how. Cindy had, as usual, shone on her assignment. She'd arranged for the kids to have an introductory lesson at a tae kwon do studio and then be videotaped while sparring against a blue screen. Meanwhile, she'd contacted an animation studio in Toluca Lake to retouch the video to make it look as if the kids were slaying dragons and demons. The finished product would then be ready in time for Serenity's birthday party in two weeks.

What's getting a kid to take a bath compared to that?

Finally, A.M. shooed the beauty contingent away. "Okay, we're starting, I'll kill Platinum later. You ready?"

Bronwyn nodded. "Three, two, one, and . . ."

"We're here at world-famous Universal Studios for another *Platinum Nanny* challenge," she told the camera, and then pointed to the far end of the street. "Contestants, take a look at this."

At the other end of the set, a double line of black sport-utility vehicles rolled in their direction. There were four of them, complete with a sound track, as vintage Platinum rock and roll pounded from their open windows. They came to a stop directly in front of the contestants.

"Ladies, some people call Los Angeles a car culture. I call it the world's most dangerous place to drive," A.M. declared. "Not only are there hundreds of miles of jam-packed freeways, but we've also got some of the most lunatic drivers on the planet. As Platinum's nanny, you're going to spend a considerable amount of time behind the wheel. Taking the kids to lessons, picking up pizza in Santa Monica . . . you haven't really lived until you've spent all day in a car with three feuding kids."

"I hate to drive," Veronique muttered. "In Paris I always take zee Metro."

"This challenge will test all the skills you'll need, and more," A.M. continued. "In the backseat of these SUVs, you'll find life-size crash test dummies made up to look like Platinum's kids. You'll be driving them through an obstacle course right here on the famous movie sets of Universal Studios. The fastest ones through the course stay in the competition. Finish last? Have a pleasant life."

Kiley felt her mouth go dry. She'd only had her driver's

license for six months. And driving in La Crosse was a piece of cake; big traffic was when a train came through downtown on its way to Iowa and the railroad gates backed things up for a few hundred yards.

"We're going to send you off at thirty-second intervals," A.M. explained. "Veronique, you start. Then Cindy. Then Kiley. Tamika, you're last."

"Thanks a lot," Tamika said.

"It's to your advantage," A.M. told her. "You can learn from their mistakes."

"They got the dummies in the kids' clothes," Tamika remarked, peering into the SUV next to Kiley's. "Now that's freaky."

"One more thing," A.M. called. "If the crash test dummies hit their heads, you get penalized five minutes."

A driver in full NASCAR gear helped Kiley behind the wheel and helped her put on the crash helmet and driving gloves. She turned the key. A Platinum song wailed from the sound system at earsplitting volume. She tried to turn it down. The knob turned, but the volume didn't change. The other girls' sound systems competed with Kiley's; it was deafening.

A.M. held a bullhorn to her mouth. "Veronique, ready?"

The French girl waved one arm out the window.

"And . . . go!"

The black SUV leaped forward, smoke pouring from the exhaust as Veronique roared down the first street and smoked into a hard right turn.

"Cindy, ready?"

Cindy waved.

"And . . . go!"

Cindy took her cue from Veronique and sped down the first street so fast that Kiley grimaced, afraid she'd collide with the far wall. But she managed to brake enough to whip around the corner. Then, she too was gone.

"Kiley, ready?"

Kiley had a hard time taking her white-knuckled hand off the steering wheel to signal yes. But she did it.

"And . . . go!"

Kiley accelerated as fast as she dared. In ten scary seconds she was at the far end of the street and executing the same hard right-hand turn she'd seen Cindy and Veronique do. The movie set street changed from Manhattan to the Wild West, complete with horses tied to hitching posts and cowboys passing time in front of the local saloon.

So far, so good.

That's when all hell broke loose.

Suddenly, the cowboys pulled guns from their holsters and started blasting her. *Blam! Blam! Blam!* Kiley instinctively weaved the SUV to and fro in an effort to avoid the shots. Then something red spattered on her windshield, and she realized the "bullets" were only paintballs—annoying, but not deadly. But she had no time to think, because there was a quick right turn, and a left turn, and then suddenly she was on a dirt road filled with dozens of granite boulders. Kiley mashed the brake pedal, swerving in what felt like slo-mo. In her rearview mirror, she saw Tamika's SUV gaining on her.

Faster, she told herself, flinging the steering wheel from left to right. But then, a five-foot-high boulder blocked her way. She couldn't stop.

She screamed and slammed into it.

It broke into a zillion pieces like the movie-prop, papier-mâché boulder that it was. Kiley realized too late that she'd wasted precious time, that she could have powered right down the street, boulders be damned. Which is exactly what Tamika was doing, now that she'd seen Kiley crunch a "boulder" to smithereens.

Grimly, Kiley followed a huge arrow and turned to the left. She was now on a street that had been made to look like small-town USA—almost like Main Street in La Crosse. GO RAVENS! STATE BASKETBALL CHAMPS! A banner was strung from building to building. But there wasn't time to take in the surroundings, because Tamika had powered her SUV practically alongside Kiley's. Bad news, Kiley knew, because it meant that her best friend in the competition had made up nearly thirty seconds.

Just below the banner was a broad puddle, maybe twenty feet across. Kiley and Tamika reached it at the same time. Splash! The two SUVs blew into what turned out to be a three-foot-deep pool of water.

Kiley and Tamika roared out of the water neck and neck. Both girls raced toward yet another sharp right turn. Kiley gripped the wheel. She was on the right side; she had position. But Tamika was edging ahead of her. Kiley knew that to have any chance, she had to reach that corner first.

She floored the SUV; Tamika did the same a split second later.

That was when disaster struck for the girl who knew better than anyone how to drive in Los Angeles, since she was from Southern California.

As Tamika braked to turn, her SUV hit a slick spot on the street and slid a bit to the left. She tried to correct the skid, but went too far. A moment later—Kiley saw the whole thing in her rearview mirror—Tamika was in a dangerous three-hundred-sixty-degree spin. She didn't hit anything, fortunately, but did come to rest under an overhang from a mock storefront. And when she tried to get her SUV back into the race, it wouldn't move. She was stuck. Kiley, who'd slowed to make sure Tamika was okay, saw her friend slam her arm against the side panel in frustration.

Kiley exhaled. All she had to do was finish the obstacle course. She was sad that the person she'd beaten was Tamika—why couldn't it be that bitch Veronique?—but it meant she would survive another day, and that's what it was all about.

27

Kiley slid her eyes to Cindy and Veronique; the three were in Platinum's living room, seated in identical white-on-white chairs. They were the only *Platinum Nanny* candidates left, after Tamika's departure.

They'd been told to meet at six p.m. sharp for a preview of the next day's challenge. But that hour had come and gone. It was already 6:15, and they were the only ones in the white room. No producers. No film crew. No A.M. No Platinum. Not even Kiley's mother, who'd been taken away by a production assistant to a Topanga Canyon herbalist who specialized in panic disorders.

"I guess they're running behind," Kiley said tentatively.

"Gee, you think?" Cindy asked, her tone withering. She drummed her fingers on the armrest of her chair. "You should feel good that you got this far, Kiley."

"What's that supposed to mean?"

"It means you are, how do you say in English, a gimmick," said Veronique. She pronounced the word *gee-meek*.

"You don't know that," Kiley replied, holding her ground.

"Please," Cindy scoffed. "They're never going to give this gig to a seventeen-year-old kid. The liability issues alone stagger the mind."

Kiley searched for a stinging comeback, but couldn't fashion one.

But she's wrong, I can still win. And I'd have friends here, too. I had such a fantastic time at the pier with Lydia and Esme. I'd have a whole new life. I'd be a California resident and I'd get into Scripps and—

Suddenly, A.M. strode into the room. But to Kiley's surprise, no camera crew trailed her.

"Ladies," she began, her brow furrowed so deeply that the creases looked like irrigation ditches. "We've got a bit of a problem."

"Define 'a bit,' " Cindy said warily.

A.M. cleared her throat. "The network has decided to go in another direction."

"Shit." Veronique cussed in English for once, pulled a cigarette out of her purse, and fired it up.

Kiley didn't understand. "What does that mean, exactly?"

"It means the show is cancelled, you ignorant cheesehead," Cindy snapped. She glared at the producer. "Game over, right?"

"Something along those lines," A.M. agreed. "Thank you all for participating."

"Son of a goddamn bitch," Cindy seethed.

"Wait. How can it be over? It hasn't even started!" Kiley was stunned. She'd been close. So close.

"The network did the usual," A.M. explained. "Put together some segments, brought in focus groups, had them watch what we were going to put on the air. Bottom line: The test audiences in Burbank didn't respond to it. The network says they might burn off a few episodes in the summer and then do an interview with Platinum or something, one of those 'shows that never made it' thingies. I'm sorry, guys. This is bad news for me, too, but it's on to the next. It was fun while it lasted and all that. We'll pay your airfare home, of course."

"There is no next for me," Kiley said. She dug the nails of her right hand into the flesh of her left hand to keep from sobbing.

"Come on, Kiley," A.M. began, her voice more exasperated than kind. "You had an all-expenses-paid, kick-ass adventure. Didn't you?"

Kiley couldn't bring herself to nod.

"You didn't actually think you were going to win, did you?" A.M. asked.

Veronique stood. "I need a limo to the airport."

"Limo? Gimme a break," A.M. scoffed. "No budget for limos. Share a cab."

"Fine," Cindy told her. "Eat me very much."

She and Veronique stomped out a moment before Platinum stumbled into the room from the other direction. Her hair was a mess. There were dark smudges of mascara under her eyes. She held an open bottle of champagne.

"Hey, no hard feelings, okay?" she asked Kiley, slurring her words slightly. "Want some?"

Kiley shook her head. "No. Thanks."

"Whatever." Platinum took a swig from the bottle.

Kiley knew she should do what Cindy and Veronique had just done: leave. She should pack, meet up with her mom, and go to the airport. She'd be back in La Crosse in time for the eleven o'clock news. But depression made her legs feel leaden. "I just . . . I don't know what to say."

"Cheer up. You weren't going to win. Cindy was."

So, Cindy had been right; everyone knew but her. And Veronique had been right; she had just been a gimmick all along. She'd been the small-town, underage cheesehead chick there for comic relief.

"It's so—so unethical," she told Platinum.

The rock star shrugged. "I'm suffering too. Because *someone* in this room couldn't *shit* a decent reality show."

A.M. bristled. "That is crap and you know it, Platinum."

"Oh yeah?" Platinum challenged. "Who said: 'Change your image, Platinum. Go for classy, Platinum'?" the singer mocked. "This is all your fault, you tight-ass bitch."

"Well, screw you and the bottle you rode in on, you sorry over-the-hill sack of shit," A.M. shot back.

"Get the hell out of my house!" Platinum flung the champagne bottle at A.M.'s head. A.M. ducked; the bottle crashed in a lethal confetti against the wall, champagne spewing everywhere.

A.M. fled. Platinum watched her hasty departure, then wiped her mouth with the back of her hand. "I can't stand that bitch," she told Kiley. "She hasn't gotten laid since Woodstock."

Whatever. Kiley cleared her throat. "Umm . . . do you know if my mom is back from Topanga?"

"I'm not really drunk, you know."

"I asked you—"

"Yeah, I heard you. I'm nuts, not deaf." She gazed at the remains of the champagne bottle. "I need another one. We can share. What the hell, you got screwed today, too."

Before Kiley could respond, Serenity stepped into the living room. "Mom, where did the stupid maid put my pink shirt?"

"Shit," Platinum mumbled, and buried her head in her hands.

Kiley watched Serenity stare at her mother; for the briefest instant, the girl looked her age—lost and scared. Kiley knew how it felt to have a drunken parent; she'd seen her father that way enough times. It was terrible.

"Come on, Serenity," Kiley told the girl. "I'll help you find it."

Serenity didn't budge, just eyed her mother. "Is she stoned, drunk, or both?"

"She's just not feeling good," Kiley said.

"Gimme a break, don't lie to me," Serenity spat. "I want my pink shirt. *I want my pink shirt!*" Her voice rose to a pitch that would injure canine eardrums.

Mrs. Cleveland came running into the room. "I found it in the kitchen, sweetie," she told Serenity. "Come on with me." The little girl allowed herself to be ushered out of the room.

Platinum peeked out from behind her hands. "There's no pink shirt in the kitchen. Mrs. Cleveland saves my ass all the time."

"I figured." Kiley licked her dry lips. "Well, I'll just be going, then."

"Yeah." Platinum raked a hand through her messy hair. "Sorry you missed your fifteen minutes of fame, Kelly."

"Kiley. I never *wanted* my fifteen minutes. I *wanted* the job."

"Why the hell would anyone *want* to be my nanny?"

Kiley sighed. "It doesn't matter anymore. Bye."

Kiley was halfway to the door when Platinum called to her. "Hey, I still need a nanny."

Kiley stopped. "What?"

"You were great with my kid just now—don't think I didn't notice."

The tiniest bubble of hope began to percolate in Kiley's stomach. "I can have the job? Really?"

"Yeah, you can have the freaking job. But the first thing you have to do is get me some more champagne. Pick up the house phone. Tell Mrs. Cleveland I want the Taittingers. If she doesn't answer, go to the kitchen and find it in the fridge. Is that so tough?"

"No."

Platinum smiled. "Good girl. Welcome to my world."

Kiley couldn't help it. She actually grabbed Platinum and hugged her. "Oh my God, this is so fantastic!"

"Off me," Platinum mumbled into Kiley's shoulder.

Kiley backed away. "Sorry. I'm just so . . . this is great."

"There's still some stuff to work out. Your mother is even more whacked-out than I am. You really think she's ready to make me your guardian?"

"Maybe if you talk to her."

Platinum gave a brittle laugh. "I have my own loony mother to deal with. Plus, I'm about to get hammered. You're on your own."

Kiley squared her shoulders with resolve. "Okay, I can do that. What do I have to lose? I'll talk to her. The worst thing she can say is"—Kiley and Platinum said it at the same time—"No."

• • •

173

"No. Absolutely not." Mrs. McCann strode past her daughter to retrieve her suitcase from the guesthouse bedroom.

"But, Mom. You can't say no," Kiley implored as she followed her mother. "What did we do all of this for, if you were going to say no anyway?"

Kiley's mother found the suitcase and hoisted it onto one of the twin beds. "I wanted to meet her. Now that I have, I will never make that . . . *woman* your guardian, Kiley. I don't trust her."

"Then why did you tell me to win, Mom? Why?"

"Because I trust you."

Kiley shook her head. "I'm totally confused."

Mrs. McCann pressed a hand to her slender chest. "I know I have some . . . issues, Kiley. I get nervous. Anxious. But that doesn't make me stupid."

"I never said—"

Her mother raised a palm to stop Kiley midsentence. "Listen to me, honey. You know Mr. Bartlett, right?"

Kiley sighed with impatience. "He owns the Derby, where you waitress. But what does that have to do with—"

Her mother raised her hand again. "Mr. Bartlett always brags on his son, Sam, how Sam started at the U when he was only seventeen. So before we came out here, I asked Mr. Bartlett about who was in charge of Sam when he was at school, you know, before he turned eighteen. And Mr. Bartlett said: Sam. I didn't understand. But it's something called . . . it starts with an *e*. What the heck was it, a something minor—"

"You mean an emancipated minor?" Kiley asked, incredulous.

"That's it."

"You'd let me do that? Be a legal adult, even though I'm still seventeen?"

Mrs. McCann put her hand over her daughter's. "Kiley. When we were seniors at La Crosse High School, my best friend Arletta and I said we would go to Florida when we graduated. I don't know why we picked there—because it's warm, I guess. We were gonna get an apartment on the beach. Meet rich boys with yachts. Live the high life. You betcha."

"I never knew you wanted to live in Florida."

"It was a dream." Her mother got up, went to the bedroom window, and stared outside for a moment. "Anyhow, Arletta went. I still get Christmas cards from her."

"And you didn't."

Mrs. McCann turned back to her daughter and crossed her arms. "I can't help who I am, Kiley. Little things turn into big things and make me nervous. I know that. I hate it about myself, but . . ." Her hands fluttered in the air. "I don't want the same thing to happen to you."

"You'll let me stay? Really?"

Her mother nodded. "I can't give you your ocean, Kiley, but it's right out there." She gestured toward the window. "Get it for yourself."

The love welled up inside Kiley; she gave her mother a fierce hug. "Thank you, Mom. Thank you so much."

"You're welcome so much." Mrs. McCann pulled far enough away to look into her daughter's eyes. "Don't let fear hold you back, Kiley. Hear me?"

Kiley's voice caught in her throat. "What about . . . Dad?"

Kiley watched her mother's mouth settle into a grim line of determination. "I'll take care of him."

Suddenly, the impossibility of what she wanted hit Kiley in the gut. Who was she kidding? This was her mother she was talking to, a woman who, no matter how well intentioned, couldn't make it inside the Scripps Institution for a tour without hyperventilating.

Kiley shook her head. "No. You can't. *I* can't. You'd have to fly back to Wisconsin by yourself. Face Dad. I wouldn't be there to help you. Forget it. What was I thinking? I must be the most selfish person on the—"

"Kiley, listen to me." Mrs. McCann took her daughter by the shoulders and stared into her eyes. "You are not letting my problems hold you back."

"But—"

"I can do this, Kiley. I *am* doing it. Not just for you. For both of us."

28

DAILY SCHEDULE FOR MARTINA AND JIMMY

(Lydia—talk to me with questions.—Anya)

6:30—Wake children. Shower, dress. Apply SPF 30 sunblock to all exposed skin.

6:45—Fast walk around property. Make sure children wear proper shoes.

7:00—Breakfast. Hot flax cereal, bananas, soy milk.

7:30—Read front section of <u>Los Angeles Times</u>. Quiz children on current events.

8:30—Chess on computer. Please supervise.

10:30—Russian tutor. Address is on bulletin board in study. Make sure children tape session for later review.

12:00–Lunch. No sweets, fried food, or milk products.

12:30–Educational video game, children's choice.

1:00–Tennis lesson. If Jimmy says he has stomachache, do not believe him.

Lydia sagged against the stucco wall in the family room. There was a lot more on the list, but she just couldn't face it right now. Anya *had* to be joking. Any kid would go nuts with this kind of schedule. Plus, she'd go insane if she had to enforce it. Where was the fun?

Anya rushed past Lydia. "You didn't hear door?"

No, she hadn't. Evidently her aunt Kat was home with her cousins. She stuffed the list into the back pocket of Kat's purloined Seven jeans.

Lydia followed Anya; Anya opened the heavy front door to Kat and the kids. The two women embraced; then Kat smiled and held her arms out to Lydia. "Lydia. I can't get over it. You look just like your mom did when she was a teenager."

Kat held Lydia in a warm hug, startled again to see how much her aunt looked like her big sister, Lydia's mom. It made Lydia miss her mother—whom, saint complex aside, she actually liked.

"It's great to see you, too, Aunt Kat," Lydia said.

"Now that I'm really back, we'll have to sit down and you'll fill me in on my insane sister," Kat said. "She's not the best correspondent. But now . . ." She stepped to the side and gestured to her children. "You guys were too young to remember the last time you saw her, but this is your cousin, Lydia. Lydia, this is Jimmy and Martina."

Lydia stared at her cousins, trying not to let her surprise—not in a good way—show on her face. She vaguely recalled meeting them, right before she'd left for the Amazon. They'd been toddlers then, and eight-and-a-half-year-old Lydia hadn't paid much attention.

Jimmy was the elder of the two, having just finished sixth grade. Martina was supposed to be two grades behind him. But she was one of those girls who'd reached puberty probably not just first in her class, but first in her school. She was already five feet tall, and the brassiere that she wore under her very over-sized Hello Kitty sweatshirt definitely was not for training. The rest of her ensemble was equally baggy—jeans and a floppy hat. A curtain of lank brown hair nearly hid her face. But there wasn't much face to see in any event, since Martina's gaze was focused on the Moorish-tile floor.

Neither cousin acknowledged Lydia's presence.

"Well, nice to see y'all again!" Lydia said, in an effort to break the ice. "We're going to have a blast together. Did y'all have fun at camp?"

Lydia waited. Nothing. Were they deaf and no one had warned her? If not, their manners were appalling. Hadn't they learned how to greet someone from their own tribe? She plunged on. "I helped the cook make those cookies you like."

"I hope you didn't put in any milk." Martina broke her silence in a small voice, but it was still directed at the floor. "I'm lactose intolerant. So is my brother. Right, Jimmy?"

Jimmy shrugged his agreement.

"So, how nice for the cousins to be together again!" Aunt Kat exclaimed, with what was obviously false enthusiasm.

Anya frowned, as if she knew what a poor showing her

children were making. "Stand up straight, Martina," she scolded. The girl barely adjusted her hunched posture.

"When can we eat?" Jimmy asked.

"Now," Anya said. "Cook made your favorite, grilled soy cheese on sprouted wheat toast."

"That's not my favorite," Jimmy said.

"Well, Lydia will find you something else," Kat said. She put her arms around her kids. "I missed you guys so much. Let's go to the kitchen. You can tell us everything that happened at camp."

"You are too indulgent with them, Kat," Anya chastised.

Lydia brought up the rear of the procession to the kitchen. It was abundantly clear who wore the loincloth in this family, who was the nice mom and who was the strict mom. Or maybe Russians just had a different theory of how to bring up children.

Dinner was already on the table, the plates covered by restaurant-style metal crowns to maintain their heat. A silver platter of home-baked cookies sat on the sideboard. Lydia found a chair as Jimmy zeroed in on the cookies.

"Hurray!" he cried, ignoring the covered main dishes.

"After dinner," Anya insisted.

"Oh, come on, sweetie," Kat wheedled. "Just this once. It's a celebration."

Jimmy took this as permission and stuffed a cookie into his mouth. Martina grabbed one in each hand. Anya scowled again and retreated to a far corner of the kitchen, arms crossed.

"You want one?" Jimmy asked Lydia.

"Sure." Lydia took one and bit into it. It tasted like roasted, dried sand. She choked out a "Not bad."

"Come on, children. At least drink soy milk," Anya implored from her corner.

"Lydia?" Aunt Kat asked. "Would you please get the kids some soy milk?"

Lydia stared at her blankly. Didn't the kids have legs and feet?

"You're the nanny," Kat reminded her.

"Right!" Lydia stood, red-faced. She'd forgotten completely that she was supposed to be on the job. "I'm the nanny. Sorry."

She found glasses in a cupboard and a half-gallon of soy milk in the fridge. As she poured two glasses of milk, she asked her cousins how they'd gotten their names.

"Tennis, duh," Jimmy explained. "Martina for Martina Navratilova, Jimmy for Jimmy Connors. If you haven't heard of them, it's because they're really old now."

"So do y'all like tennis?" Lydia asked, determined to find something that would result in a discussion that lasted more than three sentences.

"No, I hate it," Jimmy declared. "I suck."

Anya frowned. "Not to use that language. The problem is you do not practice. You think all things should come easy to you."

"Just because you play doesn't mean I should have to," Jimmy shot back sullenly. "I don't even want a tennis coach."

"You are lazy boy," Anya scolded. "How did Anya Kuriakova have lazy boy?"

Jeez, Lydia thought, *isn't this the happy bunch.* She made another stab at connecting with her cousins. "How about you, Martina? Do you like tennis?"

She shook her head.

"Another sport?"

Martina shook her head again.

"Then what do you like to do?"

Martina shrugged.

"Tell Lydia how you like to draw, sweetie," Kat coaxed.

Martina shot a panicked look at her brother.

"My sister is kinda shy," Jimmy explained. "Until you get to know her, but she's really nice."

Well, at least the kids liked each other. That was a start, anyway.

"Tell your cousin about art, Martina," Anya prompted. "It was your one high mark in school."

"Anya . . . why don't you and I go upstairs and unpack?" Kat asked. "We can leave the kids with Lydia to get reacquainted."

"Good idea," Anya agreed.

"Um, Anya, about your list?" Lydia began. "It seems a little . . . rigid."

"Parent says, children do," Anya declared.

Kat took her partner's hand. "We'll talk about it later," she promised Lydia. Then the moms beat a hasty retreat. Lydia knew very well that it wasn't necessary for Kat to unpack her own things—there'd be plenty of household help in the morning. *Why don't you and I go upstairs* had to be code for "Let's go get naked and funky." Fine. Whatever floated their outrigger canoe.

As soon as the moms were gone, the kids descended on the cookies again.

"Hey, let's go outside," Lydia suggested; listening to them chew was not her idea of a good time.

182

"I know," Jimmy groaned, "we have to take a brisk walk around the property."

So. Jimmy had been treated to Mean Mom's summer list already. "No, we'll find something more fun to do," Lydia promised.

Jimmy's eyes slid to her. "Did Momma Anya give you the list?"

"Yep."

"We had a list last summer, too," Jimmy said. "I *hate* that list."

Martina nodded her agreement.

Well, Lydia thought, *at least it was signs of life.*

"We can take a few little liberties with it," Lydia decided.

"What if you get fired?" Jimmy asked.

What if she did? No way was she going back to the Amazon. But no, Aunt Kat wouldn't fire her. But just in case . . . "We don't necessarily have to tell the moms exactly what you do every day. Do we?"

Wide-eyed, both kids shook their heads.

"Great!" Lydia jumped up. "Let's go."

"If we go out we need sunblock," Martina whispered.

"The sun's going down. You'll be fine," Lydia said, leading the way.

"But I'm still hungry," Jimmy complained.

How annoying. "Fine." Lydia opened the large cupboard door where Kat and Anya stowed their junk food out of harm's way. She stood on tiptoes and peered inside. "Ding Dongs? Doritos? Hostess Ho Hos? Caramel corn? What's your pleasure?"

"Caramel corn?" Jimmy's eyes grew wide. "I *love* caramel corn."

"Caramel corn is made with milk," Martina reminded him.

"A little milk never hurt anyone, sweetie," Lydia assured her. She snagged the bag and used it to lure the kids out the door. There, they stood around for a while. Lydia suggested tennis. No. Paddle tennis. Nope. Shuffleboard. Forget it. Bike riding on the driveway. Neither kid knew how to ride.

In desperation, she suggested that they go swimming.

"We can't." Martina shook her head vehemently. "We just ate."

"Um, can I have the caramel corn?" Jimmy asked. Lydia tossed it to him. He tore into the bag and took a huge mouthful.

"Oh well, Martina," Lydia said. "Clearly no one told you about the cookie exception to the no-swim rule. See, cookies don't count as actual food. Same thing with caramel corn."

The kids stared at her, unsure how to respond.

"That was a joke," Lydia told them. "Anyway, that no-swimming-after-you-eat thing only applies to, like, Olympic athletes. Back in the Amazon where I used to live, people eat and then swim all the time. No one dies."

Jimmy chewed another fistful of caramel corn, leaving sticky crumbs all over his face. "That's right. Momma Kat said you lived in the Amazon. That's so cool."

"More like hot," Lydia quipped. "Anyway, let's get in the water and I'll tell you all about it. There are suits in the cabanas, right?"

"I don't want to swim." Martina hung back.

Her brother went to her. "It's okay," he said quietly. "There's no one here."

Martina's eyes cut to Lydia. "*She's* here."

"Well, yeah. Anyway, I want to swim. When's the next time you'll get to go after you ate? If Momma Anya knew, she'd kill us." He took another handful of caramel corn and trudged toward one cabana.

Reluctantly, Martina went into the other one. Lydia decided to wait until her cousin was in her suit before she went in, since Martina was obviously so self-conscious about her body.

So. Her cousins were weird. Shy, scared, and as low-energy as children could be while still registering a pulse. Lydia was going to have to do something about that.

"Wait. Are you saying that where you used to live, girls walked around *naked*?"

Lydia smiled at Martina. "Definitely. Totally naked. All the time."

She'd been paddling around the deep end with her cousin, talking about everyday life in the rain forest, and exaggerating wildly for dramatic effect. But nothing seemed to interest Martina until she started in on the dressing, dating, and mating habits of the natives. As for Jimmy, he was in the shallow end, alternately chasing a floating action toy and stopping to chomp on the caramel corn.

"I'd rather die than go naked," Martina confided. Her body was covered by an exceptionally unflattering two-piece swimsuit with a purple blouson top that fell loosely over her chest and stomach.

"If you grew up that way, it would seem normal," Lydia said. "Of course, in Amazonia, girls start getting their breasts at, like, nine."

Martina's eyes grew huge. "Really? That's even younger than me."

"Really. Sometimes even at *eight*," Lydia went on. It was a total whopper, but it wasn't like the kid would research the truth. "Not only that, girls there don't really have to be afraid of anyone dissing them, either. They're the queens of every village. And they know all the secrets of the rain forest, too."

Martina paddled to the edge of the pool and held on to the overhang. For the first time, her voice was animated. "Like what?"

"Well, like potions that can make people do what you want them to do. Or stop them from doing what you don't want them to do."

"I don't get it."

"I'll show you sometime. If you want."

Martina shook her head. "Nah. I might get hurt."

Fine. Swell. Martina was a wuss, and Jimmy wasn't much better. Irritated at the prospect of another hour with them, Lydia climbed out of the pool and went for her towel. On the way, she passed a wooden planter full of potted wildflowers. A slug crawled along the base of the stems.

"Hey Martina, check this out!" Lydia called.

The girl looked up. When she did, Lydia grabbed the slug, flipped it eight feet into the air, and let it drop . . . directly into her mouth.

"Mmm, tender!" Lydia pronounced as she chewed.

"Eww!" Martina shrieked with a lung capacity Lydia hadn't known she possessed. "She just ate a worm! Jimmy! She ate a worm!"

This got Jimmy's attention in a hurry, as Lydia had hoped it would. The boy hustled over to his sister. "She did?"

"Alive!" Martina squealed. "She ate it!"

"They're a lot better roasted," Lydia confided.

Jimmy clambered out of the pool and ran over to Lydia. "Open your mouth so I can see," he demanded.

Lydia opened her mouth and stuck her tongue out. There was nothing there. "Swallowed it," she explained.

"I don't believe you," Jimmy scoffed. "You didn't eat a worm."

"You're right. It wasn't a worm." She saw another slug, this one making its way up a pansy shoot. "Watch and learn."

She picked up the new slug, flipped it even higher into the air than the first, and again caught it in her mouth like a piece of popcorn. She chewed ostentatiously and swallowed with relish. "Yep. No worms. Two slugs."

Her cousins stared at her, as she feigned licking slug juice from her fingers. At least she had their attention now. And no one had barfed, either. Not from watching her eat her snack, or from a bit of milk in the caramel corn.

So far, so good.

29

Off in the distance, the Santa Monica Pier looked like a fairy-land, the Ferris wheel brightly lit against the night sky. Whispers of music and salty sea air wafted on the breeze.

Kiley stood alone by the water's edge, a mile north of the pier on deserted Will Rogers Beach. What struck her most were the contrasts: the buzz of traffic behind her on the Pacific Coast Highway, the waves splashing against the shoreline. And her on the shore, between the two. It was the ocean and a dream that had lured her to California. Her mother had just freed her to follow them both. So it seemed somehow right to come here alone and think about her future.

What would it be like to be nanny to the children of a famous—albeit thoroughly whacked-out—rock star? How would she manage in the fall, when school started? She had to get top grades and score well on the SATs if she had any hope at all of getting into Scripps. Could she do that and be Platinum's nanny at the same time? It was what she wanted, but it felt overwhelming.

She took her shoes off and stepped into the water. It was surprisingly chilly for July—her toes squished into the cold sand. What had her literature teacher said in tenth grade? The longest journey begins with a single step. Well, she'd taken that step, halfway across the country to a completely different world.

She cupped her hands into the briny water and splashed it over her face. Which was just so wussy. And safe. What a safe, wussy girl from La Crosse, Wisconsin, would do.

Damn. What if you could take the girl out of Wisconsin but you couldn't take Wisconsin out of the girl? How would she ever make it in California, go to Bel Air High, live with an insane superstar?

Kiley pulled a PayDay bar Serenity had given her out of her jean jacket's pocket, then put the jacket on the sand and sat on it, bringing her knees to her chin. She tore open the wrapper and bit into the candy.

What was going on back in La Crosse that very minute? Was Nina asleep, or had she taken the night job at Pizza-Neatsa? Was her mom serving eggs to truckers at the restaurant? Was her dad passed out in front of the TV?

God, all she had was questions, questions, and more questions. She polished off the PayDay and stuck the wrapper in her pocket so that she could throw it away later. She wasn't about to litter the beach of *her* ocean.

"My ocean," Kiley whispered aloud. "I *will* go to Scripps. I *will* make it happen."

A little demon on her shoulder told her she was crazy, that she'd be back in La Crosse with Nina, asking kids if they wanted extra cheese on their pizza, inside of a week.

No. Screw that. She was not her mom. She was not going to be afraid.

With that thought, Kiley stood up. Stripped off her clothes. Then, clad only in her Kmart underwear, she waded into the ocean. *Her* ocean. Ducked her head under and came up whooping with the sheer exhilaration of it.

It felt good. No. It felt great. And most of all, it felt right.

30

Esme sat on the living room couch of her guesthouse, staring at the damned phone. The one that didn't ring. The number that Junior didn't call back. She'd tried him four times in the past two days. So her suspicions had been on target. Junior didn't love her anymore. Couldn't he just be man enough to tell her to her face?

It wasn't so bad during the day when she was busy with the girls. Everything was new to them—ice makers, escalators, even riding in the car. Both girls had gotten carsick more than once; Esme now kept barf bags, bottled water, baby wipes, and mints in the Audi's glove compartment.

Sometimes it seemed as though they were adjusting rapidly to life in America. But they were also capable of world-class melt-downs. One of those happened that morning. Diane had called from a Cedars-Sinai board meeting to say that two ornate, hand-carved dollhouses had just been delivered from a craftsman in Colorado. Could Esme show them to the girls, then call to report their reaction?

Esme was thrilled, sure that Easton and Weston would adore the miniature houses. Instead, the girls had lost it. Weston screamed that the houses were ugly, then Easton bellowed the same thing, then both girls started throwing their clothes and toys on their floor and out of their room. They hated their new parents, they hated America, and they wanted to go home to Colombia *right now*.

Esme tried to reason with them, but the girls were beyond reason. They swept books off their bookcases. They flung their newly framed family photos at the mirror above their Joseph Wahl dresser.

Esme was frozen by the onslaught. Short of physically holding them down, how was she supposed to stop them from wrecking the place, or even hurting themselves? She knew instinctively that yelling would only backfire.

Then her eyes lit on two tattered cloth baby dolls that had fallen next to their bed. These were the only items the girls had brought with them from Colombia. Even as the twins were on their rampage, Esme calmly picked up the dolls and began to rock them in her arms, softly singing a Spanish lullaby.

After a while, Weston stopped to listen. Then, Easton did too. Five minutes later, they were sound asleep at her feet. Esme had continued to sing, imagining what these two small souls had already experienced in their short lives. No wonder they were confused and overwhelmed. Hell, *she* was confused and overwhelmed.

When Esme reported all this to their mother, Diane seemed remarkably unfazed and supportive. "I've read some things about children from other cultures adapting," she'd said. "It was really helpful. I'll have copies made for you, okay?" Then she asked Esme to take the girls, when they awakened, to the Page Museum at the La Brea Tar Pits. Diane thought it might calm them down.

And it had. The girls brought their baby dolls, and it kept them relatively calm. They were fascinated by the giant fossils from the Ice Age, and had hung on every word as Esme translated the information from the exhibits. Then they walked through the outdoor park to see the life-size replicas of saber-toothed cats and mammoths. As Esme explained it all to them, they in turn explained it to their dolls.

Score one for Diane, Esme mused. Just when Esme thought she had Diane pegged as shallow, Diane proved herself anything but.

By the time they got home, the mess in the room had been cleaned up, but the girls were exhausted and whiny. They were supposed to work for an hour with their new English tutor, a bilingual education professor at UCLA. Why they needed a tutor, Esme couldn't understand. They were making good progress in English already. But Diane had left a note saying that if Esme felt the girls were too tired, she could cancel.

Score another point for Diane.

Maybe Esme had only imagined that Diane objected to her flirtation with Jonathan. Perhaps Esme was just so class-conscious that she imagined friction when there wasn't any. She just didn't know anymore.

She didn't know about Jonathan, either. Esme did not want to think about him. But it seemed as if the harder she tried to *not* think about him, the more she thought about him. And even though she knew it was ridiculous, Esme worried that maybe Junior was some kind of clairvoyant mind reader; that he already knew that Esme wanted Jonathan in a way that no girl with a boyfriend should ever want another guy. Especially not the son of her employers.

No. She would not think about him another moment. She eyed the long thank-you list on the coffee table, and the pile of engraved Goldhagen note cards. She'd only completed half of them.

Ugh. Not tonight. Instead, she went into her bedroom and undressed, putting on an ivory silk nightgown and matching robe that an aunt had given her the previous Christmas. Then she puttered around for a while and got out her manicure kit before she clicked on the small TV to watch an *ER* rerun.

Cross-legged on the bed, she filed her nails while that hot doctor from Bosnia made time with a Latina nurse. Did she have to be Latina? It reminded her too much of—

What was that? Someone at the front door?

She turned down the TV and listened.

Tap-tap-tap. Knuckles on wood.

Esme went to the door and opened it. Jonathan stood there smiling at her.

Her heart shouted, "Yes!" She told it to shut up.

"I'm not allowed to have male guests," she said stiffly.

"I'm not a guest. I live here."

"No," Esme said. "You live *there.*" She pointed in the direction of the mansion.

Jonathan smiled. "If you want to get technical. Are you going to invite me in?"

She gestured him in with one hand, smoothing the neckline

of her robe more modestly around her throat with the other. He seemed to fill up the living room.

"I've always liked this little place."

"I don't think your mother would want you here." Esme's mouth was so dry she could barely speak.

"Diane's not my mom," Jonathan said.

Esme was taken aback. "Of course she is."

"Nope. My mother is an attorney in New York," Jonathan filled her in. "Diane was a line producer on one of my dad's TV shows; she got promoted to trophy wife two years ago."

Well, so much for Esme's theory that Diane didn't want the nanny getting too chummy with her son. Esme had completely mistaken the nature of their relationship.

"Besides, they took the kids to Aunt Claire's in Pacific Palisades for a sleepover with their cousins. Then they went to a fund-raiser thing at Kehillat Israel. They won't be checking on you." He picked up the list of adoption present givers and gazed at it ruefully. "Tonight's fun activity?"

"Not really," Esme admitted.

"Good. You're supposed to be off duty."

The bird cuckooed from the wall clock. Jonathan glanced at it. "Hey, it's on time."

"So?" Esme asked.

"So it wasn't before. I noticed when the real estate agent walked us through, because I thought it was such a cool old clock."

"I fixed it. Temporarily," Esme said. "The bellow tops need replacing."

"You know how to fix a clock? Very resourceful."

Esme shrugged. "Family trait. Necessity is a mother."

"The only thing that's a necessity for my father and Diane is the Yellow Pages, a cell phone, and their credit cards. But I didn't come to discuss family traits."

"Why, then?"

"Passion." He took a step toward her.

She took a step backward. "What are you talking about?"

"Your passion. Tattoos. I want one."

Oh. That's what he meant. She felt like a fool.

"I'm not giving you a tattoo."

"Yeah, you are. Right here."

He lifted the right sleeve of his T-shirt and bared a tanned, muscular bicep. There was an ink circle on it.

Esme's brows rose. "And when do you plan to tell your par— Diane and your father that the nanny gave you a tattoo?"

"I wasn't planning on telling them. Were you?"

"No. Because I'm not doing it."

He smiled. "You're the artist, I'm the canvas. Right, Esme?"

The way he said her name. Like a caress, lips trailing across her stomach, her thighs. She had never found her name beautiful until that very minute.

"Esme," he whispered again, staring at her lips.

She couldn't back away, didn't want to. "If I make a mistake—"

"You won't."

She cleared her throat, trying to be businesslike. "Fine. Let's get started. Go into the kitchen. What do you want the tattoo to say?"

Jonathan led the way to her small kitchen. "No words. Other than that, you're the artist."

"This is crazy, Jonathan."

"Don't you ever want that, Esme, to just be crazy? To get carried away?"

"No."

His eyes said he knew she was lying. How easily she could get lost in that ocean blue, caught in its undertow.

"It's just a tattoo," she forced herself to say.

"Ah, all business," he teased. "Fine. I pay the going rate for a Castaneda original."

His offer of money broke the spell. Thank God.

"You don't pay me shit," Esme warned. "I'm getting my stuff. Boil some water on the stove, please."

Moments later, Esme returned carrying a coffin-shaped box in her arms. Jonathan had put a pot of water on the stove, with the gas flame turned up high. "Count Dracula?" Jonathan asked when he saw the box.

"Don't joke, I'm the one who'll have the needle. Sit, please."

Jonathan sat backward on a kitchen chair, bicep exposed. Esme took a bottle of rubbing alcohol from her box, poured some on a cotton ball, then swabbed his bicep. She followed that with the prescription cleanser pHisoHex, then more rubbing alcohol.

"You're thorough," Jonathan observed. "No germ could survive that onslaught."

"I'd prefer not to give you an infection, if you don't mind. A *cholo* I know went to this guy on Van Nuys Boulevard to get his girlfriend's name on his back. He ended up septic in County General."

"A *cholo*?" Jonathan echoed.

"What? You want to know his name?" Esme asked. "You don't know him." She unwrapped a new disposable razor and

197

carefully shaved Jonathan's bicep, though no hair was visible. They were so close she could feel his breath, sweet and minty, on her cheek. "Tell me what you want."

"You."

Her heart jumped. "What?"

"I already told you, Esme. You decide."

She flipped through her stencils, the predesigned tattoo forms she'd created. Then she stood. "I'll be right back. I have to get deodorant."

"What the hell for?"

"To attach the stencil to your arm," she explained. "When I pull the stencil away, it leaves a colored outline of the tattoo. Then I fill it in with color."

He shook his head. "No stencil. You think Van Gogh used a cheat sheet?"

"Maybe if he did, he wouldn't have cut off his stupid ear," Esme shot back.

"No stencil."

Esme pursed her lips. "Don't say I didn't warn you."

For the next several minutes, Esme was all work—preparing her small cups of ink, getting her needles and tubes sterilized for her tattoo machine, and concentrating on the spot where Jonathan wanted his body art. Already, a design was taking shape in her mind. Something that he would never forget. But it would be difficult to execute without a stencil.

She slipped on her rubber gloves and started up the machine. "Don't hold your breath or you might pass out."

"I never—"

She sliced into his flesh.

"Shit! That hurts!"

"Stay still!"

She knew her needle wasn't penetrating more than a sixteenth of an inch below his skin, but there were still plenty of nerves in the epidermis. She'd learned that from experience.

"You okay?" she asked, wiping up some blood with a sterile gauze pad as she applied a circle of black to Jonathan's bicep.

"Yes," he managed, through gritted teeth.

She kept working. Half the circle was done in five minutes, the other half in three, as she found her touch. It was amazing—though there was nothing more than black ink in his skin, she could picture exactly how the tattoo would look. She hoped he'd be as pleased with the reality as she was with the fantasy.

"What is it?" he asked.

"It says B-R-I-T-N-E-Y. Hold still."

On she worked. Filling in red, blue, the base. Crisscrossing black metallic lines to indicate the support beams from a dark center. It was magnificent. No one else in Los Angeles would have a tattoo of a Ferris wheel.

Jonathan tried to see the design, but the angle of his arm made it impossible. "Come on, Esme. Tell me—"

"You'll see soon enough. It's a—"

A huge crash cut off Esme's answer. She spun around just in time to see two high school guys barge into the kitchen, having busted through the front door. It took a moment for Esme to place them—Freddie and Victor, two members of Los Locos. She'd often seen them hanging out in Junior's living room.

"Goddamn right he'll see!" Freddie spat, legs splayed, leather jacket open over his muscle shirt. Victor glowered at her.

Instantly, Jonathan was out of the chair. "How'd you get up here?"

"Your gate's broken, man," Victor sneered. "Ain't keeping the riffraff out. What you doing with this *linda* in her night-clothes, eh?"

Jonathan tensed, ready if they made a move. "She's giving me a tattoo."

"She ain't giving you shit," Victor spat. "But I know what you wanna give her. We saw you together, the other night, eh. At the pier in Santa Monica. How you gonna go disrespecting Junior like that?"

Esme felt sick. The lowrider that had passed them while they were waiting for the valet. The boys who had yelled something out the window at her. It had been them, Esme now realized. Freddie and Victor. Her mind raced. She'd seen this before—gang members out to protect the honor of another member. So what if Junior wasn't in the life anymore? These boys would do anything for him. With their fists, with their shivs, with their Glocks. They would die for him.

31

Victor gave Jonathan a long once-over, from head to feet and back again, then lifted his eyebrows at Esme. "Does Junior know this white boy is at your crib?"

Esme could see he already knew the answer. She decided to tough it out; begging for mercy would only make things worse. "I dunno. Does Junior know you two *children* are here?"

Victor stabbed a finger at Esme. "Watch your mouth." He jerked his head at Jonathan. "And you, asshole? Sit the hell down."

"Look, you two need to leave." Jonathan's voice was steady.

In a flash, Freddie grabbed Esme and twisted her arm behind her back, while Victor stepped between them and Jonathan, his smirk daring Jonathan to take a swing at him. "I said *sit.*"

Jonathan sat. "Leave her alone, man. You got a problem, take it up with me."

"I don't think so, gringo," Freddie said, but released Esme anyway.

She got right in his face. "You want my cell phone, Victor?"

"Why the hell would I want your cell?"

"To call Junior, you asshole," Esme spat. " 'Cause my boyfriend's gonna kill you when he finds out what you're doing."

Esme saw a twitch of doubt in Freddie's eyes as he looked at Victor. Then it was gone. "Let's end this shit and get out of here before they fix that damn gate, man."

It happened so fast: Jonathan burst out of his chair and lunged at Freddie. But Freddie was too quick, sidestepping him as Victor grabbed Jonathan from behind. Esme cried, "No!" But she knew if she intervened, these two *cholos* could kill them both.

Freddie punched Jonathan twice to the face, then hard in the gut. Jonathan snapped over, grunting with pain, the wind knocked out of him. Blood poured from his nose.

"This is just a warning," Freddie said, dark eyes gleaming. "Stay away from Junior's lady, or next time, I make you wish you were never born."

"Get out of here!" Esme screamed at them. "Get out!"

Freddie pointed at Jonathan. "Remember my words, gringo." With that, the two guys sauntered out.

Esme rushed to Jonathan. "Are you okay?"

Jonathan found a dish towel and wiped the blood off his face. "Damn."

"Sit," Esme told Jonathan. "Put your head back."

"Got any ice?" he asked as he followed her instructions.

"Not yet. Don't move." She got a cotton ball from her tattoo kit, and poured something out of a small plastic bottle onto it.

"What are you doing?"

"Colostrum. It will stop the bleeding." She stuffed the cotton up his bleeding nostril.

"What the hell is colostrum?"

"A milk by-product," Esme said, peering at his nose. "It works better than ice."

"Swell."

She took the bloody towel and tossed it into the garbage, then got some ice from the freezer and wrapped it in another one. She put it on his left eye. "Hold that there. For the next hour."

Wincing, he put his hand over the ice.

"I'm so sorry, Jonathan."

"Interesting company you keep."

"I don't—" She couldn't possibly explain. "Never mind."

He touched his nose, and looked at his finger in surprise. The bleeding really had stopped. "Who's Junior?"

Esme was ashamed. She could feel heat rush to her face.

"My boyfriend."

He lowered his head so that he could see her through his right eye. "You didn't mention that you had one of those."

"Leave it, or your eye is going to look like an eggplant," Esme said. "Maybe we should talk about your girlfriend, the one at the tennis court."

"Mackenzie? We were over a long time ago."

Esme remembered the awful moment when the toilet spewed, how the girl had stood behind Jonathan, snaking an arm around his waist. "You'd better tell *Mackenzie* that."

"She's not my girlfriend, Esme," he insisted. "Don't change the subject. This boyfriend of yours hangs with those lowlifes?"

"You don't know anything about it," Esme insisted, on the defensive.

"Right. That's why I'm asking you."

"He used to be in their gang," Esme reluctantly explained.

"He got out. But he takes care of them when no one else will. They look up to him."

"Does the boyfriend have a name?"

"Junior," Esme told him.

"So this Junior was a bad guy who is now a good guy but still looks out for the bad guys even though he's a good guy?"

"Something like that."

"Shit."

Esme folded her arms. "How can you say that?"

"Because it means I would probably like him." He moved the ice again and peered at her. "And I don't want to like him. Because I want to steal his girlfriend."

Esme frowned. "Why do you say stupid things? You could get a million girls, beautiful rich girls, like, like Tennis Girl."

"Her name is Mackenzie."

"You know, I don't give a shit what her name is!" She whirled back to him. "You think I'm exotic, is that it? A poor Latina girl? That get you all hot?"

"Don't underestimate yourself, Esme." He stood. "I'll take the ice with me, if you don't mind."

"You can take anything you want in this damn house. It belongs to your parents, anyway," Esme said crossly.

"Except you," Jonathan added. "I've never known anyone quite like you before."

"There are thousands of girls like me, Jonathan." She peered at his left eye. "It's turning purple. Put the ice back on it. What will you tell your parents?"

"That I got clocked by a stray tennis ball."

Guilt washed over Esme. "It isn't right. It isn't fair. Those *cholos* punched you out because of—"

"Shhh." He put a single finger on her lips. "Not important." He twisted his bicep so that he could see the half-finished tattoo. "What was it supposed to be, anyway?"

"Nothing," Esme said.

"Yeah, well, let's call it 'To be continued.' " He started toward the front door.

"I doubt it."

"I don't."

As he started to open the door, Esme called to him. "I really am very sorry that this happened. I will make sure that it doesn't happen again."

He turned to her. "Yeah? How?"

"I'll take care of it."

"Esme." That voice again, saying her name like a prayer. "What I'm feeling is . . . I swear. I'm not playing you."

Then he left, heading for the big house.

32

Kiley and Serenity sat on a chaise longue by the adult pool at the Brentwood Hills Country Club. Platinum's daughter pored through a copy of *Star,* commenting on every celebrity that she knew.

"Pink. She did a duet with my mom, she's nice." Page-flip. "That's Cher. I saw her backstage in Las Vegas. When she made her hair blond she was just trying to copy my mom." Page-flip. "Christina. You know her?"

"Not personally," Kiley said, smiling.

"Obviously," Serenity said.

Kiley nodded, ignoring the insulting tone. "But I like her music."

"Do you think I look like her?"

"I don't know. What do you think?"

"I think I asked a question and you answered with another question which means it wasn't an answer."

"What do you say we go over to the family pool and swim?" Kiley suggested, anxious to cut off this line of discussion.

"No. I'm hungry." Serenity put a hand to her forehead to block the sun's glare, and then peered around. "Where's a waiter?"

"Mrs. Cleveland asked me to have you home at twelve-thirty for dinner," Kiley reminded her. "It's already a quarter to eleven."

"What are you talking about?" Serenity challenged. "Dinner is at night."

Kiley chuckled. "Not where I'm from in Wisconsin, it's not. The farmers get up early—their big meal is in the middle of the day. That's called dinner."

"What do you call dinner at night?"

"Supper."

"That's stupid. I'm hungry and I want to eat." Serenity spotted a waiter and waved one hand at him. "Excuse me? Over here, please!"

"Serenity . . ."

But the waiter was already getting out his order pad. Stuck, Kiley speed-dialed Platinum on her cell. Her boss picked up on the third ring.

"What?"

Kiley was taken aback. "It's me. Kiley."

"I know that. What do you want? I'm busy."

"Sorry," Kiley said hastily. "Serenity's hungry and would like to eat at the country club, but Mrs. Cleveland said—"

"That's why you called?" Platinum sounded incredulous. "Because Serenity is hungry?"

"Um . . . yes?"

"Goddammit, Kiley! I'm in the studio. There are eight musicians, three backup singers, two engineers, and three producers standing here with their thumbs up their ass while you're calling to discuss when, where, and what my hungry daughter should eat!"

Kiley's face burned. "I'm sorry. I didn't know—"

"Jesus. If you're not grown-up enough to handle the gig, Kiley, do me a big favor and quit."

The line went dead. Kiley turned to see that Serenity was deep into her order with the cute waiter: a focaccia and an Oreo milk shake.

"You want anything, Kiley?" Serenity asked, as if they were adult friends hanging out for the day.

Kiley shook her head, and the waiter trotted off as the little girl flipped open the magazine again, this time to the *Star* Style and Error page.

"Paris Hilton," Serenity opined. "I hate her. She made a sex tape. That's the only reason she got famous."

Kiley blinked at Serenity's words. Then she ripped the magazine from Serenity's hands.

"Hey! Give it back!"

"I really don't want to hear you talking like that," Kiley said. "Remember what I told you about my job, Serenity? When you're with me, I'm in charge."

Serenity folded her arms defiantly. "Says who? I'm in charge of me. You can be in charge of doodyhead."

"Well, *Sid* is at his therapist. But when I'm with him, I'm in charge of him, too."

"He has to have therapy because he wets the bed. If you're so in charge of him, make him not pee when he sleeps."

208

"He doesn't do it on purpose, sweetie." Not knowing what else to do, Kiley offered Serenity the magazine again. The girl took it, and all was instantly forgiven.

"Let's rate how pretty they are and if they have cool clothes. 'Kay?" Serenity asked. She lay back on the chaise like a movie star, and pushed her sunglasses up into her hair. "Paris Hilton. Zero for pretty and zero for cool outfit. Avril Lavigne. Zero and zero. Hilary Duff. Zero and double zero. Your turn."

Kiley was sure she should be doing something much more Mary Poppins–esque than rating the looks and clothing of the stars in *Star.* But then, if Mary Poppins had been in charge of Serenity, maybe the famed movie nanny would have been on trial for aggravated assault instead of floating around the skies of London under her umbrella.

Kiley's cell rang. She was tempted to ignore it. It could easily be Platinum, firing her. But what if her boss was trying to reach her for another reason? If she didn't pick up, she'd probably get fired for that. Either way, she was screwed. She looked at her phone and didn't recognize the incoming digits. Whew.

"Hello?"

"Kiley?"

"Yes."

"It's Esme Castaneda."

Kiley exhaled with relief that it was her friend instead of her boss. "Esme! I've been meaning to call you. I got the job!"

"That's wonderful. Congratulations."

"It's been a while. How'd it go after we left you at the party the other night? With that guy Jonathan?"

"Good. But . . ."

209

Only now did it register with Kiley how odd and tense Esme sounded. "Hey, are you okay?"

"Yeah. Just . . . something happened last night. With Jonathan."

"Good something or bad something?"

"Bad," Esme admitted.

"What?"

"It's complicated, I—"

Kiley felt Serenity tug at her arm. "Who's on the phone?" the girl demanded.

"A friend, okay?" Kiley got up and took a few paces away to protect her privacy. She saw the waiter on the other side of the pool, returning with a tray in his hands—Serenity's focaccia and milk shake.

But that's not what got Kiley's attention. Instead, it was the guy who'd just climbed to the top of the diving board.

It was Tom Chappelle. *That* Tom. Of course, he looked perfect in his surfer Jams. Like something out of a dream. His eyes caught hers, and Kiley saw that he recognized her. He smiled. This was her chance. All she had to do was drift over there and make some joke, like "Hi, long time no see" or—

"You there, Kiley?" Esme asked. "Maybe I shouldn't have called—"

"No, no, of course I'm here," Kiley insisted. She forced herself to turn her back on the pool, and on Tom. "What happened to Jonathan?"

"It's complicated," Esme said. "Can you meet me later? For coffee?"

"Sure." Kiley nibbled on a cuticle and checked to see if Tom was still on the diving board. He wasn't. But then Kiley saw him in the pool, his buff arms cutting through the water in a firm freestyle. When he reached the edge of the pool, he stopped and looked at Kiley again. This time, he waved.

Oh my God, oh my God, oh my God.

Kiley waved back.

"These friends of my boyfriend punched Jonathan and—"

That got Kiley's attention. She pulled her gaze from Tom. "They *what*?"

"I'll explain when I see you," Esme said. "What time do you get off?"

Kiley considered. Platinum had said that she'd be back from the studio around six. "How about if I meet you at seven-thirty. At the Coffee Bean in Beverly Hills?"

"Great," Esme agreed. "And Kiley?"

"Yeah?"

"Thank you."

"You're welcome." Kiley disconnected the call and turned quickly, hoping to see Tom waiting by the side of the pool.

Nope. He was gone.

Esme got to the Coffee Bean forty-five minutes early. By seven-thirty, she was jangling from espresso refills and had bitten off all her lipstick, with second, third, and fourth thoughts about having called Kiley. She barely knew her. But she didn't have the nerve to call her best friend, Jorge. Jorge hated Junior; she hadn't even spoken to Jorge since she'd started this job. Her girlfriends from the Echo were out of the question. If she'd told them that two *cholos* had caught her with a rich white boy, they'd say it served Esme right. In fact, that Freddie and Victor should have jacked her up as well as the boy. Jacked her up good, not no jab-jab to the face kinda shit.

But the way Jonathan had looked at her when he said, *I want to steal his girlfriend.* The way it had made her feel then—the way it made her feel now.

Esme raked her fingers through her hair and checked the door for the umpteenth time for Kiley. *If I just tell him that I'm not interested, that I'm in love with Junior, if I'm never alone with him . . .*

But she wanted to be alone with him. That was the problem.

That morning, Jonathan had stopped by when she'd been playing with the kids in the sandbox. He'd asked if she was all right. She, who the *cholos* had barely touched! Meanwhile, his eye was every shade of purple and his nose was swollen, but he assured her that he was okay. He even joked how he must have really strong bones since he hadn't broken anything. He invited her to come with him to Venice that night, to hear a band he liked. But she'd declined; she had something else she had to do that evening. Short of quitting her nanny job, it was the only way she could ensure that Jonathan would never be at risk again because of her.

God. How stupid was she to want this boy? She had to fight it. Go back to Junior. And make sure those damn *cholos* paid for what they did to Jonathan.

Kiley pushed through the door; Esme waved. A moment later, Kiley slid into the empty seat across the table.

"Do you want coffee?" Esme asked.

"I'm good." Kiley leaned forward across the table. "So, what happened?"

Esme told her everything.

"God." Kiley sank back in her chair. "How is he?"

"His face is swollen, his eye is black, his chest is sore," Esme said. "That's it."

212

"It could have been a lot worse," Kiley pointed out.

"Next time it will be. Next time, they'll kill him. Me too."

Kiley hesitated. "That's hyperbole. Right?"

Esme realized that in Kiley's world, such a statement would be an exaggeration. But she'd merely been stating the truth.

"What about the police?" Kiley asked. "Can't you get a restraining order or something?"

"Are you kidding?" The word "police" made Esme sick with fear in a way that Kiley could never understand. "No police."

"But why?" Kiley asked. "If the guys come again they'll get arrested and—"

"I *said* no police!" Esme insisted. "I know what I gotta do. Tell my boyfriend. He'll deal with them. With me, too, probably. But that's the way it has to be."

"Deal with them how?" Kiley asked warily.

Esme shook her head. Her new friend understood nothing about her world. But Esme had reached out to Kiley, and Kiley had come through for her, so Esme figured that she had to try.

"In my neighborhood, we take care of our own problems. We never go to the cops. It would be like . . . like turning against your own family."

Kiley nodded. "Got it."

"My boyfriend, Junior. He's a *patrón*," Esme went on. "He's not in the life—I mean, in a gang anymore—but all the *cholos* respect him. If they thought they were doing this to protect his honor, *he* needs to be the one to set them straight. But . . ."

"What?" Kiley urged her.

"I don't know how he'll react. He might blame me. Shit, he

213

should blame me," Esme added bitterly. She put her head in her hands.

Kiley reached across the table to touch Esme's arm. "That's a crock. You didn't do anything wrong."

Esme raised her eyes. "That might not be the way Junior sees it. I know this is a lot to ask, Kiley, but . . . will you come with me to tell him? I'll understand if you say no," she added quickly.

Kiley didn't hesitate. "Of course I'll come."

Esme felt so grateful. This girl barely knew her, yet was willing to stand by her the same way a homie would.

"When?" Kiley asked. "Now?"

"Yeah."

"We should call Lydia," Kiley said.

Esme hesitated. "I was really rude to her at the pier."

Kiley waved a hand in the air. "Friends piss each other off all the time. It doesn't mean anything. Call her. There's strength in numbers."

True, Esme thought. *Especially since the only kind of backup she was going to get from Kiley was emotional.*

Esme got out her cell and punched in Lydia's number. But all she got was voice mail. She left a message that she hoped would make sense: what happened, that she and Kiley were going to Junior's. When Kiley urged Esme to leave Junior's address, Esme did, even though it seemed ridiculous.

She put her cell back in her purse. "Ready?"

"Let's do it."

Together, they headed for the parking lot.

33

Esme pulled the Goldhagens' Audi into the gravel driveway of Junior's house.

"*This* is where your boyfriend lives?" Kiley asked.

Esme could see that her new friend was trying to cover her shock. She understood why. The route to Junior's had taken them through the heart of Echo Park—past the seedy bars, the addicts looking for a mark, the gangstas claiming their turf. Kiley had gaped at the bodegas and taco stands, the low-riders, and the *cholos* in the street. As imposing as the sights were the smells: rice and beans from a hundred kitchens, flavored ices from pushcarts, sweat and perfume from passersby, even the rotting apricots from a lone tree that choked on car fumes but still managed to bear fruit. When Kiley had rolled up the windows and locked the car doors, Esme had tried not to feel insulted. There was probably nothing within a hundred thousand miles of La Crosse, Wisconsin, that looked remotely like the Echo.

"Uh-huh."

"Did you live around here, too?" Kiley asked.

"Yeah." Esme turned off the ignition, relieved there were no cars in front of the house but Junior's. He was probably home alone. "You coming or not?"

"I'm coming."

Together, they approached the barred front door. Esme got out her key. But before she could put it in the first lock, the door swung open. Junior stood in the doorway, hands on hips, a scowl on his face. He wore baggy jeans, and a muscle tee covered by an open black shirt that Esme had bought for him because she'd always loved the way he looked in black: tough, powerful, fearless.

He spoke before Esme could open her mouth. "I know. So get inside. Hold on." He pointed at Kiley. "Who the hell is she?"

"My friend," Esme explained. "Her name is Kiley."

Kiley managed a wan smile. "Hi."

"Why you bring her here, Esme?" Junior demanded.

"Like I said, she's my friend." Esme forced a toughness that she didn't feel. "You got a problem with that, Junior?"

A muscle jumped in Junior's jaw. "Both of you get inside. You wanna get yourself *killed*?"

The small living room was neat, as always. A Mexican shawl covered the threadbare couch. There was a Tecate can on the coffee table. The TV was tuned to ESPN.

Junior locked the door, then nodded at Kiley. "Make yourself comfortable." He jerked his head at Esme to follow him into the bedroom.

Esme gulped as she followed him into the bedroom that she knew so well. Junior had never hit her. He hadn't been that kind of guy in a long time. But he looked mad. Very, very mad.

"Sit." Junior pointed to the bed. She did. He leaned against the dresser and folded his arms. "Why I have to hear about this from those *cholos,* Esme, eh?"

"I didn't do anything wrong," Esme insisted.

"They told me. You didn't."

"Don't make this about me, Junior. What did you do to them?"

"Nothing," Junior replied.

Esme was incredulous. "Noth—"

"Yet. I wanted to see if you'd be woman enough to tell me the truth."

Esme looked down at her feet, unable to meet his eyes.

"What about how you can't have male visitors in your guest-house, eh?" Junior went on. "Or don't this white boy have *cojones*?"

"He lives on the property," Esme reminded Junior. "It's his family."

"And that party in Santa Monica? That family property, too?"

Esme stood, hands on her hips. "You got those homies spying for you, Junior? It was a party! I went with Kiley—that girl in the living room—and another girl. The guy—Jonathan—he was giving me a ride home because he lives there. Whatever your boys told you, it's bull."

217

"Why you do something so stupid, Esme?"

"What was stupid, going to a party? Giving someone a tattoo? You're the one who told me to get out of the Echo—"

Junior smiled mirthlessly. "Shit. This how you handle your two-week trial period? You care more about this boy than you do about your job?"

Esme flushed.

"You with him?" Junior asked, incredulous.

Esme knew what "with" meant. She shook her head. Even if she had feelings for Jonathan, she hadn't acted on them and was never going to act on them. She went to Junior and put her hand to his cheek. "What do you want from me? I call, you don't even call me back."

"To give you a chance, Esme. You on the phone with me every day, how you gonna ever get the Echo out of your blood?"

Esme felt so small. That was why Junior was pushing her away. He thought he was doing her a favor. At the moment, she really, truly hated herself. But she pushed that feeling away, too. She was here to talk about justice.

"What you going to do about Freddie and Victor?" she asked.

"I'll take care of it, Esme."

"They can't go around punching out a guy just because they see me with him. You know what they'll do next time. So I'm asking you again, Junior, what you going to do about it?"

"Yo, Junior! Qué pasa?"

Esme froze. She recognized the voice calling from the living room.

Freddie.

Junior opened the bedroom door. Freddie and Victor stood

in the middle of the living room. Kiley was still on the couch, frozen like a wax statue at Madame Tussaud's on Hollywood Boulevard.

Freddie stabbed a finger at Esme. "Saw your candy-ass Beverly Hills car in the driveway," he sneered. "How many times you do the white boy to get that ride, eh?"

"Shut up," Junior snapped at him. "You and Victor, you did wrong."

Victor's mouth fell open. "What you say? We go to Esme to warn her, and find her with that boy, eh. How we supposed to do when she's disrespecting you like that?"

"You tell me before, not after," Junior said, his voice steely. "I take care of my own business. Which makes you two my business."

"What?" Esme saw a muscle jump in Freddie's neck.

"You dish it out like a man, you got to take it like a man, eh," Junior said. He walked over to Freddie, pumping a fist against his other open palm. "Put your hands behind your back, *cholo*."

Freddie's eyes cut to Victor. "This is bullshit, man."

"We did right by you, Junior," Victor insisted.

"You next, Victor. Put your hands behind your back. One punch each."

"Screw this shit. We're outta here." Freddie spun around and loped for the door. Victor followed.

"You leave now, I'll find you!" Junior threatened.

Freddie and Victor just kept walking.

"Here's the address," the cabdriver told Lydia. He craned around to her. "You sure you don't need me to wait?"

"No, but thanks," Lydia said. She knew it was the right house; she recognized the Goldhagens' Audi in the driveway. Not because she'd ever seen it before, but because of the vanity license plate: GLDHGN3.

"Suit yourself," said the cabbie. "This is a tough neighborhood."

She'd heard that before. When she'd told X where she wanted to go, he jokingly said that no way was he driving there at night. More important, he had to schlep the moms to the NOW national convention at the Century Plaza Hotel.

She took a cab instead. But the truth was, on the ride to the Echo, Lydia found herself more excited than scared. She got Latino culture. The same thing went on in Amazonia. Forget what she'd told Martina, about girls in the rain forest being powerful queens of the villages. Amazonia was all about patriarchy. It wasn't so many years ago that the warriors believed it their right to kidnap any woman they wanted as a wife and to dine on anyone who stood in their way. Oh sure, things were changing—even the Amas had given up cannibalism. But the kidnap-the-wife thing and the take-a-young-virgin-as-a-prize thing still existed in some remote villages. Lydia had learned well how to protect herself in strange environments.

Lydia paid her fare, grabbed her purse, and headed for Junior's front door. At the same time, the door swung open and two young Latino guys came barreling out. When they saw blond Lydia, they stopped to leer at her.

"*Ay yo* trip!" the shorter one called to his friend. Then his eyes snapped back to Lydia. "Hey, *rubia*. You a friend of Esme's?"

"*Tengo nunca idea,*" said the other one. "*Probablemente una otra puta!*"

Lydia understood enough Spanish to realize that the guy had basically just called Esme a whore. "You really shouldn't go around calling my friend a bad name," she said. "Especially since a *puta* is the only girl you could get."

"Why, you little—"

"That's them, Lydia!"

Lydia looked up. Esme was calling to her from the front stoop; Kiley stood just behind her. "Those are the assholes that jacked up Jonathan!"

The taller of the two guys cupped his hands and shouted, "Screw you, Esme!"

"Shee-it," the other one added, scanning Lydia up and down. Then both swaggered menacingly in her direction.

Lydia made a snap decision. As the guys brushed past her, she put the short straw she'd been cradling in her right hand to her mouth and blew into it. Instantly, the two guys were enveloped in a dusty gray herbal mist. She stepped back as they coughed violently, then clutched at their throats.

"Enjoy your paralysis," Lydia said brightly.

"What the fu—?" the taller one gasped. Then he crumpled to the ground. A moment later, so did his friend. They lay there, frozen, their eyes dark pools of fear.

Lydia knelt so that her lips were inches from their ears. "Y'all look so cute, laid out like that. Don't worry, you can breathe. And you'll be fine in a half hour. But if you go near Esme or her friends ever again, I've got other stuff that'll close your windpipe tighter than a python's belly around a monkey. I've seen it. It isn't a pretty death."

She patted the cheek of the guy nearest to her, and then

straightened up to find Esme and Kiley standing on the other side of her frozen victims. They looked almost as stunned as the guys did.

"Hey, y'all," Lydia greeted them. "Just step over the trash. And let's get the hell out of here."

34

The next morning, Lydia and Esme were lolling on chaises at the Brentwood Hills Country Club, reading *Vogue* and *L.A. Weekly* respectively. Between them were three frosty glasses of iced ginseng tea. As for Kiley, she was with the kids—all of them, even Martina—at the shallow end of the country club's family pool.

Lydia had been the one to determine that all three families had memberships at the club and to suggest a group outing. Of course, it hadn't been on Anya's little To Do list. But thus far Lydia had ignored said list completely. The strategy appeared to be working out quite well.

The biggest challenge for the expedition had been Martina, who refused to don a bathing suit in public. But Lydia had a flash of brilliance—if Martina wore a dance leotard under her bathing suit, it would flatten out her breasts. When the idea worked, Martina almost wept with gratitude. Then Lydia coaxed the girl into a floral tankini that was, if not hip, at least decent looking. Though the long-term goal was still to get the kid comfortable with her body—she could only imagine how absurd Amazonian tribeswomen would have considered American body image nonsense—she was delighted that her cousin could pull it together sufficiently to swim in a pool with strangers.

As Lydia watched, Kiley launched a Goldhagen twin in a frilly pink one-piece off her shoulders; the girl chortled with joy as she hit the water. "Which one is that?" Lydia asked Esme.

"Easton," Esme replied. "She decided this morning that she only wants to wear pink. But Weston hates pink."

"Gee, she caught on to being a Bel Air kid fast," Lydia said, laughing.

"It's not funny," Esme said. "Diane Goldhagen thinks it's cute, so this morning she had me pack away Easton's clothes that aren't pink. By the time Easton decides to like other colors again, those clothes will be too small on her."

"Why can't Weston wear them in the meantime?"

"Diane says that Easton is the more dominant twin, so having Weston in Easton's rejected clothes might damage her psyche. Or some such bullshit."

Lydia smiled. "When I was a kid, I used to get away with stuff like that, too."

"Loco," Esme pronounced.

"The rich are different, sweetie." Lydia stretched again. She felt great. There really was nothing like temporarily paralyzing the enemy of a friend—by rain forest definition, your enemy too—to create a bonding experience. The night before, on the drive home from Echo Park, Lydia had explained to her friends about the vial of powdered herbs that she kept on her person at all times, the way another girl might carry pepper spray. These herbs had been given to her by an Ama shaman. Lydia suspected curare. She promised to show them some of the other great stuff she'd brought back—stuff that had a lot of spiritual power. Her friends had been suitably impressed by her offer.

A handsome dark-haired guy in Ray-Bans and blue Jams strolled by, drink in hand. He smiled at Lydia. She smiled back. Yep, things were looking up.

But the guy kept going. It made Lydia realize that while she had new friends and the quasi-lifestyle of the rich and famous, she still lacked bucks and boys. The bucks part would take concerted effort to correct. But the boys part? Well, it was time to do more than flirt with passing strangers.

She peered around the pool, on the lookout for the cute lifeguard, Scott Lyman. Sure, he was long on looks and short on brains. But she wasn't hunting for a future winner of the Nobel Prize for astrophysics. She had other physics in mind. She didn't spot him. Well, he'd show up eventually. One thing a girl learned in the Amazon, where the mail was air-dropped once a month and you sometimes had to fish a whole day if you wanted dinner that night, was the virtue of patience.

"I never saw a natural blond tan like you do," Esme told Lydia.

"It's a gift," Lydia said.

Esme nodded. She wanted to talk more about what happened at Junior's, but felt so self-conscious. She cleared her throat. "About last night . . ."

225

"Satisfying, wasn't it?" Lydia asked.

"Yeah, actually, it was," Esme agreed. "How those two *cholos* hit the ground. What else do you have in your bag of tricks?"

"Oh honey, I've got potions for just about everything." Lydia was rubbing sunscreen onto her thighs; she closed the lid and put it down. "Like say you want a certain boy to be your BF, I've got a potion that will make him drop to his knees and worship at your shrine."

"What's a BF?"

"Teen mag–speak for boyfriend."

"I've never heard it in my life," Esme said.

"Really?" Lydia sighed. "I still have a long way to go." She leaned toward Esme on one elbow. "So, what's up with you and this guy, Junior?"

Good question. Esme pulled a clip out of her bag and twisted her hair up, just for something to do. Her relationship with Junior was impossible to explain. But after what Lydia had done for her, how could she not?

"Junior is a great guy."

"Not great enough to keep you from wanting to jump Jonathan."

"Just because you have a feeling doesn't mean you act on it."

Lydia flexed her legs, pointing her toes toward the pool, where the kids were still cavorting with Kiley. "True. Yesterday I wanted to kill Martina for being such a weenie. But there she is, alive and well."

Esme shrugged. "Exactly."

"Still, there's a lot to be said for lust," Lydia mused. "Have you ever seen squirrel monkeys go at it?"

226

Esme almost choked on her iced tea. "No."

"They just love sex, they do it all the time in mating season. They get it on with someone new just to be friendly, or because they discovered a new fruit tree. And they're totally promiscuous, too. But the males are unbelievably dominant, so that kind of sucks."

Esme stared at her. "You spent way too much time in the jungle."

"I agree. So, are you madly in love with Junior?"

A week ago, that question would have been easy for Esme to answer. Now she wasn't as certain. "I wouldn't be sleeping with him if I didn't love him," she declared.

Lydia leaned toward Esme. "That's like a rule?"

"Yes. It's called morality. We're not squirrel monkeys."

"The Amas aren't averse to group gropes. They think that's pretty moral. It's all relative," Lydia said breezily. "So what do you love about this guy?"

Didn't this girl ever know when to back off? Apparently not.
"I feel safe with him."

"See, I think that's a bad thing." Lydia shook her head. "At our age, love should make you feel like you're skydiving without a parachute. That's why it's fun."

"How would you know anything about how love should make you feel? Or skydiving, for that matter?" Esme shot back. "You've been living in the rain forest for the last eight years!"

"I have a vivid imagination. The question is, when you see Junior, are you so happy you feel like you're filled with helium? Do you tell him your secrets? Do you have common goals and interests?"

"What is this, a test?"

"Yeah," Lydia admitted. "From *Cosmopolitan*. 'How Do You Know If You're Really, Truly in Love?' "

Esme knew this much: she did not have sex with a boy unless she loved him. But did she still love Junior, really, truly? She'd been so flattered when he'd started paying attention to her. He was such a big deal in the Echo. He'd given her status. Power. What was wrong with—

"How come Junior never came outside last night?" Lydia asked, interrupting Esme's thoughts. "Was he going to let those two guys just walk away?"

"Of course not. But in the Echo, you don't do your business in public. Junior would never take them down on the street like you did."

"But he called you? When you got home?"

Esme nodded, guarded.

"What'd he say?"

"That he wanted me to meet him tonight. At a club in Alhambra."

"Well, that's good, I guess. Let me know how it goes. Jonathan is walking hot. If you're not interested, I might go for him."

Esme shrugged. "Do what you want." She tried to mean it.

"Liar," Lydia said.

"You can be very irritating."

"It's part of my charm." She squirted more sunblock into her hand. "On second thought, forget what I said. There's nothing lower than a boy thief."

"Jonathan and I are just friends," Esme insisted.

"Uh-uh." Lydia wagged a playful finger at Esme. "It's not nice to fool a girl who paralyzed your enemies."

Esme slapped her forehead with her palm. Lydia was impossible. And yet Esme couldn't help liking her anyway. She swung her legs off the chaise. "I'm going swimming. You coming?"

Lydia turned her face to the sun and closed her eyes. "Nah. My mascara isn't waterproof."

35

As Esme went to the pool, Martina padded past her, dripping water all the way back to Lydia.

Lydia opened one eye when the girl got between her and the sun. "Having fun, sweetie?"

Martina nodded and wrapped a towel around her wet body, sarong-style. Lydia had taught her that maneuver, too. "A lot. But Serenity is kind of spoiled. She bosses everyone around."

"Maybe she doesn't get enough attention at home," Lydia guessed. "After all, she's only got one mom."

Martina's face brightened. "That's true. Can Jimmy and I eat here, as long as we don't get dairy or sugar or fried food?"

"Oh hell, I'd go for cheese fries and ice cream if I was you, sweet pea. By the way, I told the moms I'd have you home by one o'clock, but that gives us plenty of time. Why don't you order a sundae with extra whipped cream."

"For dessert?"

"Nah, life is short. Eat dessert first," Lydia decreed. "Want me to call the waiter?"

"You're not going to order worms, are you?" Martina joked.

"Well, aren't you loosening up," Lydia marveled. She leaned over and tapped Martina on the back. "Go back to the pool. I'll order for y'all, and holler when it gets here."

"Okay. I'm really glad you're here, Lydia."

Martina shyly dropped the wet towel and returned to the other kids. Lydia watched her depart, pleased with Martina's progress. Having a protégée could be fun.

"Er, excuse me?"

Lydia turned; a thirtyish blond woman in yes-I-have-a-personal-trainer-who-comes-to-my-house-five-days-a-week shape was standing to the other side of her chaise.

"Yes?" Lydia asked.

"I couldn't help noticing how good you were with that girl," the woman said. "Are you her nanny?"

"Yep."

"We had this Swiss au pair for a year. She ran off last week with my friend's husband. What a nightmare," the woman said. "May I?" She indicated the chaise next to Lydia.

Lydia nodded, and the woman sat down.

"Before that," she went on, "we went the illegal alien route. Lovely woman. But we gave her a ticket to visit relatives in New York and she never came back. Before that . . . well, it doesn't matter. I'm Evelyn Bowers." She held out her hand.

Lydia shook it briefly. "Lydia Chandler."

"Wherever did your boss find you, Lydia?"

"In the Amazon basin," Lydia said.

Evelyn laughed. "And a sense of humor, too. Who do you work for, if you don't mind my asking?"

"Kat Carpenter and her—"

"Kat Carpenter? I know her. I mean, I don't know her, but doesn't she do tennis commentary on ESPN? She's quite good." Evelyn leaned closer. "Do you mind if I ask what she's paying you?"

"Yes," Lydia said. "I do mind."

Evelyn touched a well-manicured hand to her clavicle. "God, I'm sorry. I know how rude that must have sounded." She reached for a Dooney & Bourke handbag that Lydia had admired on Rodeo Drive, and dug out a gold business-card holder. Then, looking both ways as if she was making a drug deal, she palmed off a card on Lydia.

"However much it is, I'll double it," she whispered. "Think about it and call me." Then, in a much louder voice, "Lovely to have met you, Lydia!"

She stood, mouthed "Think about it" once more, and strode off toward the clubhouse, her Charles David sandals skittering on the poolside tile.

Lydia examined the card. It was elegant in its simplicity. *Evelyn Bowers—Publicist* and a 310 phone number in raised script on oyster-colored onionskin parchment.

Double the pay. How intriguing. But what could she do? Kat was her aunt. It was because of Kat that she was here in Los Angeles, not piloting that damn launch up and down the—

"Hey, beautiful."

Lydia glanced up. There stood Scott the lifeguard, wearing white trunks that set off the deep tan stretched across his rippling muscles. He crouched by her chaise.

Lydia smiled at him. Well, well. It was about time.

"Been good?" he asked, and then nudged his chin toward the departing Evelyn. "She just offer you a gig?"

Lydia raised her eyebrows in surprise. "How'd you know?"

"Welcome to nanny poaching heaven," Scott said. "This place is worse than the child care center at Yoga Booty. I know this chick from Wyoming who got three offers in thirty-five minutes, right where you're sitting. The people she worked for ended up giving her a Lotus. Sweet ride."

"You mean she got to drive it?" Lydia asked.

"No, babe. They bought it for her. Next time you come, bring your calculator and a legal pad, and auction yourself off to the highest bidder." He let a tanned hand brush her thigh. "Maybe it'd be me."

Jeez. It took him long enough to get to the point.

"Maybe. Is my phone number still on your ass?"

"A friend scrubbed it off. If you know what I mean."

"Close friend, female variety," Lydia translated.

"A man's gotta do what a man's gotta do." He shrugged and splayed his fingers on Lydia's thigh. "If you know what I mean."

Lydia peered at the hand. And the body connected to it. "Is it my imagination, or did you get a lot more tan since the last time I saw you?"

"Spray-on," Scott confided. "I was doing a lifeguard calendar, had to go for the glow." He admired his own biceps, flexing the muscles. "It's the bomb, huh?"

"Not really," Lydia replied. "Too orange."

His fingers edged north. "Maybe you could help wash it off."

"Did you ever have sex in the shower? What's that like?"

"You're a strange girl. But you're still damn hot."

233

"Good to know," Lydia said.

"So. Lovely Lydia. You still want to hook up?"

Maybe a couple of days ago, yes. But now? Lydia sighed. "I don't think so."

Scott put his hands over his heart. "Don't say that."

"See, here's the thing. I've never had sex before."

Scott's jaw fell open. "Don't tell me you're a—"

"A virgin, yes," Lydia admitted. "I'm dying to end it, too. I thought you could be the one, because you are obviously an excellent physical specimen."

Scott looked confused. "Yeah . . ."

"From a purely physical point of view, you'd be a good candidate. I planned to overlook the fact that the things you say are so banal and trite. But you really do talk a lot, don't you."

He wriggled his eyebrows. "You saying you want me to talk dirty to you in the shower?"

Lydia sighed again. He just didn't get it. Her prince would know when to shut up.

"Scott, though it pains me to say this, our moment has come and gone."

"Too weird for me, babe." He stood and strutted off.

Well, he hadn't seemed insulted. That was good. But Lydia suspected it was because he really hadn't followed much of what she'd said. What the hell. She'd held out this long. She could last a few more days.

She retrieved Evelyn Bowers's business card from under her chaise and regarded it again. Then she grinned. Scott Lyman might be dumber than a bag of goat hair. But something he'd said had just put a very smart idea into her head.

36

With Weston next door in her room playing with Legos, Esme sat on the patchwork-patterned love seat in Easton's room reading *Goodnight Moon* to her. Even though the child couldn't follow it in English, Esme translated enough into Spanish to hold her interest.

"Me book!" Easton cried in English, and took the book out of Esme's hands. She started to invent a tale in Spanish that went along with the artwork. It didn't have much to do with the original story, but it was very cute, and it allowed Esme's mind to wander. To Junior. To what he'd told her on the phone the night before.

He'd seen from the living room window what Lydia had done to the two *cholos*. *"That was some weird-ass shit,"* he'd said. He'd dragged the boys inside; it took Victor and Freddie almost an hour to feel halfway normal.

Junior hadn't sounded mad, that was a good thing. And he'd

asked her out, to the Granada Club in Alhambra. They'd been there many times. It was elegant, Junior loved to dance, and the salsa didn't quit until the wee hours of the morning.

Still, anxiety had gnawed at her all day. She tried to cover—especially with Kiley and Lydia—but there were moments when the weight of it nearly overwhelmed her. Junior. Jonathan. What if the Goldhagens had security cameras monitoring her place? Or what if Diane decided that Esme was competition, and bad for family bonding? This was supposed to be a two-week trial period. Diane could easily decide that the trial hadn't worked out.

The ironic thing was, she was starting to enjoy the job. She liked the twins, and felt a certain stranger-in-a-strange-land kinship with them. It let her look at America with fresh eyes. For example, she'd taken them that afternoon from the country club to an art therapist in Mar Vista who was supposed to help them grieve for their left-behind life in Colombia. But the session was a bust: the shrink had an Xbox in her waiting room from which the girls could not be pried away.

Next on the afternoon's schedule was a visit to the Goldhagen cousins in Pacific Palisades. The family had an estate only slightly smaller than Diane and Steve's; there was a huge trampoline and a pool with a waterslide in their three-acre backyard. The cousins were ages eight and ten. Whatever they did, the twins wanted to do, especially Easton. So when the cousins went down the slide headfirst, Easton had followed them, though her swimming skills were rudimentary at best. Fortunately, Esme had put a life vest on her just in case.

Both girls had fallen asleep on the ride home. When she awakened them, they demanded chocolate ice cream for dinner.

Esme tried to say they could have it for dessert, but Easton refused to eat anything else. Knowing that Diane would tell her to let them eat whatever they wanted to eat, Esme had served up the ice cream. Not good parenting, but Esme knew that her opinion really didn't matter.

"Where Yon-o-tin?" Easton asked.

Esme told her in Spanish that her big brother was praying—she realized she wasn't sure of the Spanish word for synagogue. Jonathan had gone with his parents to Sinai Temple in Westwood for a folk rock end-of-Shabbat havdalah service. Esme was glad he wasn't home.

"Oye, Esme. Yo estoy finido con la cuenta. Tu lees ahora. Bien?" Easton pushed the slim volume back into Esme's hands.

"Sure, I'll read," Esme told her. It was her habit now to repeat everything in Spanish and English. "Five more minutes, then you both brush your teeth before bedtime. Where was I?"

She turned the page. But before she could begin to read, Easton had scrambled off the love seat. "Yon-o-tin!" she shouted.

"Yon-o-tin" was standing in the doorway, dressed for religious services. His eye was still three shades of purple.

"You're supposed to be at temple," Esme said.

"Yeah, I was." A smile played at the corners of his mouth. "But the prayer book was weird—there was this girl's face on every page—long dark hair, great eyes, really beautiful. You might know her."

Esme felt as if she was melting, exactly as Lydia had described love at the country club. But she tried to keep her face impassive. "I'm working," she reported.

"Plus," he went on, ignoring her, "I was overcome with this primal need for ice cream. And I know the best place."

237

"Ice cream!" Easton shouted, and Weston joined in. "Ice cream, ice cream! *Más* ice cream!"

"Hey, they can say it in English!" Jonathan exclaimed.

"And they had plenty for dinner," Esme added pointedly.

But the girls kept squealing. "Ice cream, ice cream!" They started jumping up and down, and Jonathan joined in on a three-way vocal chorus. "Ice cream! Ice cream!"

It *was* funny. And she had hours before she had to meet Junior. Her smile told them that she relented.

"Okay, girls, *vámonos!*" He scooped the twins up and carried them downstairs, Esme right behind them.

"Where are we going?" she asked as Jonathan headed out the front door with the girls.

"You'll see."

They piled into the Audi, since it had car seats for the girls in the back. Jonathan drove. He started singing an old Beatles tune, "Hello Goodbye." The song had very simple lyrics, and the twins began coming in on the words they recognized: *Yes. No. High. Low. Goodbye. Hello.*

"Rapid English via the Beatles?" Esme asked archly.

"Whatever works." He gazed at the twins in his rearview mirror. "And now, little ladies, we are going to Hollywood!"

The ice cream store was called Mashti Malone's, on La Brea Avenue, and it was jammed with beautiful people. While Jonathan held each girl by the hand, Esme read and translated the flavors scrawled on a large chalkboard. There was rose water, saffron, and orange blossom. "Do they even have chocolate?" she asked.

Jonathan pointed. "Different menu. Over there. Bitter chocolate, white chocolate, orange zest chocolate."

"The girls will have whatever is closest to just plain choco-late," Esme said.

Jonathan got macadamia mango. Esme went for crème brûlée. The twins got chocolate cones; they ended up wearing as much as they were eating. Esme thought it was the best ice cream she'd ever tasted.

"*Es doloroso?*" Weston asked shyly, pointing to her big brother's discolored eye.

"No," he assured her. "*Es bueno.*"

"It doesn't look very *bueno*," Esme said.

"Hey, I've been telling people it happened in a fight with Colin Farrell outside House of Blues. Everyone's very im-pressed." He waited a beat. "You're not laughing."

"Maybe because I know the truth." She wiped the corner of Easton's cone where the chocolate was dripping.

"In that case, maybe I can guilt-jerk you into finishing my tattoo."

"Get someone else to do it."

"You can't let another artist finish your masterpiece. Be-sides . . ." He lifted the sleeve of his T-shirt. "Right now it looks like a woman's breast."

Esme chuckled. "One that's very round and very fake."

His eyes met hers. "It's a Ferris wheel, isn't it? What you were drawing."

She nodded.

"Then you're the only one who can finish it."

His voice did the craziest things to her. Suddenly, she had a dreadful thought. "Your parents must be back from synagogue. I didn't leave a note. I didn't think—"

"No problem." Jonathan flipped open his cell and called

home. No one answered. He left a message. "There. We're cool."

Maybe. But Esme was anxious to go, just in case Diane was angry that she'd taken the girls out without permission. Easton held Jonathan's hand, she held Weston's, and they went out to the parking lot where they'd left the Audi.

It had a flat tire. Damn. Now they'd be even later.

"No sweat," Jonathan assured her. "I'll call Triple-A."

"That'll take forever."

"Nah. The weather's fine, there isn't much traffic. They'll be here in a flash." He pulled out his cell.

Esme grabbed his hand before he could call AAA. "Don't bother. I can change it."

"Come on, seriously. Changing a tire on an Audi is a bitch."

Esme gave him a level look. "You mean, before I disable the self-leveling suspension and inflate the collapsible spare, or after?"

"Jeez. Is there anything you *can't* do?"

"Yes. I can't go back and leave a note for your stepmother," Esme hissed. Why had she been so stupid as to go out with him and take the girls? This boy brought out the worst in her. When she was with him, it was like she lost her mind.

"My keen powers of observation tell me that you're irritated," Jonathan remarked.

"It doesn't matter."

"It *does* matter." He took her wrist. "How you feel, how we feel . . . it's *all* that matters."

"In your world, maybe," she told him and pulled her wrist away. "I'm changing the tire. Watch the girls, please."

240

"Esme." He caught her arm again. "This is silly. It'll take forty-five minutes, easy."

"I bet I can do it in twenty."

"You're on. And you're also crazy. We'll do it together."

Esme spied a bench by the fence a few feet from them; she told the girls to sit there and not move. For once they obeyed without an argument. Jonathan popped the trunk and took out the jack.

"What do I get if I win the bet?"

"Whatever you want," Esme said distractedly. The evening was fading; she dug into the trunk for a flashlight.

"Excellent," Jonathan said, pleased. "And what do you get if you win?"

"Anything *I* want." She jutted her chin upward and forced herself to lie. "And what I want is for you to leave me alone."

37

Esme had worn the pink sweater because it was Junior's favorite, and painted her lips the same color. Her perfume was the one he'd bought her for her last birthday. He'd see that she was trying, that she was still the girl he'd fallen in love with. They could work it all out, she was certain of it.

Two and a half hours after she'd changed the tire on the Audi in fourteen minutes—and won her bet with Jonathan—she nervously pulled the Audi into an open parking place on First Street in Alhambra, a mostly Latino neighborhood east of the Echo. Before she could turn off the engine, she could hear and feel hot salsa pour from the open door of the club.

At least she didn't have the added worry of Diane's anger. When they'd gotten the girls home, the Goldhagens were in the family room with another couple, sipping brandy from snifters. The men were smoking cigars, probably Cuban. Diane hadn't said a word about Esme and Jonathan's impromptu excursion.

But then it seemed as if maybe Diane had already had a couple of brandies herself.

Esme and Jonathan put the girls to bed, then Esme had departed. Jonathan had clearly wanted the evening to continue, but she shut him down. And out.

She crossed the street to the club; a line of revelers snaked from the front door. There was Junior, tough and cool, leaning against a lamppost. "Hey." He took her elbow. "I'm glad you're here. Let's go for a drive."

"A drive?" Esme was confused. "You don't want to dance?"

"Changed my mind." He took her hand and led her to his pride and joy—a classic yellow Dodge Charger with a 357 Hemi engine he had modified himself. Ten minutes later, they were cruising west on the 10 freeway toward downtown. For a long time, neither spoke. The thick silence between them felt unbridgeable.

"It's like you been away from the Echo for a long time, eh?" he asked, eyes on the road.

"Yeah."

How could she deny it? It was only days, but it felt like a lifetime. No matter how tense she found herself, she knew that there were some things she was already getting used to: living in a beautiful house, driving a fabulous car, going to the country club. When she or the kids got hungry, she liked ordering what they wanted and signing the tab to the Goldhagens' account. And she liked her new friends, Lydia and Kiley, maybe because they were as much outsiders in Beverly Hills as she was.

She didn't say any of that. Instead she said, *"The Echo es mi casa."*

243

"Not anymore, Esme." He shifted lanes and zoomed past a lumbering tractor-trailer.

"Of course it is," she insisted. "Just because I work over there—"

"Your parents *work* there," Junior interrupted. "You *live* there."

"No. I *stay* there. That doesn't make it home."

"You're always good with words, Esme, but it's bullshit, eh. Everything is changing." His quick glance tore at her.

"It's only a trial period, remember?" she reminded him.

"Well, you sure as hell got yourself into the shit during your damn trial period. I hear about you at some richie-rich party with a gringo. My boys go to talk to you—and find you with that same guy!"

"His name is Jonathan. And he's not . . . we're not . . ."

"Then why was he in your kitchen when you're in your nightclothes, and you're giving him a tattoo, eh?"

"It wasn't like—"

Junior waved a hand to silence her. "I'm not finished. Then your loco friend and her little potion—whatever that shit was that laid those boys out—she must be loco, Esme. You think they won't come back and give her worse?"

"No. Because you—"

"Jesus, Esme. Don't you get it? Los Locos has a grudge on for all of you. You, this rich gringo, your girlfriend. Shit. What a mess you made."

Stung, she stared out the window, watching downtown pass by on the right. In the distance, she could see the floodlit Hollywood sign up in the hills. "You told me to take this job, Junior."

"Yeah? Well, I didn't expect you to start a war."

244

He gripped the wheel tightly, accelerated, and shot around another truck, veering off the freeway at Vermont Avenue. They motored over surface streets until he started them back east on the freeway toward Alhambra again. "It comes down to this, Esme. You have to make a choice."

"What do you mean?"

"You can't live with one foot in their world and one in mine."

"But you said—"

"I know what I said. But you see what's happening. You want to be responsible for what goes down next?" Junior asked. "Do you?"

Esme gulped. "No."

"So you figure it out. When this trial period is over, either come home or leave home. You got to choose, Esme."

She shook her head. "No."

"Listen to me. I think I can talk Los Locos from going after you or your friends. But only if you are home with me or gone from here. If they see that freaking Audi in the Echo one more time—"

"My family is in the Echo," Esme said stonily. "Mama and Papa."

"See them at work." Junior's voice was hard. "Or come home and be who you were. You quit, it's like all this shit never happened. Esme, you can't have both."

She felt lost, abandoned. "You love me, Junior?"

He cursed under his breath again. "How you want to do me, Esme? You want me to lay my heart at your feet so you can walk over it to Bel Air, eh?"

She shook her head, miserable. "I can't do this."

His voice grew gentle. "Yeah, you can." He reached over and

touched a lock of her hair. "You've always been special, Esme. You shine."

Junior dropped Esme at her car. She had every intention of driving back to Bel Air. But she found herself pulling to a stop in front of her friend Jorge's house, two blocks from her own. It was the nicest place in the area.

Jorge's bedroom was on the main floor in front; his light was on. She rapped gently on the window; it took a moment for him to move the shade and peer out. Then it fell into place again.

A few moments later, he came outside. Esme was on the porch stoop, lost in thought. Silently, he sat next to her. Esme's mother had asked more than once why Jorge wasn't more than her best friend. Jorge was medium height and skinny, with beautiful hazel eyes that seemed to take in everything. He was brilliant and talented, he had morals, and he came from a good and educated family. Why hadn't they hooked up?

Esme didn't know, really. She didn't want to believe that Jorge wasn't macho enough, because she didn't like what it said about her. She preferred to think that she didn't want to risk messing up their friendship.

"You just happened to be in the neighborhood?" he asked her. A lowrider trolled by, Fat Joe's "Lean Back" booming from its sound system. Esme waited for it to pass.

"I was out with Junior." She didn't mention Jonathan. But she did tell him about Junior's ultimatum.

"Well, this is one of the few times that he and I actually agree about something."

"You were supposed to tell me he's full of shit, eh."

"You know where that came from?" Jorge asked.

246

Esme had no idea what he was talking about. "What?"

"That 'eh' thing at the end of a sentence," Jorge said. "It comes from *esa,* which comes from S.A. Which stands for Spanish American. You know. On some form where it said Caucasian, African American, Other. We're the Other."

She cut her eyes at him. "Does everything have to be political with you?"

"Pretty much. Anyway," Jorge went on, "you already know how I feel about Junior."

Esme nodded. She raised her knees to her chin and circled them with her arms.

"Junior, those other *cholos,* they're going nowhere but jail or the grave," Jorge went on. "That's the gangsta life."

"It's mine, too," Esme declared.

Jorge folded his arms. "If you say so."

She leaned her head on her knees. "I hate it when you do that."

"Do what?"

"Act like you always know better."

"I do know better," he said. "You think your parents work six days a week for those people, smile 'yes' and 'no' and 'whatever you say,' wash their clothes and scrub their toilets, so you can be a gangbanger *chica*?"

"You know I'm not a . . . Jorge, this is making me crazy." Esme rubbed her temples. "You told me I should stay in the Echo until college just like you're—"

"Not if it means you're with Junior," he interrupted.

"I'm not going to do anything stupid just because he's my boyfriend. Besides, I can take care of myself."

"Oh, you're all macho now?"

247

She gave him a stony look. "Yes."

"You hooked up with Junior for his power, Esme. If you felt so strong on your own, you would have cut him loose a long time ago."

Was that true? Esme stood and shivered in the cool night air. "You always know better, huh."

He stood too. "Only one thing I know for sure, Esme."

She gazed up into his beautiful hazel eyes. "What?"

"Wherever you go, *esa,* there you are."

He hugged her. She hugged him back. Then she turned and walked back to the Audi.

Five minutes later, she was two blocks away—in the driveway of her parents' rented bungalow, the Audi's motor running, her history washing over her. She longed to spend the night in her own scarred bed with the lumpy mattress and the street sounds and smells and sirens wailing in through the barred windows. But was that really what she wanted? Or was she brave enough to move forward on her own?

With one hand on her memories and the other on the wheel, she pulled out of the driveway and away from the Echo, knowing full well that if she kept going, she could never really come home again.

38

"Hate it. Hate it. Out of style. Send it to Dakota Fanning. Too small. Gag me."

One by one, Kiley held up the outfits that had once occupied Serenity's closet and were now strewn across the girl's canopy bed. One by one, Serenity had ordered their demise. They were going shopping that afternoon at Nordstrom's. Serenity had decreed that her wardrobe be pruned prior to the expedition. The three piles of clothes already on the floor were evidence of the ruthlessness of her triage.

"Okay, that's it for the bed," Kiley told the girl, who sat in her white sandalwood rocker. She went to the walk-in closet and took out the last items remaining—two pairs of DKNY Kids jeans, and two Patricia Field custom-designed dresses—one a floral print with a scalloped hem and a sheer overslip, the other a black sequin with spaghetti straps. Kiley couldn't imagine where a girl Serenity's age could possibly wear such clothes.

"You really want to chuck everything but these?" she asked Serenity.

"Yep. Call the maid to take it all away."

"To Goodwill?" Kiley asked. She was aghast at the girl's acquisitiveness but pleased that someone was going to get an outstanding new wardrobe at a rock-bottom thrift store price.

"I don't care. Can we go now? I'm gonna get so much cool stuff. I'm getting silk thongs, like about twenty of them."

"You're kind of young for thongs." Kiley went to the piles of clothes and started to separate them further—the shirts to one side, pants to another, skirts and dresses to another. "Can you help me, please?"

Serenity ignored her. "My mom says I can wear whatever I want. It's how I express myself. That's why I have an unlimited budget."

Kiley thought that was fortuitous, since Serenity planned to buy Madonna's entire English Roses girls' clothing collection, designed to go with her children's book, at Nordstrom's. After that, they were heading for Celine's on Montana Avenue. Serenity had explained that Madonna's daughter, Lourdes, always wore a certain two-hundred-dollar rhinestone belt that she'd purchased at Celine's.

Platinum had accounts at both stores, so Kiley's sole responsibility would be to supervise. Kiley didn't even have to wait around for a receipt. Platinum herself had wanted to take her daughter, but had been called into the studio even though it was a Sunday. The duet she was doing with someone from Destiny's Child for a CD called *Dueling Divas* wasn't going well, because the divas were really dueling.

"Did your mom put *any* limits on what you could buy?" Kiley asked. She pushed the separated piles farther apart, hoping to save some work for the people at Goodwill.

"Yep." Serenity rocked hard in her chair. "No white. Because if it's white I'd be copying her. You think my mom is pretty?"

"Very," Kiley said.

"Is your mom pretty?"

"Very."

Kiley's gaze landed on an empty plastic toy box, similar to the one in their garage at home where her father kept his tools. It gave her a sudden longing for La Crosse, her house, especially her parents. At moments like these, when Serenity was dominating her life, her reasons for coming to California and taking this job seemed remote.

"I have a great idea, for after we go shopping," Kiley said as she packed clothes for Goodwill into the toy box. "Let's go to the ocean."

Serenity looked at Kiley as if she was crazy. "If you want to swim, we can go to the country club."

"Not to swim," Kiley said, putting more of Serenity's discarded outfits into the box. "Just to hang out. Or to build a sand castle."

Serenity made a face. "I hate the ocean."

Kiley was astonished. "Why?"

"It's yucky," Serenity decreed. "Fish poop in it. All that sand. Plus there aren't any waiters. Get the jeans out of my closet. I want new ones."

So much for that great notion.

Serenity tapped one foot impatiently. "Umm, the jeans?"

When Kiley didn't move fast enough, she charged into her closet, tossed out the jeans, and reappeared. "Let's talk about boys. Do you have a boyfriend?"

"Yep," Kiley fibbed. "His name is Tom Chappelle and he's a gorgeous model."

Serenity's eyes grew huge. "Really?"

"No, not really. I met him, though."

"Did you ask him to be your boyfriend?"

Before Kiley could respond, Sid stomped into the room, ranting. "I hate that asshole!"

"What asshole?" Kiley asked absentmindedly. When she stooped to retrieve the jeans, she uncovered a black How & Wen capelet that had somehow ended up under Serenity's bed. It still had its price tag: $263.

"Jeff Greenberg, that's who," Sid thundered. "My damn male mentor. Who doesn't know a thing about Yu-Gi-Oh."

"Hi."

A guy appeared in the doorway, short and cute, with cropped blond hair and round glasses. "I'm the damn male mentor."

"What *is* a male mentor?" Kiley asked.

"Sid's therapist said he needed more positive male role models in his life. Platinum hired me yesterday," Jeff explained. "I'm a psych grad student, UCLA."

"That makes you a male mentor?"

"Got me," Jeff said. "Anyway, my psych prof recommended me and it pays a whole lot better than being a TA. Platinum said she'd tell you about me."

"She didn't."

"You're the nanny, right?"

Kiley nodded. "Yep."

"Well, call her," Jeff suggested. He sat on Serenity's bed.

Great idea. I remember what happened the last time I did that. She nearly took my head off.

"He wants to take me to a bullshit Dodgers game," Sid seethed to his sister. "I hate baseball."

"Don't say bullshit," Kiley corrected him.

"Fine. Stupid bullshit."

"Dickweed," Serenity said, getting in on it.

"Bee-otch!"

Suddenly, Kiley smacked her palm against one of the posters of Serenity's bed. The sound reverberated like a gunshot. "Stop it!" she thundered. "Both of you!"

The two stunned kids stared at her. So did the male mentor. "New policy. Every day that you don't use any swearwords, I'll give you a reward," Kiley offered. "How about that?"

"Like what?" Sid asked warily.

"Like . . . Mrs. Cleveland's candy box," Kiley said.

Both children burst out laughing.

"We get that whenever we want." Serenity chortled.

"Okay, well, I'll think of something and we'll talk about it later," Kiley said, mostly because it occurred to her that both kids got pretty much anything they wanted already.

Jeff checked his watch. "You've got tae kwon do in twenty minutes, Sid. Before we go to the game. Get a move on."

"Just a sec, Sid," Kiley instructed. She went to the in-house intercom system and buzzed Mrs. Cleveland. The older woman confirmed that Jeff Greenberg was indeed Sid's male mentor.

"Okay, thanks." Kiley clicked off. "You're cleared for take-off, guys."

"But I don't want to go," Sid said with a pout.

"Come on," Jeff urged. "I'll buy you a Dodger dog and a beer."

Sid's face lit up. "Sweet!"

"*Root* beer." Jeff cuffed Sid lightly on the back of the head and followed the boy out the door.

"Call the driver," Serenity told Kiley when they were gone. She headed for her bathroom. "I'll be right back. I need lip gloss."

Before Kiley could decide whether to inform the girl that almost-eight-year-olds customarily did not wear lip gloss, her cell rang.

"Hello?"

"Hey Kiley. It's Lydia."

"Hi, what's up?" Kiley sat on the bed. She'd deal with Serenity's makeup issues another time.

"You have to work tonight?"

"I'm off at seven until Tuesday morning, actually. I was thinking of calling you and Esme. I thought maybe you guys would like to take a drive to the ocean. And after that, we could see *The Ten* at—"

"That stuff can wait," Lydia interrupted. "I have the most fantastic idea in the history of fantastic ideas, swear to God, but I have to tell y'all in person. Can you meet me at my house tonight? Around eight? Esme already said yes."

Well, she could go to the ocean later. And to a late movie. "Fine, I'm in."

"Excellent. And forget the movie. We're going clubbing and getting crazy. Come looking hot, girl."

Kiley laughed. "I don't think I do 'hot' but I'll work on it. Later."

As she hung up, Serenity came out of the bathroom wearing mascara and blush, and carrying a vial of Lip Venom.

"Where did you get that makeup?" Kiley asked.

"My mom's dressing room. She's got tons of it. All the cosmetic companies give her stuff for free."

"Well, you shouldn't take it without asking."

With a knowing look, Serenity tossed the lip gloss to Kiley, who caught it without thinking. "Here," said the girl. "You need it a lot more than I do."

39

It was like a dream come true—Lydia was having company. Not Ama tribeswomen who'd spend the evening telling stories about their ancestors and peeling skin off roasted snakes, but actual girlfriends with whom to talk and dish. Drinks and bottled water from the main house were chilling in the fridge; purloined junk food was out on the living room table. A borrowed Modest Mouse CD from the moms (who turned out to have surprisingly good musical taste) played on the sound system.

She even had some decent clothes, having talked Kat into loaning her a Club Monaco leopard-print coatdress that she'd left unbuttoned all the way up her thighs. She'd also snagged a red pony-hair Christian Dior gambler bag, from which dangled the cutest gold-toned rhinestone dice. She hadn't exactly asked, just seen it in Kat's closet and couldn't resist. Well, she was certain she could sneak it back without her aunt realizing that it had been gone.

The evening activities were set. Oksana the Russian tennis player had no hard feelings about her failed seduction of Lydia. In fact, at Lydia's behest, she'd called the Silverbird in Los Feliz and made sure that Lydia plus two were on the guest list for the afterparty of the Pixies concert. The band was playing at the Wilshire Theater, and due at the club by midnight.

Everything was in place. Now, if only the other girls would agree with her plan.

Esme showed up first, a bit subdued. There was obviously something on her mind, but she wouldn't talk about it. She accepted a Coke; they chatted about their kids until Kiley showed up breathless, apologizing left, right, and sideways about being late.

Kiley explained how, when she'd showered in prep for the evening, she'd come out of the bathroom to find Serenity watching TV in her guesthouse, dressed to thrill in one of her new outfits. If Kiley was going clubbing, so was Serenity.

"That's sweet," Lydia said, "in a sick and twisted kind of way."

Kiley plopped down on the love seat catty-corner to Lydia. "I'll go with sick and twisted. The kid is desperate for attention. I promised I'd spend some time with her tomorrow and then walked her back to the main house."

"Tomorrow is your day off," Esme pointed out.

"I'm going to the beach tomorrow," Kiley stated. "So I'll take the kid with me; it'll do her good." She reached for some chips from the bowl on the table. "Besides, there wasn't one cussword out of her all afternoon. That's a big deal."

Lydia took that as her cue. "Speaking of big deals . . . how would y'all like to make some money?"

"Legally?" Kiley quipped between chips.

"Well, my notion won't involve a pimp or prison time." Lydia quickly told the other girls about the conversation she'd had with Evelyn Bowers at the country club pool.

"You're going to work for her?" Kiley asked.

"What does that have to do with us?" Esme added.

"No, I'm not taking the offer and it has everything to do with you," Lydia replied. "I called her today. She told me she has three other friends desperate for decent nannies. Trust me. When this woman uses the word 'desperate,' she means *desperate*."

Esme looked bewildered. "You want us to find her a nanny?"

"Think bigger," Lydia urged. "Think: we place educated, attractive nannies with rich families in Beverly Hills and Bel Air. We take a big fat finder's fee. Plus a percentage of their earnings."

Kiley took a thoughtful sip of her Coke. "It's a great idea."

"I know!" Lydia agreed.

"But you should have had it, like, forty years ago," Kiley added. "You have a computer here?"

Lydia nodded. "In my bedroom. I have no clue how it works."

"I'll teach you sometime," Kiley offered, and led the girls to the bedroom, logged on to Google, and Googled the words "nanny agency" and "Los Angeles" in the same search. There were 4,710 hits.

Esme whistled. "That's what I call steep comp."

Lydia was undaunted. "Try 'restaurant' and 'Los Angeles,' " she instructed.

Kiley shrugged and clicked away. There were more than two million Google entries.

"Reduce that by ninety-five percent for duplication," Lydia declared, "and you're still talking a hundred thousand restaurants in this town. But according to *Jane* magazine, the hip places always seem to be brand new."

"It's not the same," Esme insisted. "People have to eat three times a day. They only hire a nanny once. If they're lucky."

Lydia grinned. "So we make sure they get lucky. We don't want to be the biggest agency. Just the best, most exclusive, and most expensive. When rich people pay more for something, they think it's worth more." She ushered her friends back to the living room as she spoke.

"I don't know . . ." Esme shook her head.

"Okay, take my mom, before she lost her mind and moved to the Amazon." Lydia paced the floor like a lawyer in front of a jury. "She always shopped at Neiman Marcus, even though she could get the same white T-shirt at Sears for a fifth of the money. Where do you think Diane Goldhagen shops?"

"Fred Segal, Barney's, Harry Winston," Esme reported. "I've seen the bags."

Lydia nodded. "I rest my case."

Kiley sat back down on the love seat. "So . . . we'd cater to the *way* upscale trade. Something I know nothing about."

Lydia waved this off. "Fake it."

But Esme wasn't convinced. "Maybe it will work and maybe it won't. But why do you need us? It's your idea."

"Because every potential nanny I know is five feet tall, naked, and has a stick through her upper lip. I don't know anyone I could recommend. Yet."

Kiley sipped thoughtfully from her Coke. "Actually, I have a friend back in La Crosse who'd kill for a job like mine. I think."

Lydia whirled around. "See, that's what I'm talking about!" Her eyes flew from Kiley to Esme and back again. "I'm brilliant, right?"

Esme still seemed doubtful. "People say things they don't mean all the time. How do you know these people would pay us for this service?"

"Well, my new best friend Evelyn gave me the numbers of her three desperate friends," Lydia explained. "I called them and said I charged a thousand bucks for the perfect nanny. Half when they start, half after four weeks of nanny-bonding bliss. None of them batted an eyelash."

"Amazing," Kiley said.

"What if something goes wrong?" Esme asked. "Would we be responsible?"

"My uncle in Dallas is a lawyer," Lydia said. "He'll handle all that for us. We'll get releases. Come on, Esme. You're local. You must know someone who'd like a job with a rich family. Right?"

"You saw where I come from," Esme said stiffly.

"So?" Lydia asked. "You should see where I come from."

"Do these families really want a nanny from Echo Park?" Esme asked.

"The Goldhagens wanted you," Kiley pointed out.

"That's an exception. They knew my parents."

"Fine," Lydia said, waving a hand through the air. "If it turns out some of our clients are snobs, we'll find them a nanny with some tight-ass pedigree, charge them double, and laugh all the way to the shoe department at Barney's."

"Maybe." Esme almost smiled.

"You know, I actually think it could work," Kiley said. "I'll call my friend Nina in the morning."

"Excellent!" Lydia jumped up and hugged her friends. "Y'all, this is so exciting. I'll be right back."

Lydia went to the kitchen and returned with three coffee cups and a bottle of Cristal champagne she'd found in the moms' basement fridge.

"I don't really drink," Esme demurred.

"Tonight you do." Lydia popped the cork and poured three cups full of champagne. She handed one to each of her friends, and hoisted her own in the air. "A toast."

"To actual glasses," Kiley cracked.

"From Tiffany's," Lydia added.

Esme smiled. "And I want to say . . ." She hesitated.

"You must know you can tell us anything by now," Lydia encouraged.

Esme nodded. "That's just it. I want to thank you both. What you did for me . . ."

"That's what friends are for," Kiley said, smiling.

"You have to admit, we are three very unlikely friends," Esme pointed out.

"That's part of what makes it so great." Kiley hoisted her cup.

Esme hoisted hers. "To new friendships."

"Now you're getting into the spirit of things," Lydia said approvingly.

"And new guys," Kiley added.

"Excellent addition," Lydia said. She raised her cup, too. "To new friendships and to new ventures, business and otherwise." She clinked her cup against theirs. "Ladies, this is the beginning of everything."

epilogue

"Hola, ustedes están escuchando a 91.9 FM, KVCR, alma del barrio, la música latina la más mejor en Los Angeles. La hora es dos, pero la noche está bastante joven."

The music started up again. Esme kept the beat by tapping a finger on the steering wheel as she turned the Audi onto Bel Air Terrace, where the Goldhagens lived. She was coming from the Pixies afterparty at the Silverbird; she'd been there with Lydia and Kiley. Though the band had just played a long concert, they'd jammed for the invited audience of three hundred. Esme had enjoyed their infectious, fun sound. But it still couldn't touch Latin music.

She clicked the new remote control device that opened the Goldhagens' front gate, which finally was working properly. It struck her that it had been only eight days since she and Junior had been surrounded by the Bel Air police in this exact spot.

Just eight days. Then, she'd been with Junior. Now, she was

alone. Then, the gate had been closed. Now it opened. *Maybe it's some kind of metaphor,* she thought. As she wound the car up the driveway to the six-car, heated-and-air-conditioned garage, the chant of crickets and the scent of orange blossoms wafted through her open window.

She pulled up in front of the garage, where she'd been told to always park the Audi. For a moment, she just sat there. Was this really her new life? Had she done the right thing? Had Junior done her a favor? Well, if he had, if she was going to stay in this world, then she'd damn well make the most of it. That meant not running to Jonathan Goldhagen. He would play her as if she was his new toy. When he tired of her, he'd be on to the next.

And yet, all night long, every five or ten minutes, she'd seen him. Only it was never really him—just the turn of a head, a smile, the line of a profile.

She took off her shoes—too many hours on cheap stiletto heels—reached for her purse, and opened the Audi door.

"Esme?"

A whisper on the orange blossom–scented breeze. Jonathan. She'd know his voice anywhere. He walked up to her.

"Did you just get home, too?" she asked.

He shook his head. "I was on the upper terrace contemplating the meaning of life. I heard the gate open." He cocked his chin toward the shoes dangling from her finger. "Fun night?"

She nodded. There was an awkward beat of silence. His eye was less bruised, but it still looked like a relief map done in eggplant. "Your eye," she said.

He touched it lightly. "Almost healed. Like it never happened."

"Only it did."

"That's not the part I remember."

264

"What is?"

"How much I wanted to do this," he whispered.

It began as the gentlest of kisses, but went on and on until the world spun away. It was the kiss she'd been wanting from the first moment she'd seen him, when her sandals had been soaked in raw sewage. She was tired of thinking, sick of denying her feelings. If this was wrong, it was wrong. If she got hurt, she got hurt. All she knew was that right now, right this minute, this perfect kiss from this boy was what she wanted.

It wasn't safe, like with Junior. It was dangerous, a whole different kind of danger from the kind of life she'd always known. She stepped off the cliff, into free fall.

And she didn't care.

The Silverbird Lounge was still hopping, and Lydia was having the time of her life. A mosh pit of dancers undulated to the music as the club's famous mechanical silver birds swooped overhead at breakneck speed.

She'd called X, who was out at some gay club in West Hollywood; he said he'd swing by to pick her up. Even with three drinks in the past three hours, she felt fine. She had discovered a new beverage of choice—a California Condor, which consisted of Jamaican rum, Kahlua, Red Bull, milk, and a splash of eggnog. Her first one had been procured for her by the Pixies' sound man, the second by the deejay, and the third by an unattractive but interesting guy who claimed to write for *Rolling Stone* and offered a late-night tour of that magazine's Los Angeles offices. Lydia accepted the drink but declined the tour. Dancing was too much fun.

"Last groove, so shake what your momma gave you," the

deejay growled, and segued into They Might Be Giants' "Man, It's So Loud in Here." Lydia was in the middle of the dance floor; all around her people sang along at the top of their lungs. Lydia didn't know the song, but she rocked out anyway.

"Lydia!"

She heared someone calling her name over the music, turned, and spotted X waving at her near the bar; she had to snake through the crowd to reach him. He was with another guy who had the rangy look of an athlete. Easily six foot two, the new guy had light brown hair that flopped boyishly onto his forehead, and a deep cleft in his chin. He looked like the actor who played Clark Kent on the TV show that her cousin Jimmy loved, *Smallville*. What was the actor's name? Welling. Tom Welling.

So, X had found himself a gay Tom Welling. Lucky X.

"Hey," Lydia said. She lifted the sweaty hair from the back of her neck. "Thanks for coming for me. I had the most fantastic time."

"Glad to hear it," X said. "I've been doing pretty swell myself." He touched his friend on the forearm. "Billy, meet Lydia Chandler. Lydia, Billy Martin."

"A pleasure," Billy said, shaking hands with Lydia. It wasn't the dead fish handshake that she kept running into in Los Angeles, either. "Good party?"

"Excellent," Lydia replied. "How long y'all been here?"

"About ten minutes," Billy replied. "You were having so much fun out there we didn't want to stop you."

"Excuse me, you two," X interjected. "The men's room calls. If I don't fall in love, I'll be back shortly."

X headed off. Billy smiled at Lydia. "How long are you back

in America? X said you've had quite an interesting past eight years."

"A week."

Billy leaned against the bar. "Weird to be back, isn't it? Some things cool, some things so bizarre you can't really believe you're American."

"Exactly." Lydia was impressed by how perceptive this guy was. Did gay guys corner the market on cool?

"I was raised in about six different countries myself," Billy went on. "Mozambique, Germany, Thailand, Canada, Liberia. And here."

"Missionary parents?"

"State Department. Foreign Service officers. It was always the strangest thing to come home. Like it never *is* home."

Again, Lydia was impressed. "X has really good taste," she said.

He looked confused. "Not following."

"You're smart, interesting, and on a *Cosmopolitan* Hot or Not quiz, you'd be off the chart. If I was a guy, I'd go for you in a New York minute."

"Oh yeah?"

Lydia shrugged. "Even if you're bi, I am not a boy poacher. I like X way too much to—"

"Whoa." He put his hand on her arm. "I like X, too."

Lydia shrugged. "Exactly my point."

"The same way you like him," Billy added.

It took Lydia a beat. "You mean you're not—?"

Billy laughed. "X has been my friend since we were little kids in Redondo Beach. He's one of the world's great guys; he stayed in touch wherever my family went. If I was gay, I'd definitely go for him. But I'm not."

"You're straight," Lydia clarified.

He grinned. "Last time I checked."

Well, well, well. Would wonders never cease?

And then, it dawned on Lydia. "Wait. Did X bring you here to meet me?"

"Yup."

"I'll have to thank him."

"Me too."

"So . . . Billy. That's short for William?"

"Yup."

William. As in *Prince* William. Maybe it was a sign.

Life was *so* looking up.

Kiley stood near the corner of Hollywood and Vine and punched her mom's cell number into her phone. There was still plenty of traffic flowing by, and lots of people on the street: partygoers and club kids from the evening before, a street preacher reciting Ecclesiastes at the top of his lungs, a cluster of young high school kids standing around eating five-bucks-a-Styrofoam-plate Chinese food. A guy in full Star Wars regalia, a gay couple in leather chaps where one guy led the other by a dog leash, and a young woman wearing a Miss America–style evening gown and silver tiara with mascara tracks down her cheeks.

Kiley loved it, all of it—the insanity and the glitter and the hype. Even after hours of dancing at the Silverbird, she wasn't ready to pack it in and go home to Platinum's guesthouse. She'd torn out the movie ad from *L.A. Weekly;* a quick check revealed that *The Ten* was playing a late-night show at Grauman's Chinese Theatre. Short of a sex change operation, it was the most un-Wisconsin thing in the world she could think of doing—going to see a movie at two in the morning. Alone.

Which was exactly why she was going to do it.

"Hello?"

"Mom? Hi, it's me! Are you busy?" She'd called her mom at the restaurant, where she worked graveyard shift on weekends.

"Some truckers just left, now it's pretty empty," her mother said. "How are you, sweetie?"

"Fine. I—"

"What? Where are you? It's so noisy I can hardly hear you."

"Just a sec." There was a twenty-four-hour donut shop behind Kiley. She ducked inside. It was empty save for a drunk at one table, drooling into a chipped cup. "Mom? Can you hear me better now?"

"Much. What time is it there?"

"Two or so. I haven't gone to bed yet. I went out with some friends. Dancing."

"That sounds like fun."

"They went home but I'm not sleepy," Kiley went on. "So I'm going to the movies."

"At this time of night? *Alone?*" The anxiety in her mom's voice was palpable.

"Of course not. With some other friends," Kiley lied. Anything to keep her mom from going off. "How are you?"

"Good."

"No panic attacks?"

Instead of answering, her mother said, "They laid off two dozen people from the brewery. Isn't that terrible?"

Kiley's stomach sank. If her dad was out of work, she'd have to . . .

"Did Dad lose his job?"

"No, no, he's okay. His friend Hal got the ax, and they've got a new baby. It's so sad."

"Is Dad—?"

Kiley didn't need to fill in the word "drinking." Her mother would understand the question.

"Not too bad. Is the job going okay?"

"Yeah. The kids are spoiled rotten, though. Mom, do you know what Nina's doing this summer?"

"Working at Pizza-Neatsa, last I heard. Why?"

"Nothing, I'll call her later."

"You come in or go out?" An older Asian man in a white apron—obviously the proprietor of the donut shop—accosted Kiley.

"Coffee to go, please," she told him. He shuffled off.

"What?" her mother asked.

"Nothing. Mom, who are your favorite movie stars in the whole world?"

"Gracious! Did you meet some movie stars?"

"I'm about to stroll down the Walk of Fame—you know, where the stars put their handprints in the cement—and I've got a disposable camera."

"I'd have to say . . . Clint Eastwood? Or Geena Davis?"

"I'll see what I can do."

"Are you getting enough sleep?" Mrs. McCann asked.

"Plenty."

"I don't think you should be out at this time of night, Kiley. What if you run into a drug addict? What if someone grabs your purse?"

"You trust me. Remember?" Kiley reminded her mom.

"Yes, sweetie. I do."

Kiley's heart swelled with love for her mother. "I miss you, Mom."

"We miss you too, honey."

Kiley said her goodbyes and hung up. Homesickness washed over her. She looked around the dingy donut shop. What was she doing, alone at two in the morning in a crazy neighborhood? So many bad things could happen. What if—

"Coffee!" The Asian man thrust a Styrofoam cup at her. "One dollar! Now! Before you run 'way!"

She dug a buck out of her purse and gave it to him. Then she pushed out of his shop and stood there, coffee in hand. She didn't have to do this. She could go back to Platinum's.

No. No retreat, no surrender. She was not going to make her choices out of fear. Period.

With new resolve, she purchased a guide map to the Walk of Fame at a newsstand, and the disposable camera she'd told her mom she already had. Along the left side of the map was a key to the stars' names. She found Clint Eastwood and Geena Davis. Four minutes' walk—dodging late-night pedestrians all the way—took her to Eastwood's imprints on the sidewalk. *Snap.* Another thirty seconds, and she was at Geena Davis's square of sidewalk. *Snap.* Just for fun, she leaned over and put her own hands atop the actress's imprint. They dwarfed hers. She vowed to get the photos developed and on the way to her mother on Monday.

Now, where was the theater? She checked the map—it was two blocks away; she started walking. The late-night summer street scene had grown even more festive. This was yet another Los Angeles, a city that she found was like a diamond, with all

271

these different facets—the mansions of Beverly Hills and Bel Air, the bright lights and hip clubs of Sunset Strip, the seedy, touristy gaudiness of Hollywood and Vine, even Echo Park, where you needed an ambassador to explain the rules of the game.

And the beach—from the pristine sands of Malibu to the funky asphalt boardwalk in Venice. Beyond it all, the Pacific. Her ocean. Tomorrow she'd figure out a way to take Serenity there, to show her the magic and mystery. Maybe it would help her escape the ever-present anxiety of living with a crazy mom, just as it had once helped Kiley, and was helping her still.

Kiley snapped some photos of Grauman's Chinese Theatre for her mother. The place was done in a kitschy Asian theme, complete with a stone courtyard and Chinese pagoda. A historical marker announced that it was one of the oldest movie houses in the city. For big movies like *The Ten,* it frequently offered showings around the clock.

Kiley joined the short line of ticket buyers. In front of her was a talkative family of tourists from the Philippines that was happy to babble to Kiley about how jet lag was keeping them awake. Behind her was a cluster of high school students in letter and cheerleader jackets from someplace called La Crescenta.

The line edged forward. At the front was a lone guy in jeans and a tennis shirt. He paid his money and bought his ticket, then filed away to the left.

Kiley froze.

Holy shit. It couldn't be. But it was.

Tom Chappelle. *That* guy.

He saw her. Didn't move. Didn't show any expression. Kiley felt stupid. She'd probably only fantasized that he'd recognized her at the country club pool.

But then he smiled, and walked toward her. She turned to see if some other, much cuter girl was standing just behind her. No. Only the high school kids.

"Hi," he said as he approached. "I'm—"

"Tom," she filled in. "From the hotel."

He cocked his head sideways. "I know how weird this sounds, but for the past few days, I feel like I keep seeing you."

Kiley tried to look casual and cool. "Do you always buy a ticket to your own movie?"

"It's my first one," he confessed. "I was at opening night at the Grove. But I wanted to experience it with a real audience. And I didn't want to run into anyone I know."

Kiley laughed. "Busted."

He scratched the sexy day's growth of beard on his chin. "Actually, I don't know you. You ran away from me at the Hotel Bel-Air like I had a contagious disease."

"Uh . . . " Kiley could not think of one clever thing to say.

"So, why don't we start over, how about it?" He held out his hand. "Hi. I'm Tom Chappelle."

"Kiley McCann." She shook his hand. Only this time, she kept her hand in his.

"You here alone or do I have to give your hand to some other guy?" Tom asked.

And then, all the witty gods smiled down upon Kiley McCann.

"It belongs to me, actually," she said. "But I could loan it to you during the movie. For a price."

He smiled as she edged up to the ticket window and bought her ticket. "Which is?"

"A cup of coffee. Afterward. There's a donut place down the street where the owner doesn't trust me."

"You strike a hard bargain, Kiley McCann."

"Call me Krazy," she said. "With a *K*. All my friends do."

About the Author

Raised in Bel Air, Melody Mayer is the oldest daughter of a fourth-generation Hollywood family and has outlasted countless nannies. This is her first novel.

Poor girls. Rich boys. Richer girls.

Friends with Benefits

A Nannies Novel

coming May 2006

Win a SPA day!

Kiley, Lydia, and Esme
think that being a nanny in
Beverly Hills will be the ultimate
glamour job. But they quickly find out
that watching spoiled rich kids isn't all about tanning
at the beach and partying at Hollywood hot spots.

The Nannies

Tell us what your most **challenging** nanny or baby-sitting **experience** was and how you **handled it.**

One grand-prize winner
will win a Spa Day for two.
Three runners-up
will win a gift certificate to their favorite
cosmetics store!

ENTER NOW!

Log on to **www.randomhouse.com/teens** for complete rules and details.

NO PURCHASE NECESSARY. Entries must be mailed separately and received by Random House no later than December 31, 2005. LIMIT ONE ENTRY PER PERSON. The grand prize and 3 runners-up prizes (a gift certificate for a make-up store) will be awarded on the basis of originality, style and creativity. Contest is open to legal residents of the fifty (50) United States and the District of Columbia, and Canada, excluding the Province of Quebec, who are between the ages of 8 and 25 on September 13, 2005. Void where prohibited or restricted by law.

Delacorte
Press

RHCB